The Day Will Come

BERYL MATTHEWS

Allison & Busby Limited
12 Fitzroy Mews
London W1T 6DW
allisonandbusby.com

First published in Great Britain by Allison & Busby in 2015.
This paperback edition published by Allison & Busby in 2016.

A CIP catalogue record for this book is available from
the British Library.

10 9 8 7 6 5 4 3 2 1

ISBN 978-0-7490-1992-1

Typeset in 10.55/15.55 pt Sabon by
Allison & Busby Ltd.

The paper used for this Allison & Busby publication
has been produced from trees that have been legally sourced
from well-managed and credibly certified forests.

Printed and bound by
CPI Group (UK) Ltd, Croydon, CR0 4YY

Chapter One

London, Ealing 1940

There was silence in the packed cinema as the newsreel reported on the disaster of Dunkirk. They were making it seem like a victory, as it was for the smiling faces of the rescued men. The fact that so many men had been snatched from the beaches was something to be relieved about, Grace knew that, but her Brian hadn't been one of those men. Her kind, loving husband of only a year wouldn't be coming home. He'd had such enthusiasm for life, and it tore her apart to know she would never see his ready smile again, or hear his laughter. He hadn't deserved to die like that.

Clasping her hands tightly together she looked down, unable to watch the screen any longer. It hurt too much. She shouldn't have come, but her friend had said that the distraction of watching a film would do her good. Well, Helen had forgotten about the newsreel.

Someone touched her arm and she lifted her head, relieved to see the lights were on for the interval.

'Sorry about that, Grace. I didn't think they would show that in such detail. Are you all right?'

Grace grimaced. 'Not really. Thank heavens that's finished!'

'It's a bloody mess, isn't it? What do you think will happen now?' Helen asked. 'Hitler's taken France, so are we next?'

'I don't believe there is any doubt about that. We're vulnerable and will need breathing space to recover, but whether we get it is anyone's guess.'

'There's one thing in our favour, though. We are an island, so he won't be able to march across our border.'

'That's true, but he can fly over the Channel.'

Helen muttered something rude as the lights dimmed, and the main film began to run.

With her emotions and thoughts still in turmoil with shock, what was showing on the screen did not register with Grace. It was a relief when the film ended and they were able to walk in the fresh air.

'I'm thinking of joining the forces,' Helen said, looking at Grace.

'What branch of the services?'

'I don't mind which one. I feel I've got to do something useful. What about you?'

Grace took a deep breath. 'I don't know. My mind is all a jumble, at the moment. I can't think straight.'

'That's understandable.' Helen slipped her hand through her friend's arm. 'I expect you want to stay in your job. My work at the library isn't important, so I could be called upon to do some kind of war work. If I act now, I might be able to choose what I will do.'

'I know you're right.' Grace's voice trembled, and she paused to gain control of her emotions. 'Brian had such plans for when the war was over. We would save hard, buy a small house somewhere away from London, so our children could have open fields to run in. The war wouldn't last more than a year, he'd said confidently. Well, it didn't for him. Now those dreams are shattered, and I'm left to face whatever is to come without him.'

'It's a terrible disaster, and there are thousands of families suffering the same grief.' Helen gripped her friend's arm, and shook it gently. 'But you are strong, Grace. You'll get through this. We all will. We have to! There is a different kind of life facing us, and come what may, we have to deal with it.'

'As long as it isn't speaking German,' Grace remarked, dryly. 'I never could get on with that language.'

Helen stopped and faced her friend, a smile of relief on her face. 'That sounds more like you. That's not going to happen. We will all fight to our last breath to keep Hitler from adding this country to his conquests.'

'Of course we will,' Grace agreed. Helen's mouth was set in a stubborn line. Many had already given their lives, including her Brian, so they couldn't sit back and do nothing. 'So, let's assume I do leave my job, what can I do?'

They started walking again and Helen said, 'That's

something we are both going to have to decide – and quickly. I want to do something where I can make a difference. Women can't join a fighting unit, and I'm not cut out to be a nurse, or something like that.'

'Neither am I. So, let's think what we are good at.'

'Well, you're a good secretary and could look after a colonel.'

Grace laughed for the first time in days. 'I doubt that would happen. If I joined any of the forces I would probably end up in a typing pool. You might be able to work as an interpreter. Your grandmother is French, and you speak the language fluently.'

'That's a possibility, I suppose. I'll look into that. Gran is devastated by the fall of France, as you can imagine.'

They fell silent, lost in their own troubled thoughts. At twenty-three, Grace was a year older than Helen, and living next door to each other they had been friends from toddlers. In temperament and looks, they were opposites: Grace was fair with blue eyes, calm and unflappable by nature; Helen was dark, with brown eyes, and prone to rapid swings in emotions. Somehow, their differences had helped to forge a strong friendship. When Grace was being too cautious, Helen would urge her on, and Grace would calm her friend down when she was being too impulsive. It worked for them and they respected each other's qualities and opinions.

'Let's talk about this tomorrow after work,' Grace said when they reached their homes.

'Good idea. See you at seven.'

* * *

Grace's parents were still up and they smiled anxiously as she walked in.

'Did you enjoy the pictures?' her father asked.

'It was good,' she lied, hoping they wouldn't ask her what it was about. 'Would you like me to make you a cup of tea?'

'No, thanks, dear. We've just had one,' her mother replied. 'We've been waiting up for you.'

'Oh, you needn't have done that.'

'We want to talk to you.' Her father's expression was serious. 'Sit down for a moment.'

She knew they were upset by Brian's death, and worried about her, so she sat down and waited.

Her father began hesitantly. 'We know it's too soon to ask you this, but we are living in dangerous times, and . . . well . . . what are you going to do now, Grace? Will you stay in your job with the lawyers?'

'I would like to, of course. I have always been so happy there. Helen and I have been talking about that, and with the way things are, we feel we really should do something worthwhile – something that will make a difference.' Her eyes brimmed with tears and she blinked to clear them away. 'Brian and all those other men must not have died for nothing.'

'Such a terrible waste of young lives and it is only just beginning.' Her mother wiped her eyes. 'We are so sorry about Brian, my dear, he was a fine boy.'

'Yes, he was. We were very fond of him. Grace is right, though; their sacrifice mustn't be in vain. Hitler is just across the Channel and we could be next on his list to conquer. It's going to be up to each one of us to pull together if we are to survive.'

Grace gave her mother an anxious look. 'Why don't you go and stay with Aunt Sybil in Wales, Mum? It might be safer than London.'

Her mother looked horrified. 'I'm not going to run away and leave you two here! Whatever is to come, we will face it together.'

'It could get rough, Jean.'

'I know that, Ted. You are doing vital work at the engineering firm, and you won't leave that. If I went away I would be worrying all the time about you and Grace. I'm not leaving!'

Ted knew his wife well enough not to keep arguing with her. Once she made her mind up, then nothing would shift her. Not even a regiment of German soldiers marching up the street.

'I'm going to make enquiries about the Women's Voluntary Service in the morning. I might be able to make myself useful with them.' Jean turned to her daughter and asked, 'What about you, dear? Lawyers are still going to be needed, so will you stay in your job?'

'I want to, of course. The problem is, I've been there since I left college, so what else could I do?'

'Your skill and experience as a personal secretary won't be ignored. Also, you do speak French, and that could be useful.'

'I don't know that my French is good enough, Dad.'

'I've heard you chatting with Helen and it sounds

pretty good to me,' he remarked, smiling with affection at his beloved daughter. 'Why don't you go and have a talk with a recruitment officer. He might be able to suggest something that will suit you.'

'I just don't know what to do,' she told her father. 'Losing Brian in this terrible way has turned my world upside down. All our plans for the future have vanished. I'm angry! I'm not sure I could stay in a comfortable job and not do something to help. Helen feels the same, and we are meeting tomorrow evening to discuss our options.'

'Don't make any hasty decisions,' her mother told her. 'Don't forget that Mr Meredith will be lost without you, and it might not be easy for him to find another secretary. I expect a lot of girls will be joining the forces now.'

'I know. He's been good to me and I wouldn't want to let him down.' She yawned and stood up. 'That's another problem for tomorrow.'

There was an atmosphere at the office when Grace arrived. They all knew that her husband had been killed in France, and had given her their support and understanding. The concern on her colleagues' faces showed that something else was happening.

There wasn't time to ask because her boss, James Meredith, called for her the moment she arrived. She collected her notebook, went to his office, and sat down, pencil poised ready to take dictation.

He didn't say anything while he studied papers on his desk, and she waited, quite used to this. James Meredith was a bright, up-and-coming lawyer, who was gaining an excellent reputation. She didn't know his age, but guessed him to be no more than thirty. When Grace had joined the firm of lawyers at the age of sixteen, she had started in the typing pool. Her efficiency with typing, shorthand, organisation skills and French had soon been noticed. James had promoted her to be his personal secretary. She loved working with him.

He pushed the papers away and sat back, a gentle smile on his face. 'Good morning, Grace. How are you feeling today?'

'I'm fine, thank you, sir,' she replied, returning his smile.

He nodded. 'You would make a good lawyer. You hide your feelings well.'

'I've had a good teacher.'

Laughter shone in his grey eyes. 'I'll take that as a compliment.'

'It was meant as one.' She watched him carefully. He usually set to work immediately, but that wasn't happening today. Something other than work was on his mind, which wasn't surprising with the country facing disaster and invasion. In the time she had worked for him, she had come to know his every mood, and she had the uncomfortable feeling that she was about to get some news. News she wasn't going to like.

'You have shown courage since the loss of your husband.' He took a deep breath before continuing. 'I regret that I am about to add to your burden. As you know, I have a private pilot's licence. The air force want pilots urgently, so I have enlisted.'

Grace wasn't surprised, but it still came as a blow. A man with his abilities would be greatly needed. Being careful not to show how upset she was, she asked calmly, 'When do you leave?'

'As soon as I've handed over my cases to Mr Palmer. I will need your help to clear my desk by lunchtime.'

'We will manage that, sir.' She pinned a smile on her face, knowing how difficult this must be for him. Everything was changing so quickly, but that was something they all had to face. The man sitting opposite her was about to turn his back on a career he had worked and studied hard for. She had always liked and respected him – now her heart went out to him – and the many others who were facing similar decisions. All plans for the future were being put aside. What the future held now was the cause of much speculation. 'What do you think will happen now?' she asked.

'Well, the Germans won't find it easy to come across the Channel, so the feeling is they will come by air first. I expect that after Dunkirk they think we are already beaten, and it won't take much to finish us off.'

'Then they are wrong!' Grace's eyes glittered with defiance. 'Many thought the war wouldn't last long, but it's going to be a long, hard struggle, isn't it?'

'I'm afraid so.' James gazed into space for a moment, and then turned his attention back to Grace. 'Peter and Fredrick are also leaving at the end of the week. The two senior partners will be the only lawyers here.'

Grace knew what this meant, without her boss putting it in to words. The senior partners both had mature, faithful secretaries. No wonder there had been an air of gloom in the main office. Many of them were not going to be needed – including her. 'Do I leave at the end of the day as well, sir?'

'Yes. I'm sorry, Grace. This has come about suddenly, and you haven't had time to give it much thought, but do you have any idea what you are going to do?'

'I would like to do something worthwhile, but if I join any of the forces I could end up in an office doing routine jobs.'

'I agree.' He handed her a sealed envelope. 'Colonel Askew is a friend of mine. I told him about you, and he'll see you tomorrow at ten o'clock at the War Office. Go and see him, Grace, and give him that envelope. You are not obliged to take any job he might offer, of course, but it would be worth your while to talk to him.'

'I will, sir. Thank you very much.' Grace stared at the envelope in her hands with the colonel's name written in James Meredith's bold hand. This was so hard. She was quite overcome by his thoughtfulness in arranging this for her.

'It was the least I could do. We've worked together for about five years now, and you've been an excellent secretary.'

'Yes, we have, and I've enjoyed every day. I'll miss you, and everyone here. This war is forcing change on all of us. It's inevitable.'

'Sadly, that's true.' James pulled the pile of paperwork towards him. 'Let's deal with this lot. I need to be out of here as soon as possible.'

Chapter Two

It was a sad end to the day for Grace. Saying goodbye to James Meredith had been awful, and there had been tears from others, who, like Grace, were no longer needed. Her life had become one heartbreak after another. Somehow she had to get through this time and move on with her life, but it was going to be so hard.

Her mother always had a cup of tea waiting for her, but the welcoming smile on her face faded when she saw her daughter. 'Oh, my dear, you don't look well.'

Grace didn't move. She had held on to her emotions all day – now the dam burst. Silent tears streamed down her face.

Without a word, her mother gathered Grace in her arms, and waited. When her daughter was more composed, she made her sit down.

'Sorry, Mum,' she said, wiping the tears away. 'But it is one blow after another at the moment.'

'You don't have to apologise. Now, tell me what has happened.'

Jean's eyes clouded with sorrow as she listened to the account of Grace's day.

'I know we've all been talking about doing something to help the war effort, but after Brian's death I was really hoping I could stay in my job. I needed the stability of familiar surroundings and people, but even that has been taken from me. That might sound selfish when so many people are suffering, but I'm lost, Mum. The foundations of the life I've built up have crumbled.'

'It's upsetting to lose your job so suddenly, but it has settled one dilemma for you.'

'Has it?'

'Yes. Last night you and Helen had been talking about what you should both do. Now you are free to make that decision.'

Grace had forgotten about the letter James Meredith had given her. She took the envelope out of her bag and stared at it, and then handed it to her mother. 'James has made an appointment for me to see Colonel Askew tomorrow and give him this letter.'

'That was kind of him and shows how much he thought of you. You are going, aren't you? It might lead to something interesting.'

'I wouldn't let James down by not keeping the appointment.' Grace gave a wan smile. 'It's time to start repairing the foundations, don't you think?'

'No. It's time to make new ones, darling,' her mother said gently.

* * *

She had been waiting for two hours. Grace glanced at the clock on the wall and stifled a sigh. The colonel must have forgotten about the appointment. This was probably a waste of time, and she was tempted to leave, but that would be rude after all the trouble James Meredith had gone to. She owed it to him to stay.

Resisting the temptation to keep looking at the clock, she studied her surroundings. There were men of various ranks and services walking through the entrance with worried expressions on their faces. This wasn't surprising considering the perilous situation the country was now in. She saw only a few women; some in uniform and some in civilian clothes. She occupied herself by studying each person as they hurried past. What were they thinking? Did the safety of Britain rest on their shoulders? If it did, then they were carrying a heavy burden.

'Mrs Lincoln, thank you for waiting. I am sorry, but I was in a meeting and couldn't get away.'

Grace, lost in her thoughts, started, and leapt to her feet. The tall man standing in front of her had dark shadows of strain under his eyes, and looked as if he hadn't slept for days. She knew he was a colonel because she had made sure she had studied the various ranks before coming for the appointment. But was this the man she had come to see?

'Colonel Askew?'

He nodded. 'Please come with me.'

He turned and marched away so quickly that Grace had to almost run a couple of steps to catch up with him. The room he took her to was littered with papers, and maps were pinned to almost every surface of the walls. Her orderly mind longed to get her hands on this mess.

'Please sit down,' he ordered, as he settled behind a large oak desk. 'I've ordered refreshments. You must be hungry after that long wait.'

'Thank you, sir.' She took the letter out of her handbag and handed it across the desk. 'James Meredith asked me to give you this.'

He slit open the envelope and began reading. She could see immediately that it was not the short introduction she had expected it to be. There were three pages in James's distinctive handwriting.

The colonel read it through twice before looking up. 'James thinks highly of you, Mrs Lincoln. He stresses that you are discreet and do not gossip. Is that so?'

'I have never talked to anyone about the cases Mr Meredith has been working on.'

He nodded. 'Was your husband killed on the beaches at Dunkirk?'

Grace was taken aback by this question. What on earth had that to do with an interview for a job? As much as she objected to being asked this, she had to answer him. 'No, sir. I understand he was killed near Dunkirk. He never made it to the beaches.'

He nodded. 'I was there. It wasn't pleasant.'

Ah, so that was why he wanted to know. She clenched her hands together, wishing he would change the subject. It tore her apart to talk about it, but she wasn't going to let him see that. 'I don't suppose it was, sir.'

He was watching her intently, and when she held his gaze without wavering, he gave that nod again. She was wishing she hadn't come.

'We won't need to test your typing and shorthand skills. I can take James's word that they are excellent. Everything that goes on in this building is highly confidential. If you worked here you would have to sign the Official Secrets Act. Would you be prepared to do that?'

'Yes, sir, but I would have to know what the job is before signing anything.'

Hc picked up the telephone, dialled a number, and waited. 'Dan, come to my office at once. Leave what you're doing. I could have the answer to your problem.'

The door opened as he put the phone down, and a young soldier wheeled in a trolley. 'Refreshments for three – as ordered, sir.'

'Thank you, Corporal.'

The soldier spun smartly round and left, leaving the door open for someone to enter.

'Ah, Dan, good. This is Mrs Grace Lincoln. She comes highly recommended. Mrs Lincoln, this is Major Daniel Chester.'

Grace had risen to her feet the moment he had walked into the room and, while studying him, shook hands. He appeared to be even more exhausted than the colonel.

'Sit down, Dan, before you fall down!' the colonel ordered sharply. 'You should have taken a couple more days' leave.'

Major Chester pulled up a chair and eased himself into it, giving the colonel a disbelieving look.

'I know, I know. There isn't time for such luxuries.'

While the officers were talking, Grace poured the tea and handed round the sandwiches; then she sat down again, taking a cheese sandwich for herself.

'Thank you, Grace.' The colonel smiled for the first time. 'We may call you by your Christian name?'

'Yes, sir.' This was turning out to be a strange interview, but she was now feeling a glimmer of interest in what they might be about to offer. These men were exhausted, and obviously loaded with cares and responsibilities. If she could help them, then it could be a worthwhile job.

'We will take a short break for lunch,' Colonel Askew told them.

Major Chester eased his long legs out, grimacing slightly.

'That leg still giving you trouble, Dan?'

'It's nothing. I've been sitting too long.'

Grace refilled their cups and handed round more sandwiches.

The major smiled his thanks, and she was struck by the transformation. He was a handsome man, and younger than she had first thought. He had the bluest eyes she had ever seen, and strands of his black hair had a tendency to fall over his forehead, even though it was cut short.

'Read this.' The colonel handed him the letter, and then turned his attention back to Grace. 'Did you enjoy working for James?'

'Very much, sir,' she replied. 'I was sad to have to leave.'

'No doubt. I tried to talk him out of becoming a pilot, but was unable to do so. His mind was made up, and is well aware what he's letting himself in for. Good pilot, though, and men like him are badly needed.'

'I'm sure they are,' Grace agreed. 'He was also an exceptional lawyer, and it couldn't have been an easy decision to turn his back on a career he has studied and worked so hard for.'

Major Chester folded the letter and placed it on the desk. He looked at the colonel and nodded.

'Good,' the colonel said in reply to the silent agreement. 'Now, all we have to do is persuade Grace that you need her help.'

A wry smile crossed Daniel Chester's face when he turned to Grace. 'Would the word "desperate" do the trick?'

She couldn't help returning his smile. 'What would the desperate help entail?'

'Look after me. Organise the office, protect me from unnecessary interruptions and stay by my side. Where I go, you go. In fact, be my right-hand man. The hours will be long and unpredictable. You will get little time off, and could be away from home for long periods at a time.'

There was silence when he stopped speaking, and Grace had to resist the temptation to burst out laughing. As a job description, that was enough to put anyone off. She managed to keep a serious expression, before she said, 'When would you like me to start?'

'Right now.' Daniel was on his feet. 'Can you do that?'

'There isn't anything else I need to do today.'

The smile was back, and Grace decided it suited him. If she could help him get rid of that haunted look in his eyes, then it would be an achievement. In fact, if she could help any of these men, then that would give her a lot of satisfaction.

Dan turned to the colonel. 'Thank you, George.'

'How the hell did you do that?' he asked, amusement written all over his face. 'After that run-down of the job, I expected Grace to refuse.'

'The letter James sent you convinced me she wouldn't, and it was no good glossing over her duties. I wouldn't have been able to keep her once she found out what a tough job it was.'

The colonel nodded, serious now. 'Don't let her near anything confidential today. You know there is a procedure to go through first. You are breaking all the rules.'

'I know, and I'll see to it straight away.'

'And don't stay here all night. For heaven's sake get some rest!'

'I will.'

Colonel Askew sighed wearily. 'I've heard that before. I'm handing him over to you now, Grace. After what he's been through he needs time to recover completely. Make him stop driving himself. I don't care how you do it!'

'You're a fine one to talk, George. And stop telling my secretary what to do. Don't take any notice of him, Grace. He worries too much. Come on. I'll show you the office. That's if I can find it under all the paperwork.'

'I am your uncle, Dan. I'm entitled to worry.' The colonel smiled and held out his hand to Grace. 'Thank you for coming, and being so patient with us.'

'It has been – interesting – sir.'

'Hah! That's a polite way of putting it. I'll tell James you are going to risk working for us. Good luck.'

Dan ushered her out of the room, and as they walked along, he said, 'You haven't asked what the salary is.'

'I don't care,' she admitted honestly. 'As long as I have enough to live on, then that's all I need.'

'Oh, I'll see you have more than that. The work you will be doing will be highly confidential, and your background will be examined very carefully. I don't see any problem with that, though, because the letter James supplied was very detailed. I'll see everything is rushed through.' He glanced down at her as he opened a door for her. 'Here we are. See what you can do with this lot. There's a private washroom through that other door.'

Grace stood just inside the room and gazed around. There were files and rolled up maps everywhere – on chairs, window sills, the floor and even some papers balanced precariously on a three-dimensional globe. She had never seen such a mess!

'How do you find anything?' she asked.

'I don't. I only arrived yesterday and was given this room. This is how the previous occupant left it.'

'Why don't they make him sort it out?'

'Not possible, I'm afraid.'

She knew at once what that meant by the tone of his voice, and didn't pursue the subject. 'Then I had better make a start.'

'Thanks. I'll leave you to it while I go and get you established as a member of staff, or they won't let you in tomorrow.'

'Before you go, do you need to keep anything here? Can I bundle it up and have it moved to a basement, or wherever they keep paperwork they no longer need?'

'I'd better have a look at it first. It would be helpful if you could get it in some kind of order, so I can look through it quickly. I've never had a desk job before, and I'm going to need you to steer me through the next few weeks.'

'I'll do that, sir. You'll soon settle in.'

He grimaced. 'This isn't what I joined the army for, but it seems I have certain knowledge and skills they need at the moment. You'll be all right for a while?'

'Yes, sir.'

With a nod of satisfaction, he left.

Grace removed her jacket, rolled up her sleeves, and made straight for the two large filing cabinets right by the door. They would have to be moved further along as they were causing an obstruction. They were empty, except for an old whisky bottle and two glasses. At least she didn't have to clear them out. She opened the door and looked into the corridor. A sergeant, who appeared to be strong enough to move heavy objects, was walking by.

She called to him, smiling brightly. 'I'm sorry to bother you, Sergeant, but could you move two cabinets for me?'

'Certainly – where would you like them?'

The job was done in no time at all, and she set to work.

It was nearly three hours before the major returned, and by that time everything was neat and in date order. The bottle was in the wastepaper basket, and the glasses washed until they gleamed.

When Dan walked in, he just stood there in astonishment. 'What a transformation. You've worked wonders in such a short time!'

'Everything is sorted and in the filing cabinets. Would you like a cup of tea? I've managed to scrounge a kettle and china.'

He grinned when he saw the tray containing a tea pot, fine china, and even a plate of biscuits. 'Where did you get all that?'

'I explained what I needed to a nice female officer, and she arranged it for me.'

'Who was she?'

'I don't know, sir. She happened to be walking by.'

'I have a feeling we are going to get along quite well,' he said as he sat behind the desk, now cleared of clutter. 'I'd love a cup of tea. I've spent the last couple of hours throwing orders around, and even had to get the colonel's help. But, between us, we've managed to get you a temporary pass. The permanent one will take a few days.'

'Thank you, sir.' Grace handed him the tea, and then picked up the pass. 'Is there anything else I can do for you today?'

'No, thank you.' He sipped his tea and laid his head

against the high-backed chair. In an instant he was asleep.

Grace tiptoed to the door and locked it to stop anyone disturbing him. She removed her shoes and moved around quietly to finish some more jobs. She would stay until he woke up.

Chapter Three

'I'm wasting my breath telling you to take it easy, aren't I?' The colonel marched in, and then stopped in astonishment. 'My word, what a difference! Did that young girl do all this today?'

Dan nodded. 'And without any help from me. I'm impressed.'

George sat down. 'I only saw her because James pleaded with me to find her a job here. I had only intended to tell her I would see what I could do, and leave it at that. There was something about her, though, and after reading James's letter, I thought of you. You need help, and it looks as if she might be as efficient as James said.'

'Quite possible, but only time will tell.' Dan stood up and gazed out of the window, and then turned sharply. 'What the blazes am I doing here, Uncle? Was this also your doing?'

'As a matter of fact, it wasn't. You were called on for your knowledge of France and Germany, and for your experience of being in the front line. Don't fight against it. You are not fit for active duty.'

'As soon as I am, I'm out of here! I'm not spending this war sitting on my backside listening to a load of bureaucrats who don't know what the hell they're talking about.'

'That's harsh, and not true about everyone.'

'Sorry. I didn't mean it like that. What I'm trying to say is that we've got to learn from the past, and do things differently. The old ways and battle strategies won't work now.'

'I agree, and that's why you're here. We've got to change our ideas – and fast. We've both got battle experience and can, hopefully, be of some help.' George stood up. 'Come on. I'll buy you a pint.'

The pub was crowded, but they managed to find a quiet corner in the saloon bar.

'Are you still having nightmares?' George asked, once settled with pints in front of them.

'Not as bad, or so often. They will eventually go, I suppose. Time heals everything, they say.'

'I've read the report of your experiences, of course, but you've never talked about it. It might help if you did.'

Dan drank half of the pint in one go, put the glass down, and then said, 'Our orders were to secure a certain village, and the intelligence we received was way off. We walked into an ambush. There were a dozen of us – five of us were captured. They were a nasty lot. They didn't want to stop their advance and be bothered with prisoners.

They lined us up, and I knew what they were going to do. There was a forest area nearby, but an open field to cross before reaching it. I figured there was nothing to lose, so I sent a message along the line to make a run for it, and we took off. We heard machine-gun fire, then rifles, as a couple of Germans chased after us. I took a bullet in the leg, but it wasn't enough to stop me. Fortunately, they didn't continue the pursuit. Too eager to push on, I expect. We hid in the forest for a couple of hours, and one of the men bound my leg to stop the bleeding. We made our way to the coast, and ended up at Dunkirk. You know what that was like; you were there.'

George nodded. 'And you don't know what happened to the other prisoners?'

'We didn't stop to look. The corporal who came with us was upset, and convinced his comrades had been shot. I don't know for sure, though.'

'You saved your men by your quick thinking. It was up to the others to follow you, or stay. Only one did. It was their choice, Dan. You couldn't have done more.'

'Maybe, but it still haunts me. There should have been something I could have done.'

'At least you all got back safely.'

'I made damned sure they did! We had spent days together, walking when it was safe, and hiding when necessary.'

'A journey like that didn't do your leg any good.'

Dan drained his glass. 'They could have travelled faster by themselves. I tried – no, ordered them to leave me – but they refused.'

'Good men.'

'Yes. I was relieved to get them on one of those boats.'

'When I arrived back I stayed dockside, praying you were on one of them. I didn't recognise you at first. You looked in bad shape. I didn't know how you were still standing.'

'You didn't look too good yourself.'

'True, but we both made it, which is more than many other poor devils.'

'Like Grace Lincoln's husband. That girl is wise beyond her years. Do you know what she did today?'

The colonel shook his head, relieved he had been able to get his nephew talking about his experiences.

'When I finally got back to the office, she made me a cup of tea – and I fell asleep. It was about seven when I woke up, and she was still there. I had been having a bad dream again and the sweat was pouring off me. Without commenting, she poured me a small brandy, and waited while I drank it. Then she calmly washed up the glass and asked if there was anything else she could do for me before she left. I said that would be all for today. I asked her where on earth she had got the small bottle of brandy from. She smiled and said a sergeant had got it for her.' Dan laughed. 'She's very enterprising.'

'We must thank James for sending her to us when we see him.'

'He loves flying, but I wish he hadn't enlisted as a pilot. I hope he's going to be all right.'

'I hope we are all going to survive this war,' the colonel added.

'Amen, to that!' Dan stood up. 'Want another pint?'

'Might as well.'

By the time Grace and Helen got together that evening, it was too late to go anywhere. It was a pleasant evening, though, so they decided to head for a nearby park. There were quite a few people around, but they managed to find a seat to themselves.

'You were late arriving home, Grace. I'm itching to know what you've been doing.'

'I've had a very odd day,' she said, shaking her head.

Helen laughed. 'So have I. Tell me about yours first.'

'Well, I kept the appointment James Meredith made for me with a Colonel Askew. It turned out that James is his godson, and the major I met is the colonel's nephew. I can tell you that at one point I was wishing I hadn't gone to the meeting.'

'You obviously changed your mind. Go on. I'm intrigued.'

Grace then gave her friend a detailed account of her day.

'My word!' Helen exclaimed. 'What have you let yourself in for?'

'I haven't the faintest idea, but I couldn't turn Major Chester down. The man is not fit and needs help.'

'And they were both at Dunkirk.'

'That too.' Grace sighed sadly. 'Anyway, I'm committed now. I just hope I've done the right thing. Now, how did you get on?'

'I went to a recruitment place in the morning to see

what my options were if I joined one of the services. The officer I saw seemed to want my life history, and I couldn't see what most of the things he asked me had to do with joining the forces. Then, he suddenly switched to French. I was surprised, but it didn't faze me. You know I'm used to speaking both languages.'

'I thought they'd pick up on that,' Grace said. 'What happened then?'

'We chatted for a while, and then he stood up and marched out of the room. I was perplexed, and was wondering if I should leave when he returned with a corporal. He said this was his driver, and he would take me to see someone else. When I asked where we were going, he merely said it was only a short distance.'

'How odd!'

'It certainly was. And it got even more peculiar. The driver never said a word to me, and when we stopped he held open the car door, and told me to follow him. We went inside and he said something to the receptionist, who told me to take a seat, and someone would come for me in a moment.'

'Where were you?'

'Same as you. The War Office. Anyway, a soldier soon came for me, and I was taken to a room and left there.' Helen laughed. 'I was beginning to feel like a criminal under arrest. I was considering making a run for it, when a major came in. The questions started again, but in French all the time. We had tea and biscuits, and it was all very friendly. He asked me if I spoke any other languages, and when I said no, he smiled and told me I would soon learn, if necessary. I was there for about two hours, and he finally told me not to join any of the services or take on any other kind of work. I would hear from them soon with instructions of where to go. When I asked what the job would be, he just smiled again and said it would all be explained later. My fluency with French was greatly needed.'

'What are you going to do?'

Helen shrugged. 'Wait and see what happens. I had the feeling I was being given orders which had to be obeyed.'

'Well!' Grace said, shaking her head. 'We have both taken on jobs without knowing what on earth they entail.'

'Looks that way.'

Sleep was illusive, and after tossing and turning for ages, Grace got up, walked over to the window and gazed out. How strange it was without street lighting. The blackout was strictly enforced with wardens checking constantly. The events of the day were churning through her mind, making rest impossible. She had agreed to work for Major Chester without knowing what her duties would be. That had been silly and impulsive, going completely against her normal character. She never made hasty decisions! Brian had had to wait some time before she finally agreed to marry him.

Her sigh was ragged as the pain of loss lanced through her again. Everyone told her it would get easier with time. At the moment, that was hard to believe. She constantly told herself there were so many feeling like this, but that only made the sadness more intense. One of those suffering was clearly Daniel Chester. He had been injured in France, but something else had happened, and it was tormenting him. She had watched him sleeping, peacefully at first, and then the dreams came. It had appeared to be a mixture of anger, regret and deep sorrow but, she suspected, mostly anger. That was probably why he resented being taken off active duty. If her instincts were correct, he wanted revenge.

What a mess everything was. He'd said he needed looking after, and seeing his troubles, she knew that was true. Well, that was what she had been trained for.

Grace got back into bed. Her day had been peculiar enough, but what about Helen? After two long interviews, they had told her to wait, saying only that they would be in touch. There hadn't been the slightest indication what they wanted her for. It was all very worrying.

Stop this, she told herself sternly. The only thing either of them could do was take each day as it came, and see what happened. Sleep was needed if she was going to cope with tomorrow.

Chapter Four

'Can I help you, sir?'

Dan tore his gaze away from the assault course, and turned his head. 'You're about early, Sergeant . . . ?'

'Dickins. I saw you arrive and head this way, sir. I hadn't seen you before, so I followed to see if you needed any help. I'm the drill sergeant.'

'I was stationed here and did my training on this course.'

'I see, sir.' The sergeant studied the tall man beside him. 'I see you're wearing fatigues. Were you thinking of having a go at it again?'

'That was my idea. It's changed since I was last here. Can you take me over it?'

'How bad is the injury to your leg, sir? You were limping as you walked here.'

'Very observant of you. It isn't much, and is healed now.'

'I'm sure it is, but this is a tough course now, sir, and I wouldn't advise you dashing over it before you have the medical officer take a look at you.'

Dan turned back to the course and swore fluently under his breath. The man was talking sense, of course, but he wanted to return to active duty so bad it hurt.

'Can I have your name, sir?'

'Major Chester.'

Sergeant Dickins came to attention and saluted smartly. 'I've heard of you, Major. A corporal, Bob Higgins, came through here and said your quick thinking had saved his life in France.'

'Is he still here?'

'He was moved to another regiment last week. How can I help you, sir?'

'I need to get fit for active duty again.'

'Understood. You are going to do more harm than good if you don't go about it in the right way. Come with me and see the MO. If your leg is strong enough, I will personally see you get fit again. I'll arrange your training sessions to suit you.'

'It will have to be about this time in the mornings.'

'I'm an early riser. I can take you to the MO immediately, sir.'

'I appreciate your help, sergeant.'

Dan smiled when he saw the medical officer. 'Hello, Steve, you still here?'

The officer spun round. 'Dan! It's good to see you. Are you stationed here again?'

'I'm afraid not. Sergeant Dickins caught me about to

have a go at the assault course, and insisted I come and see you first.'

The MO raised his hands in exasperation. 'I heard about your exploits in France. You were badly injured, Dan. Good Lord, you haven't changed, have you?' He turned to the sergeant, who was watching with interest. 'He would never expect his men to do anything he couldn't do himself.'

'So I've heard, sir. I've promised to help the major get fit again, but I need you to have a look at him. Once I have your assessment of his condition, I will be able to work out a programme of exercises.'

'You've taken on quite a task, sergeant. I know Major Chester, and he's as stubborn as a mule.'

'Don't exaggerate, Steve. Are you going to examine me, or shall I just take my chance and have a go at the course?'

'You do that and you'll put yourself back in the hospital.'

Dan began to unbutton his shirt. 'Get on with it, Doc. They've given me a bloody desk job, and I'm not going to put up with that!'

'They've stuck *you* behind a desk?' Steve burst out laughing. 'Good grief, man, don't they know your reputation? Where is this desk?'

'The War Office.'

'Oh, my!' Steve was doubled over with laughter. 'That's priceless! Have you been to any meetings yet?'

Dan smirked. 'I've got my first one today. They are under the impression that I will be useful.'

'Well, I'm sure you will be . . . after you've banged

37

a few heads together.' Steve managed to control his amusement. 'Get stripped off. Let's hope you're strong enough for Sergeant Dickins to work you to exhaustion. The people at the War Office don't know what's about to hit them.'

'The colonel will be there as well.'

Both men looked at each and burst out laughing.

'Oh, oh! I would love to be a fly on the wall.' The MO shook his head, instantly serious as he began his examination.

It was nearly ten o'clock when Dan walked into the office. 'Good morning, Grace.'

'Good morning, sir.' He looked different today, more relaxed, and almost buoyant, she thought as soon as she saw him. The irritation of the day before had disappeared. Perhaps he had slept well for a change.

She handed him the morning post. 'I didn't open anything in case it was something I shouldn't see.'

He nodded and eased himself into the chair. Ignoring the letters, he picked up a folder from his desk, read the contents, and then passed them over to her. 'Sign those.'

Grace controlled a smile. That was an order, not a request, but she would have to get used to that. She was working for an army officer now, not James Meredith. Sadness for all she had lost over the last few weeks tried to engulf her, but she pushed it away ruthlessly. This was no time for self-pity.

She sat down and began to read through the forms.

'Sign them. You don't have to read every word.'

The irritation was back. 'Yes, I do, sir. Mr Meredith taught me not to sign anything without reading every word – including the small print.'

'James was always meticulous. That's what made him a good lawyer, and a safe pilot.'

'I pray he stays safe.' She looked down so he couldn't see the distress in her eyes, but he was very observant.

'You don't want to be here, do you?' he said gently.

She looked up then. 'Do any of us, sir?'

Without answering, he stood up and flexed his leg, before walking over to the window. 'I haven't any choice. Orders have to be obeyed, but you were under no such constraints. Why did you take this job? I want an honest reply, Grace.'

'I came only because James had arranged the interview for me – and I stayed because you needed help.'

Dan studied her intently. 'As simple as that?'

She nodded. 'I made my decision, and it might not have been the right one, but I'll work hard and faithfully for you.'

'I don't doubt that, and just so we understand each other, I'll be straight with you. The job might not last long because I intend to return to my regiment at the earliest opportunity.'

'I am aware of that, but all any of us can do is to take each day as it comes. We don't know what is going to happen. Hitler is only the other side of the Channel, so that is all we can do. My mother always tells us not to try and cross our bridges before we get to them.' Grace smiled. 'She has a saying for everything.'

'Sound advice, and something I should try to keep in mind.' He smiled wryly. 'All right, Grace. Let's deal with this day, and let tomorrow take care of itself, shall we?'

'An excellent idea, sir.' She handed him the signed documents.

He checked they were correct, and then said, 'Put the kettle on while I take these to the appropriate department. I won't be long.'

It only took him five minutes. 'Do you have any biscuits?' he asked, the moment he walked back in the room. 'I'm ravenous.'

'Yes, I got some from the catering manager this morning.'

She poured the tea and piled a plate with biscuits. 'Didn't you have any breakfast?'

He nodded, munching away. 'That was a long time ago.'

The door opened and the colonel swept in. 'Ah, good. I'm just in time.'

Grace poured another cup of tea for the officer.

He smiled at her, sat down and took a biscuit from the plate. 'Thanks. Dan, I popped in to see if you're ready for that meeting this afternoon? We'd better decide on our strategy.'

'I know mine already. I'm going to speak my mind.'

'So am I. But let's try not to lose our tempers, eh?'

'Don't worry, Uncle. I won't say a word out of place.'

The colonel studied his nephew with suspicion. 'What have you been up to?'

Dan laughed softly, winked at Grace, and held out his cup for a refill.

She refilled all their cups, and put the kettle on to make a fresh pot. This job had been taken in haste, without proper thought, and she had been very doubtful about it, but she was beginning to like these two men. They were both strong, determined and fighters. Just the kind this country would need in the months or years to come.

'Grace has signed all the necessary papers now, so I'm bringing her to the meeting.'

'They'll have their own recorder and might not allow her to stay,' the colonel pointed out.

Dan raised his eyebrows. 'Then I don't stay.'

'I thought you weren't going to make trouble.'

'George, I didn't ask to come here. If I'm to be of any help—'

'I know.' George held up his hand to stop Dan. 'They'll take you as you are – a man who knows what he's talking about, and a bloody fine soldier. But you're a maverick. How on earth did you manage to get a promotion?'

Dan shrugged. 'Don't ask me. I didn't ask for that either.'

'No, you didn't have to. You're a natural leader of men, and I expect that's what they recognised.'

'Well, I haven't got any bloody men to lead now, have I?'

'You will have again before this damned war is over.' The colonel turned to Grace. 'Excuse the language. Will you be embarrassed if there is an argument about you being at the meeting?'

'Not at all, sir. I am Major Chester's personal secretary. If he wants me to take notes at this meeting, then that is what I will do.'

'Right. I'll want a copy as well, Dan. They'll probably want an account of what happened in France, and how a disaster like that can be avoided in the future.'

Grace listened to the two officers, making a mental note of what they were saying. Her Brian had been out there and, in a way, it was comforting to know what he'd had to go through. She had no doubt that he had been as courageous as the two men with her. One thing was certain, though, this job wasn't going to be dull.

Time for the meeting arrived, and Grace walked into the conference room. It was dominated by a huge table, and seated around it were some twenty men, she quickly assessed. Some were in civilian suits, but the majority were high-ranking officers, representing all the services.

The colonel and the major appeared to know quite a few of them, and Grace stood slightly behind them while they were introduced to everyone else.

'Please take your seats, gentlemen,' the man at the head of the table said. 'We are pleased you have been able to join us. Your experiences in the field will be a great help.'

The colonel sat down while Dan found Grace a chair in the corner of the room.

'Major Chester, the young lady will not be allowed to stay.'

'Mrs Lincoln is my personal aide who has full clearance to handle secret information. She will be making notes for my future reference.' He then walked calmly to his place at the table.

Grace stayed where she was, aware that every eye in the room was focused on her. She flipped open her notebook, and waited, pen poised. No more was said and, as the meeting began, she was impressed. He had won that round without even raising his voice.

From then on the meeting took her whole concentration. Her instructions were to make a note of only the relevant points, and to cut out all the unnecessary chatter and arguments. Some of the things she heard shocked her, as the full import of the perilous situation the country was in became clear. Not only had precious men been lost at Dunkirk, but a huge amount of military equipment had been left behind. There was now a desperate need to rebuild and re-equip the army, as well as building up defences against anticipated attack.

After two hours, the chairman said, 'That will be all for this meeting. Thank you all for your contributions. There is no doubt that we need time, but will we be given the necessary breathing space? That is something we don't know, so we must act quickly.'

Grace remained where she was while the men began to file out of the room.

'Major Chester.' The chairman stopped him. 'You were an asset today. Your suggestions were sound, based on first-hand experience. I would like to have a copy of the notes when your . . . aide, has them ready.'

'You shall have them, sir.'

The chairman nodded, and then smiled. 'By the way,

it would be more appropriate if your secretary was in uniform.'

Grace followed the major out, wondering what he would say about that last remark. But he said nothing, and the subject wasn't mentioned for the rest of the day.

Chapter Five

'How did your day go?' Helen asked Grace when they met that evening.

'It wasn't any different from working for the lawyers. I sat in on a meeting, took notes and then typed them up. I made tea, ran errands, and looked after the major.'

'What's he like?'

'I haven't quite worked him out yet. He's a complicated man. I don't suppose you've heard anything yet, have you?' she asked, changing the subject.

'No. I'll give them a couple of weeks. If I haven't received a letter by then I think I'll join up.'

'Which one of the services do you fancy?'

'I don't mind. I'll go and have a talk to the recruitment officer again. Wish we could join up together, but I suppose you're stuck with that job.'

Grace nodded. 'I couldn't walk out now, especially after

all the trouble James took to get me in at the War Office.'

'No, of course not.' Helen sighed. 'We were always so sure of the direction our lives would take, but suddenly everything has been thrown into confusion. Ah, well, there isn't anything we can do about it tonight. What do you want to do? Go to the pictures?'

'Not really. I've had quite a hectic day. How about coming to my room? We can play records, chat and relax.'

'Perfect.'

The colonel finished reading the notes of the meeting, and then looked at Dan. 'She's good, isn't she? No wonder James thought so highly of her.'

'It's more than that. I have the feeling he sent her to us to take care of. Is he in love with her?'

'No, he's been going steady with Janet for a couple of years now, but he's been working with Grace for some time and he probably feels protective towards her. And, he wouldn't have sent anyone to us if they weren't efficient.'

'True. She's got a calm, quiet air about her, and isn't easily frightened. Did you notice that she didn't appear at all perturbed when the chairman said she couldn't stay?' Dan laughed softly. 'Her expression was composed when she flipped open her notebook. Without saying a word, she had made it clear to everyone in the room that she was staying.'

'I did, and so did everyone else. I believe that was why there was no further argument.' George finished his drink and put the glass on Dan's desk. 'She's still suffering from the death of her husband. It shows in her eyes in unguarded moments, but under that calm exterior, there's a fighter.'

'I've noticed. The chairman suggested it would be more appropriate to have her with me if she was in uniform. I don't know why he suggested that. There are plenty of civilians here, and if she joins one of the services we would never see her again. James would be furious with us!'

'Almost certainly. He can really let rip when he feels the need.' George pursed his lips. 'There might be a way to get her into uniform without losing her.'

'How?'

'The organisation called the FANY – the First Aid Nursing Yeomanry – have a women's transport service. With your injuries you could claim the need for a driver.'

'Hmm.' Dan thought the idea over, and then shook his head. 'Grace would have to volunteer for the FANY, and I'm sure she would if we asked her to. She would have to go away for training, though, and there's always the risk she wouldn't be assigned back here.'

'That is always possible, of course. I could ask James what he thought about the idea. We can make all sorts of plans, of course, but the final decision would be up to Grace. If we start trying to arrange her life for her, she would have every right to tell us what to do with the job. And I've no doubt she would do just that. She can walk out of here any time she wants to.' He looked at his nephew with an amused glint in his eyes. 'James wasn't too pleased when I told him she was working for you.'

'Oh, why?' Dan asked, innocently.

'He said you were too volatile for Grace.'

'Volatile? Where on earth did he get that idea from?'

'I wonder?' They both burst into laughter.

'You two are trying to make me into some kind of monster. You can tell James that I've calmed down since we were children. No, don't bother – I'll tell him myself!'

'You've learnt a few lessons since you were young boys, but your strong character can still overwhelm some people. There is also an added edge to you since your experiences in France. You are angry, Dan. You must deal with that or it will cloud your judgement.'

'Of course I'm angry, George! I lost too many of my men out there, and that doesn't sit well with me. I've got to get back on active duty again. I'm wasting my time here.'

'I know how you feel, but you need the breathing space to regain your full health and strength. You are still mentally fighting the enemy, so sort yourself out, and quickly. We've got a hard struggle ahead of us, and we need men like you in the field.'

Dan's expression became serious. 'We are also going to need good pilots in the near future, if my hunch is right. I wish James hadn't joined the RAF. I hope he's going to be all right. Grace told me her mother is always saying that we should take each day as it comes and not try to cross our bridges until we get to them. It's hard to do that. I don't know how to stand on the sidelines and see what happens.'

'None of us know exactly what Hitler is going to do. There's no doubt that he will be making plans to invade. When and how, we don't know yet. All we can do is strengthen our defences, and wait for him to make his move.'

'My role here is purely advisory, so I'm going to need to keep busy. I've found a friendly sergeant who is going to knock me into shape. Did you know Steve Edwards is still MO at Bordon?'

'No, I didn't. You've been down there, then?'

Dan nodded. 'I was having a look at the assault course.'

'Just looking?'

'There wasn't anyone around and I was tempted to have a go. Sergeant Dickins arrived and suggested I see the MO first.'

'So, how fit are you?'

'Quite good. With the sergeant's help, I'll be out of here in three months. I'll be going down to Hampshire three times a week, so I'll take Grace with me. I've arranged for her to have driving lessons while I'm working out.' A slow smile spread across Dan's face. 'I thought she might also like to have a go at the assault course with me.'

'Don't you dare! Teaching her to drive is good, but you leave it at that!'

'You know that's the wrong thing to say to me, Uncle.'

'The sooner you get back to your regiment, the better, Dan. You're a menace with time on your hands.' George stood up. 'Come on. You can buy me a drink.'

Major Chester was already in the office when Grace arrived at eight o'clock the next day.

'Ah, good, you're early.' He glanced down at her shoes. 'Can you walk over rough ground in those?'

'Yes, sir. They've only got a low heel, and are very comfortable.'

'Come on, then. We're going out for the day. Bring your pad. We will need a record.'

The car was waiting outside, and she got into the passenger door Dan was holding open. He slipped into the driver's seat, and Grace was surprised. Considering he had an injury to his leg she had expected him to have an official driver. He hadn't said where they were going, and she didn't ask. The major would tell her when he was ready.

She relaxed and watched the passing scenery. They were heading out of London, but as the signposts had been removed in case of invasion, she had no idea where they were heading.

They had been driving for over an hour before he spoke. 'We'll soon be at Dover. I'll tell you when I want something recorded.'

'Yes, sir.'

He glanced sideways at her. 'It will be a long and busy day. When we get back to the office, I will need the notes typed up today.'

'Understood, sir. My parents know this isn't a nine-to-five job. Oh, there's the sea!' she exclaimed.

He stopped the car so she could have a look at the view. She tried to image it crowded with landing craft. 'German losses will be enormous if they try to cross the Channel.'

Dan nodded. 'That's why I believe they will have to knock out our air force and defences first. But we've got to be prepared for anything. If they had invaded soon after Dunkirk, they would have had a better chance. For some reason Hitler didn't do that. He's given us time to rally ourselves after our losses, and that was a big mistake on his part. Now, we must get on. Do you see that castle over there?'

Grace nodded.

'That's where we are going.'

Over the next week, Grace was busy until late in the evenings. By the time she arrived home it was too late to see Helen, and all she wanted to do was have a bath and fall into bed. Major Chester attacked the inspection tour he was on as if he was going into battle. He was a power house; never flagging, even though his limp was more pronounced by the end of the day.

Grace took to wearing skirts with plenty of room in them, and flat shoes. She was determined to stay with him, no matter what the conditions were – and some were pretty rugged. He never had to wait for her as he strode around. She made sure she was always just a step behind him on his right-hand side. After the first two days he didn't even bother to look round, but gave his instructions, knowing she was there.

After a week she was fitter than she had ever been, and loved every minute of it. They would arrive back at the office around seven every evening, dusty, often dirty, and ravenous. The major would order food, and while eating, Grace would type the notes for the day. These were then distributed to the required people. Only then was the day finished.

The last day of the assignment the major was to act as advisor and observer for the Local Defence Volunteers manoeuvres. Before setting out he had made her change

51

into ATS slacks and jacket. It turned out to be a wise move. They had tramped through fields, muddy from overnight rain, hid in barns, and even jumped into a ditch to keep out of sight. It was the most fun she had ever had.

They were given strange looks when they arrived back at the War Office that evening.

'Good Lord!' George exclaimed when he met them heading for the office. 'What have you two been up to? You're covered in mud.'

Grace laughed. 'We've been on manoeuvres with the Local Defence Volunteers, sir.'

'Really Dan! Couldn't you have found Grace a nice, clean observation post?'

Dan looked at her, his eyes glinting with amusement. 'Would you have preferred that?'

'Oh no, sir. I couldn't have done my job – and I enjoyed it. In fact, I've loved the whole trip.'

'There you are, George. We've had a great time.'

George eyed them up and down again and shook his head. 'I give up! Just wait until I tell James what you are making his secretary do. And he thought she would be safe with us.' He began to walk away, calling over his shoulder, 'He wants her back when this blasted war is over – in one piece!'

They were both laughing as they reached their office.

'Put the kettle on, Grace, while I order in some sandwiches. It's going to be a very late night, I'm afraid.'

The report was long and detailed. As each page was finished, Dan checked through it, making changes here and there, and handing it back to Grace for re-typing. When the final draft was accepted, she prepared the documents for distribution.

'I don't know how I would have managed without you this week.' He stretched out his long legs and relaxed. 'I would have had to make my own notes, and then found someone to type them for me. You've done an excellent job. Thank you.'

'I've enjoyed the challenge, sir.'

'I do believe you have. It's very late, so I'll drive you home. Do you want to change first?'

She looked down at the filthy fatigues she was wearing, and shook her head. 'I'm too dirty to put on clean clothes. I'll stay as I am, and wash these before returning them to you.'

'Keep them.' He grinned. 'They suit you – and so does the mud! You might need them again, anyway. Come on, let's get you home.'

The moment the car stopped outside her house, her father appeared holding a dimmed torch.

Dan was immediately out of the car and holding the door open for Grace. 'I apologise for keeping your daughter so late, sir.'

'No need to apologise.' Grace's father peered at the tall man. 'Are you Major Chester?'

'Yes, sir.'

'Ah, it's good to meet you. Come in for a moment and have a drink with us. My wife would like to meet you.'

'That's kind of you, but I haven't cleaned up after a day tramping through fields.'

'Don't worry about that. You look fine.'

Dan laughed. 'How can you tell, sir? It's dark out here.'

Jean called from the door. 'Tell them to come in, Ted. I've saved dinner, and there's enough for two.'

Grace knew her parents were very curious about the officer she was working for, but the major probably didn't feel like being sociable after the week he'd had – especially at this time of night.

'I'm sorry, sir,' she whispered. 'They are itching to meet you. I'll tell them you have another appointment.'

He touched her arm, and she could just make out a slight shake of his head.

'Well, if you don't mind me trailing mud through your house, then I would enjoy a home-cooked meal for a change. We have been surviving on sandwiches.'

'Good, good. In you come then.'

Ted ushered them straight into the kitchen, where Jean was already busy at the stove. She turned and smiled as soon as they walked in and shook hands with Dan.

'It's good to meet you, Major Chester. I'm Jean and my husband is Ted. Do sit down. It's only stew and dumplings, but it's tasty and filling.'

'It smells delicious. And please, call me Dan.'

Grace watched her parents carefully. They gave no indication that they had noticed their dishevelled state.

'Hope you don't mind eating in the kitchen?' Jean said, as she put large plates of piping hot stew in front of them. 'There, you tuck into that.'

'Would you like a beer to go with that, Dan?' Ted asked.

'I would, thank you.'

The stew was delicious, and the dumplings light and

fluffy. Grace hadn't realised how hungry she was. Dan obviously felt the same because he had two large helpings.

'That's the best meal I've had in ages, Jean. Thank you very much.'

'I'm pleased you enjoyed it after your busy day.' She smiled at her daughter. 'I know Grace is always ready for her dinner in the evenings. You look very nice in that outfit, darling. It suits her, doesn't it, Dan?'

Grace nearly choked on a mouthful of tea, and she could sense Dan trying to control his laughter. Her mother had no intention of giving up, though.

'She was such a tomboy as a child, always climbing trees and getting into mischief. Helen, her friend, was the same, but they had to smarten up when they started work.'

'Ah, I nearly forgot,' her father said before Dan could answer. 'Helen left a message for you, Grace. She said to tell you that she's had the letter she was waiting for, and has an appointment tomorrow at the War Office.'

'Did she say what time and who with?'

'Ten o'clock with a Mr Graham, I believe.'

Grace frowned, and looked at Dan. 'I haven't heard of anyone by that name, have you?'

'Not that I can recall.'

'I expect they are interested in her fluent French,' her mother said. 'They probably want her to be an interpreter – or something.'

'Most likely. I'll try and catch her when she arrives.'

'Is your friend French?' Dan asked.

'Her grandmother is. They speak French nearly all the time.'

'Grace talks to Helen in that language sometimes,' Jean told Dan proudly. 'They chatter away and no one can understand what they are saying. They were little devils as children.'

'Grace speaks German, as well,' her father added.

'Oh, Dad! I'm not very good.'

'I wouldn't know, dear. It's all foreign to me,' Jean said and chuckled when they all laughed at the joke.

Dan stood up. 'I must be on my way. Thank you for your hospitality, and an excellent meal, Jean.'

When Grace returned to the kitchen after seeing Dan out, her mother was smiling happily. 'What a charming boy. Such lovely manners.'

'Boy! Mum, that's a full-grown, tough man!'

'Anyone from thirty down is a boy to us, dear. Remember we had you late in life, so we're getting on in years. The water's hot, so have a quick bath and get some sleep. You must be tired out. Leave those clothes out and I'll wash them for you.'

Grace kissed her parents goodnight and went up to the bathroom. What a day it had been!

Chapter Six

At seven o'clock the next morning, Dan went along to his uncle's office, knowing he would already be there.

'Morning, Dan. Finished running around, have you?'

'For the moment.' He pulled up a chair and sat down. 'Do you know a Mr Graham who works here?'

'Can't place him. Why do you want to know?'

Dan explained about Grace's friend.

'Interesting.' The colonel took a large sheet of paper out of his desk drawer and studied it for a while. 'This is a floor plan of all the offices and who occupies them. I can't see anyone by that name.'

'Perhaps he's a new arrival.'

'Must be.' George pursed his lips. 'A French grandmother, you said?'

Dan nodded. 'Are they recruiting interpreters?'

'Well, they will always be needed, and if the girl is fluent, then she could be valuable.'

'See if you can find out. I'm curious. I know Grace declared French as another language when she joined us, but I found out last night that she also knows German.'

'Does she? How good?'

'Not very, according to her.'

'Find out. That should be easy for you. You speak it like a native.' He paused for a moment. 'Is that what made you take that risky dash for the forest?'

Dan's jaw tightened before answering. 'They were speaking quietly, but I heard enough to know they didn't want to be bothered with prisoners. They couldn't let us go, and when several of them began to line up in front of us with rifles, I told the men to run. Knowing the language got us out of a couple of tight spots as we made our way to the coast. Anyway, that's in the past. We've got to prepare for what we are going to face now.'

'That's why I think you should find out how good Grace's German is. If it isn't fluent enough, then teach her. We all need to improve whatever skills we have. Never know when they might come in useful.'

'I'll do that.' Dan stood up. 'Let me know if you hear anything of interest.'

When he walked into the office, Grace was already there.

'Good morning, sir,' she smiled. 'Thank you for being so kind to my parents.'

'It was my pleasure.' He pulled a face when he saw the amount of envelopes she was busy opening. 'That has piled up while we've been busy.'

'We'll soon get through it. That heap on your desk is for immediate attention.'

They had been working steadily for about an hour, when he suddenly gave his instructions in German. For a moment, Grace was taken by surprise. She managed to quickly bring the unused language to mind, and answered – badly, she was sure. If he'd spoken to her in French she wouldn't have had to struggle so hard.

He continued in that way, while Grace answered hesitantly. It was soon apparent that he was very good.

After a while, he said, 'Your accent is terrible, Grace. We'll have to do something about that.'

The switch back to English made her sag with relief. 'I know, sir. I wasn't very good, and I haven't used it for a long time. I can read it better than speak it. You are excellent, though. Where did you learn it?'

'I lived in Germany for a few of years when I was twelve. I went to school there, and you pick things up easily at that age. My father was in the diplomatic service. He's retired now and they live in Cornwall. We will set aside at least an hour each day when we will speak only in German.'

Grace was puzzled. 'May I ask why, sir?'

'It could be useful to you in the future.'

'When the Germans invade, you mean?'

'Good Lord, no. The other way round, Grace.'

'I see.' She didn't, but he was her boss, and if he wanted to speak German, then who was she to argue? She would have to get her reference books out again.

She was busy typing when he interrupted her. 'It's

coming up to ten o'clock. Why don't you go and see if your friend has arrived?'

'Oh, thank you. I didn't realise it was that late.' She stood up quickly. 'I won't be long, sir.'

'Take all the time you need.'

Helen was already waiting when Grace arrived. Her friend was wearing a navy blue suit with a crisp white blouse.

'You do look smart,' she said as she greeted her.

'I thought I had better wear something simple. I've no idea what this is all about. I have been told to wait until someone comes for me.'

'I hope you don't have to wait as long as I did. Dad said you were seeing a Mr Graham. Is that right?'

Helen nodded. 'The letter didn't say what he's in charge of.'

'Well, you are soon going to find out. Here's your escort. Best of luck. I'll see you tonight, if I'm not too late.'

She watched until Helen had disappeared, and then hurried back to her office.

'That was quick. Did you see her?'

'Yes, but we didn't have time to talk much because they came for her almost immediately. I thought all the offices were up here, but they went down the stairs.'

'I expect they are using every available space. This place is getting crowded now.' He smiled. 'Put the kettle on. All this paperwork is making me thirsty.'

She smiled at the disgusted expression on his face. 'You'd rather be tramping through muddy fields?'

'Definitely. We are going out tomorrow morning. I'll

pick you up from your home around 5 a.m. Wear flat shoes and the slacks again.'

She stared at him, astonished. 'Five in the morning?'

'You can get up that early?'

'Of course, but where are we going? I thought your inspection tour was over?'

'This is personal. That's why we have to go so early. You'll enjoy it. Bring your office clothes to change into before we come back here.'

There wasn't time to reply because the phone rang. The major listened for a moment, and then left the office.

What was he up to now? she thought. And if this trip was personal, why was he taking her with him? What a job! She never knew what was going to happen next.

Grace couldn't wait to see Helen, so she went straight to her friend's house. 'What happened?' she asked, eagerly. 'Did they offer you a job?'

'Yes . . .' Helen hesitated. 'But I've been told I mustn't talk about it. All I can say is that I'll be working for a French section.'

'Ah, I understand. I'm in the same situation. But did you accept the job?'

'Yes, I did.' Helen smiled broadly. 'It should be interesting, and Grandmother is thrilled I'll be using my French.'

'I'll bet she is,' Grace laughed. 'She's thinking you'll be looking after the French soldiers who came over after Dunkirk, and could find yourself a nice husband among them.'

'She never gives up, does she? Anyway they asked me to volunteer for an organisation called FANY.'

'What on earth is that?'

'The First Aid Nursing Yeomanry.'

'You're going to be a nurse?' Grace was horrified.

'No. The name goes back to when it was formed years ago. The women used to help the wounded soldiers, and they went everywhere on horseback. Things have changed now, and they do all kinds of jobs.'

Grace was highly amused. 'I can just imagine you charging around on horseback. What's the uniform like?'

'Khaki, and much the same as the ATS. I don't know where I'll be stationed yet, but as soon as I get an address I shall expect a letter from you every week.'

'I'll write twice a week. I promise. Do you know when you'll be going?'

'They said within a week. We'll have a party before I leave.'

'Mum, I told you to stay in bed. I can get my own breakfast.' Grace had moved around quietly in order not to disturb her parents, only to find her mother busy in the kitchen.

'I was already awake, so I thought I'd get you something to eat before you leave. Don't you know why Dan wants you ready so early?'

'No.' Grace sighed. 'I probably won't know until we get to wherever we're going. He doesn't explain until it's necessary.'

'Ah, well, it keeps thing interesting, doesn't it? He doesn't look like a man it would be easy to disobey.'

Grace shook her head, and then sat down at the table. 'You shouldn't have gone to all this trouble, Mum. Toast would have been enough.'

'I managed to get some extra eggs from Gladys up the road. Her chickens have been laying well. You've got a long day ahead of you, so enjoy the scrambled eggs.'

She did enjoy them, and by ten minutes to five she was watching from the front window, knowing he would be right on time. The moment the car arrived, she picked up her bag and walked out before he had time to come up the path.

'Good morning, sir,' she said, brightly. 'Looks as if it might be a dry day.'

'Hoping to avoid any mud today, are you?' He held the car door open for her, and then got in himself, wasting no time in getting underway.

She was amused by his remark, and said, teasingly, 'It could be my lucky day. Mum insisted on washing the clothes, and has pressed a lovely crease in the slacks.'

He laughed softly. 'I think I can guarantee that you won't get in a mess today. Don't be too disappointed, though, because I'll almost certainly change that in a week or two.'

'Are we going to be leaving this early for some time, then?'

'Only two or three days a week. It depends how we both get on.'

Dan fell silent then, and Grace knew that was all she was going to be told.

The journey took nearly two hours, and Grace had no

idea where they were as they drove onto a military site.

The moment they were out of the car, a sergeant marched up to them and saluted the major. 'Good morning, Major Chester. Everything is ready for the young lady. Corporal Hunt is one of our best drivers. She'll be in good hands.'

Grace was looking from one man to the other. What was going on?

Another soldier marched up and saluted smartly. 'Corporal Hunt, sir.'

Dan looked down at Grace. 'Off you go. The corporal is going to teach you to drive. I'll see you in about an hour.'

She looked doubtfully at the enormous machines near them. 'A tank?'

'You can have a go at one of those later, but you'd better learn to drive a car first.'

Dan had a perfectly straight face, but the other two soldiers were having great difficulty keeping their laughter at bay.

'I see.' She looked the major straight in the eyes. They were dancing with amusement. He was enjoying this. 'And for the record, sir, can I ask what you will be doing?'

'The sergeant is going to knock me into shape. Off you go.'

As she walked away with the corporal, she whispered to the sergeant, 'Good luck!' and received a sly wink in reply.

Now they were away from the others, the corporal was laughing openly. 'Didn't the major tell you he had arranged driving lessons for you?'

'Not a word.'

'Is he easy to work for?'

'Oh, very. He's a perfect gentleman. He gives the orders and I obey them. It works well.'

They had reached a car, and the corporal held open the passenger door for her. There was still a broad smile on his face as he got in the driver's side. 'I'm going to take us to a practice ground, and then you can take over.'

'Can Major Chester do this?' she asked. 'I'm not in the forces. These clothes are borrowed.'

'We are both doing this in our own time, Miss . . .' he glanced at her left hand.

'Call me Grace.'

'And I'm Bob. As I was saying, we are doing this to help the major. He is well known here – and respected. If he wants to get fit enough to return to active duty, then we'll do what we can for him. It will also help him if you can drive.'

They pulled up on some spare ground. 'You sit in the driver's seat now. I'll run through the controls with you, and teach you to steer in a straight line first. We have plenty of space here.'

'Hello, Steve,' Dan said, when they found the MO waiting for them in the exercise hall. 'Are you going to join me?'

'No, I'm going to watch you don't overdo it. If I tell you to stop – you stop. Is that understood?'

'I'm sure Sergeant Dickins won't allow me to work too hard in the beginning.' Dan rolled up his sleeves, eager to get started.

'I hear you brought a pretty girl with you.'

'I see news still travels at the speed of light here. She's my secretary, Steve! Let's get started, Sergeant, and don't take it too easy. I need to get fit – and quickly. I need this workout, because I'm never going to regain my full mobility by sitting at the damned desk they've given me.'

'It must have some compensation, Dan. Like being given a lovely girl to work with,' the MO stated.

Dan glared at Steve. 'She's married, Doc – or was. Her husband was killed in France, and she's still grieving for him. I'm sure she will never want anything to do with another man in uniform. This is no time to form relationships, or become too attached to someone.'

'Ah, that's sad. She's so young.'

'And there are far too many like her, and there are going to be many more before this mess is over. Go and sit in the corner, Steve. We're wasting time.'

For the next hour the sergeant took Dan at his word, and worked him until he was wreathed in sweat and gasping for breath.

'Enough!' Steve came over. 'Damn you, Dan, I should have stopped you sooner. Let's have a look at that leg.'

After a thorough examination, Steve nodded. 'You don't appear to have done any damage, although that workout would have floored many men.'

'He's very strong, sir,' the sergeant said with respect in his voice.

'All right, Dan. Have a shower and change into uniform, and then we'll have breakfast. I've ordered it to be served in my office. You must be hungry by now.'

Dan stood under the spray of hot water, and closed

his eyes. He was relieved. He had been able to do more than he'd thought possible. Because he had gone so long without proper medical attention, by the time he had reached England his leg was in a mess. It had been touch and go for a while, but it had healed. If he'd lost it, his army career would have been over, and that would have devastated him.

Scrubbed clean and in full uniform again, he returned to the others. He smiled to himself when he saw Grace with them, looking smart and prim in her office clothes. He was beginning to realise that she was not the docile girl she presented to them. Her parents had helped to dispel that notion.

'How did she get on, Corporal?'

'Very well, sir. I think she will make a competent driver in no time at all.'

He nodded, and asked Grace, 'Did you enjoy learning to drive?'

'Yes, sir.' A smile tugged at the corners of her mouth. 'I can't wait to have a go at a tank.'

They all laughed, and she joined in. It felt good to laugh again. The pain was still there, of course, but she was beginning to live with it better. Brian would have wanted her to get on with her life.

'This is Steve, Grace. He's the medical officer here, and he's arranged breakfast for us.' He then turned to the two soldiers waiting to be dismissed. 'Thank you, Sergeant and Corporal. We've appreciated your help this morning.'

'Sir.' Both men saluted smartly. 'It's been a pleasure.'

'Thank you, Bob.' Grace smiled. 'I enjoyed the lesson.'

He bowed slightly. 'I look forward to the next one. Perhaps we'll take you out on the road next time.'

After a quick meal with Steve, they were on their way back to London, and as they drove along, Grace studied Dan. He appeared more relaxed after his exercise session with the sergeant. 'It was kind of you to arrange driving lessons for me, sir.' She smiled when he glanced at her. 'I enjoyed it.'

'It's a skill worth having. You never know when it might come in useful. How did your friend get on with her interview?' he asked, changing the subject.

'All right, I think. She couldn't say much about it. Everything is so secret these days, but she was able to tell me they wanted her for her fluent French, and she's had to join the First Aid Nursing Yeomanry. I've never heard of the FANY before, sir. Have you?'

'It's a volunteer organisation. Been established quite some time, I believe.'

Grace nodded. 'She'll be going away for training quite soon.'

'You'll miss her.'

'Yes, I will. We've been friends since we were toddlers.' Pushing the sad thought aside, Grace then settled down to watch how the major used the pedals while he was driving.

Chapter Seven

It was the middle of August now, and Dan was edgy. Convoys were being continually attacked, and air fields bombed. The pilots were being pushed to their limits, but when he had seen James two days ago, there hadn't been the slightest doubt in his mind that they would beat the enemy air force. Every day they were fighting for their lives, and he was still stuck to this blasted desk!

His sessions with the sergeant had gone well, and the fitter he became, the more he riled against the job he was now doing. According to the corporal, Grace was an excellent pupil. He had told Dan that she had a sharp mind, and was quick to learn. He seldom had to explain anything twice to her.

He glanced across the office where she was busy working. What was going to happen to her when he returned to his regiment? That day was fast approaching, and the problem was beginning to play on his mind. George had his own staff, so there wasn't an opportunity there, and he had been making discreet enquiries here at the War Office, but there didn't appear to be any vacancies at the moment. He had told her at the start that the job with him probably wouldn't last for long, of course, so he shouldn't be worrying about it. But he was, and he now understood why James had been so protective towards her. She had suffered a great loss, but she had kept going with courage and determination, keeping her grief a private emotion. If only he could find some way to take her with him. She was a competent driver now, but he couldn't declare that he needed a driver when he was doing everything to prove he was fit again for active service. He could run faster than Sergeant Dickins, and the man was like a hare. He was having a final training session tomorrow, and then a medical examination later in the week. They couldn't declare him unfit for duty now. He was stronger than he had ever been. Grace was going to be given a driving test by one of the transport instructors. She had been taught by the best and at least he had been able to do something for her.

It had been more than generous of them all to give of their free time like this, and to show his appreciation he was going to invite them to London for an evening at the Savoy Hotel. Grace, as well, of course. She had put up with a lot from him, and she had never complained.

'How do you feel about the test?' Dan asked Grace, as they headed out of London the next morning.

'Nervous,' she admitted. 'I hope I'm good enough, because we won't be coming here again, will we?'

'No, this is the last session for both of us.' Dan cast a quick glance at her. 'I'm fully fit again. The sergeant has done his job well. I wouldn't have made such rapid progress without him.'

'They have been very kind, and I have enjoyed the challenge of learning to drive.' She tried to keep her tone bright, but to be honest she was feeling a little sad. This wasn't just the end of the early morning trips – it was more than that. He hadn't said anything, but it didn't take a genius to know that her job with him was coming to an end. The change in him was remarkable. The limp had completely disappeared, and for such a big man, his movements were now quite graceful. She smiled to herself. That seemed a silly thing to say about a man who exuded power and strength, but that was how she saw it. And that was what the medical examiners would see. There was no doubt in her mind that he would be declared fit for active duty again.

Helen had settled into whatever she was doing, and was happy. They wrote regular long letters to each other, but never mentioned their jobs. Everyone was continually reminded not to talk, as you never knew who was listening.

Grace had been lost in thought and hadn't noticed the miles slipping away, so she was surprised when he stopped.

'You drive now,' Dan told her, getting out of the car and holding the door open for her. 'Don't look so worried. You need practice before we get there.'

Now she really was nervous. This was the last thing

she had expected him to ask her to do. He adjusted the driver's seat so she could reach the pedals. It had been pushed right back to accommodate his long legs. At five feet eight inches, she was by no means short, but he was over six feet.

'That seems right,' he said. 'Can you reach the pedals easily?'

'Yes, that feels fine. Thank you.'

He adjusted the passenger seat, and got in. 'All right, Grace. You know the way by now.'

She drew in a deep, silent breath, and started the car, concentrating hard to remember everything Bob had taught her.

'Relax,' he told her after a few miles. 'You are doing fine.'

It wasn't easy with him sitting beside her and watching every move she made, but those few words of encouragement was the only comment he made. By the time she reached the camp she was relieved, and rather pleased with herself. She didn't feel as if she had made any bad mistakes, or he would certainly have corrected her. It boded well for the test.

Bob smiled with pleasure when he saw Grace getting out of the driver's side. He saluted the major. 'How did my pupil do, sir?'

'Very well, Corporal. I felt quite safe.'

Grace gave him a disbelieving look. She had noticed his foot pressing on an imaginary brake once or twice.

He laughed softly, reading her expression accurately. 'Don't change out of the slacks straight after the test.

There's something else I want you to do before we leave.'

'Very well, sir. I'll see you in about an hour.'

'You didn't ask Major Chester what he had planned,' Bob remarked as they walked towards the car.

'I quickly learnt not to ask him questions.'

'I know,' Bob laughed. 'He tells you what to do, and you do it.'

She smiled, and nodded towards another soldier waiting by the car. 'Is that the man who is going to do the test?'

'That's right. You don't have anything to worry about. You are a good driver. All you're lacking is experience. Just forget he's there and concentrate on the driving.'

'I'll try not to let you, or myself, down.' Putting on a confident air, she walked towards the examiner.

'We'll go straight to the assault course, Sergeant.'

'Yes, sir. I've got a few volunteers who will give you a bit of competition. They are looking forward to beating an officer. All I've told them is that you are an officer who wants to see if he can still tackle the course. They don't know who you are.'

Dan grinned. 'So they think they can beat me, do they? We'll see about that. I used to be quite good at this.'

'And I'm sure you still are – now you're fit again, sir.'

'Let's not keep them waiting, then.'

There were six soldiers at the course, laughing and joking. They snapped to attention when Dan arrived.

'At ease. Thank you for volunteering to run the assault course with me. I haven't tackled it for some time, and it will be more fun to be running with others.'

The men smiled smugly, and one said, 'We're looking forward to it, sir. We don't get the chance to run against an officer.'

Dan put on a slightly worried frown as he studied the course, making the sergeant turn away to hide his grin.

'Confident bunch you've gathered together, Sergeant,' Dan remarked quietly.

'They are new here, sir, and don't know you, or your reputation of never expecting your men to do anything you can't. I can't wait to see them brought down a peg or two.'

'You really think I can do that?'

The sergeant nodded, hardly able to contain his amusement. 'Working with you over the last few weeks I've seen for myself what you can do, and I'm sure they won't find it as easy as they think it's going to be.'

'I appreciate the vote of confidence. Let's see just how fit I am, shall we?'

The sergeant faced the men. 'Right, let's get this started. Any man I see tripping, pushing or obstructing another will regret it. Is that clear?'

'Yes, Sergeant,' they chorused.

'Play fair, or I will make your lives a misery. Get ready . . . Go!'

Dan started several paces behind the enthusiastic men, pacing himself over the first few obstacles. Then, finally, feeling good, he increased his speed, overtaking one man, and then another. The sergeant was running beside them, yelling comments at the top of his voice. Not all of them complimentary.

It was only in the last few yards Dan managed to overtake the last of the men. He was bent over, gasping for breath, when the team of soldiers gathered round, moaning with exhaustion.

'Well done, sir,' one of them gasped. 'We couldn't stay with you.'

Dan grinned, straightening up, elated with the way it had gone. 'I wasn't sure I could beat you. Thanks for giving me the chance to try.'

Steve wandered up. 'That was impressive, Dan. How does the leg feel?'

'Good. It held up well.'

The soldiers were now looking at the tall officer in amazement. 'You did that with a gammy leg?' one of them asked.

'It's healed now.' Dan turned to Steve. 'What do you think, Doc, will they let me return to active duty?'

'No doubt about it. I'll send in a report as well, to make sure of it. You'll be back with your regiment by the end of the month. Your men will be relieved to see you.'

A cloud crossed Dan's face. 'I'll know some that survived, but there will be a lot of replacements I don't know.'

'They will have all heard about the exploits of Major Chester, and they will be just as relieved to see you back. No one thought it would be possible, Dan. But you always were a stubborn bastard.'

One of the soldiers whispered to the others, 'What did he do?'

'Dunno,' another replied, 'but I think the sergeant has

been hiding things from us. He damned well knew we were going to be beaten!'

All comments stopped as Grace walked into view, accompanied by the corporal and the examiner.

'Ah.' Dan strolled over. 'How did she get on, Andy?'

'I gave her the same test as a military driver, and she passed easily. I've been trying to persuade her to join the ATS, but I haven't been successful.'

Dan didn't comment on that, but smiled at Grace. 'Well done!'

'Thank you, sir.' Her eyes shone with amusement as she looked at him. 'I see you've managed to find some mud.'

'Are you jealous?' he asked, and they both laughed at the private joke. 'As it's our last visit here, and as a celebration of you passing your test, I thought you might like to have a go at the assault course with me.'

'Dan!' Steve exclaimed. 'You can't ask a girl to tackle that!'

'Why not? I'm sure she'd like to have as go. Wouldn't you?'

She eyed the monstrosity, and thought for a moment. The glint in his eyes told her he really wanted to do this. Things had obviously gone well for him today, and she could see his relief. He knew he was on his way back to active duty, so perhaps this would be a fitting way to bring their short time together to a close – with laughter. She smiled at him. 'You're on!'

He took hold of her arm and placed her in front of the first obstacle. 'I'll tell you how to deal with each stage of the course. Trust me and go for it. I won't let you hurt yourself.'

She nodded, wondering why on earth she had agreed to this.

'Run as fast as you can!'

It was bedlam. Everyone there was running beside them, shouting encouragement. The first obstacle wasn't too bad, and her balance was good when she reached the pole across the water, but there was a high wall in front of her now.

'Keep your speed up,' Dan instructed, 'and be ready to grab the top of the wall.'

When they reached it she was lifted off her feet, and thrown to the top. She made a desperate grab and held on with all her might. Suddenly, Dan was also up there with her.

'Right. Now, get your legs up.'

The yelling from the onlookers was deafening as Grace struggled to sit astride the wall. She looked down and saw the sergeant waiting on the other side, urging her to swing down.

The rest of the course was negotiated in the same way, with willing hands helping her along, and enthusiastic encouragement from all sides.

By the end, she was dirty, exhausted, and probably bruised, she thought. But it had been fun, and she had never seen Dan laughing so much.

'Well done, Grace! That was a valiant effort. I'm proud of you.'

Everyone was clustered around, having thoroughly enjoyed the sight of a girl trying to tackle their course.

She finally found enough breath to talk, and said,

'Thank you, sir. I couldn't have done it without you and the sergeant. You both practically carried me over some obstacles.'

Steve waded in and took hold of Grace's arm. 'All right, men, you've had your fun. You come with me, young lady.'

'I'll see you when we've both cleaned up.'

As Steve led her away, he shook his head. 'That was crazy, Grace.'

'I know, and I'm sure I'll regret it tomorrow.'

'You did it for Dan, didn't you?'

'I couldn't refuse. He is so happy, and it felt right to finish off with some light-hearted fun. He'll be returning to his regiment soon, won't he?'

'He's going for a full medical in two days, and there's no doubt he is now fully fit. They will have to declare him fit for active duty. Will you be transferred to another office?'

'I really don't know. That's a bridge I will have to cross when I reach it.'

'You get on well together. It will probably be a wrench to watch him walk away.'

'I expect so but, for me, the last few months have consisted of one loss after another. I'm getting used to it.' Her smile was tinged with sadness. 'I didn't want to work for him, you know. I only went to the War Office because my boss had arranged the interview for me when he joined the air force. Now, I'm sorry my time there has been so short.'

* * *

An hour later, both scrubbed clean and dressed for business, they were on their way back to London.

'I've invited everyone who has helped us to an evening at the Savoy,' Dan told Grace. 'It's next Saturday, so get out your party dress. We'll have a celebration.'

Chapter Eight

For the next three days Dan was out of the office most of the time. Grace knew he must have taken the medical, but he hadn't mentioned it. She would have known if he hadn't passed, though, because his volatile nature would have erupted. He was sweeping around like a man with a purpose, and whatever he was doing it was personal because he hadn't asked for her help.

The door opened and the colonel looked in. 'Do you know where Dan is, Grace?'

'No, sir. I haven't seen much of him this week.'

Colonel Askew shook his head. 'He should let you know where he's going. Tell him I want to see him when he shows his face.'

'I will, sir. If he doesn't come back this afternoon, I'll leave a message for him. I'm afraid he's in and out, and prowling around like a tiger.'

The colonel laughed. 'That's very apt. The Royal Hampshire Regiment are nicknamed "The Hampshire Tigers".'

'Ah, well,' Grace smiled, 'he's in the right outfit.'

'Now he's passed the medical he can't wait to rejoin them. He won't suffer any delays, either. He's probably out making sure his return is immediate.'

Now she knew, Grace thought, as the officer left. She could be out of a job after tomorrow. One thing was for sure; she wasn't going to rush into anything this time. She hadn't been thinking straight after Brian's death, but she would take time with her next move.

It was late in the afternoon when Dan swept back in to the office. 'Make some tea, Grace, and is there anything to eat in this place?'

She nodded. 'I'll find you something, sir. What would you like?'

'Anything.'

Grace soon returned with a plate of cheese sandwiches. 'This was all I could get.'

'That's fine.' He smiled as he took one from the plate. 'Thanks Grace. You're a treasure.'

By the time she had made the tea, the plate was empty. 'Would you like some more?'

He shook his head as she handed him a cup of tea.

'Colonel Askew would like to see you.'

'Right.' Dan drank the tea, and held the cup out for a refill. That disappeared just as quickly. 'I'll go and see him now.'

He swept out of the office, and Grace watched the closing door with amusement. Tiger was indeed apt.

* * *

'You wanted to see me, George?'

'Oh, you've decided to pay us a visit, have you?' He studied his nephew carefully. Even as a child, Dan had been a force to be reckoned with, and since his experiences in France and Dunkirk, that quality was even more noticeable. 'Got what you wanted, have you?'

'I'm off to Lower Barracks, Winchester, on Sunday.'

'Have you told Grace?'

'Not yet.'

'Then you had better do it today, Dan. If I'd known you were going to return to active duty so soon, I would have tried to find her a different position. Assigning her to you was a mistake.'

'No, it wasn't!' Dan exclaimed angrily. 'I told her right from the beginning that the job probably wouldn't last long. She's an intelligent girl. She understood. I've done what I could for her. She's had the very best driving instruction it's possible to get. I've also tried to find her another job here, without success. What more do you and James expect me to do? There's a bloody war on, Colonel, and I'm going back to my regiment where I belong!'

Dan surged to his feet, ready to storm out of the office and stopped in mid-stride. He was looking into the face of a girl who was not at all happy about what she had just heard.

Grace was not only furious – she was hurt, as well. Her gaze was icy as she looked at the two men. 'No one has the right to believe they can decide my future! I am quite capable of finding my own way in life, without interference from you. How dare you presume what I should, or should not, do! And you are wrong, Colonel. You didn't make a mistake – I did. James should have told me you were almost family. I didn't want to keep the appointment he had made for me, but, out of loyalty to him, I came. He also had no right to believe I needed looking after. I'm good at my job, and will make my own decisions.'

Grace stepped round Dan, picked up the telephone and dialled a number. 'General Norton, I have Major Chester for you.'

She turned and thrust the phone into Dan's hand. 'He wants to speak with you – urgently.'

As Grace swept out of the office, Dan hesitated, not wanting her to leave like this, but he was trapped. With a frustrated growl, he put the phone to his ear.

'Chester, sir.'

It turned out to be a lengthy call, and by the time Dan arrived back in his office, there was no sign of Grace. He swore fluently, and spun round, nearly crashing into his uncle.

'It's no good tearing after her, I tried to catch her, but she's gone.'

'Damn and blast!'

George grimaced. 'At least that's milder than the last lot of expletives you used. Stop fretting. Anyone would think you had formed an attachment to the girl.'

'You're letting your imagination run away with you, Uncle. She's been good while she's worked for me, and hasn't flinched, no matter what I have thrown at her. I don't want to leave with a bad feeling between us. That's all.'

'There isn't much we can do tonight, so leave it until tomorrow. She'll come back. She's too professional to leave without giving proper notice.'

Dan shook his head. 'You know I've never been able to leave things unresolved. And she's right. We have no right to interfere in her life, or try to protect her as if she was a child. If James hadn't sent her to us, would we be acting like this?'

'I doubt it. James was so insistent in his letter that we look after her, and out of our affection for him that's what we have been trying to do. A clumsy effort, as it turns out.'

'Unnecessary and unwanted, as well.' Dan prowled the office. 'I didn't see that before. She was always willing to please, tackling every task I gave her with good humour and at my side whenever I needed her. In that composed, softly spoken girl, there is a strong, independent woman. And I never saw it.'

'No, and I don't suppose James did, either. She's the perfect secretary. That's her job, and she does it well.'

Dan nodded. 'Now the real Grace has been revealed, the gloves are off, and we're in trouble.'

'I don't know how much of our argument she heard, but I think it must have been most of it, and she must have misunderstood. After all, we were only trying to be helpful.'

'She interpreted that as interfering, though. We have some explaining to do.' Dan snatched his hat from a chair and put it on. 'I'll go and find her now.'

'I'm coming with you. Neither of us is used to explaining ourselves. It might take both of us to get the job done.'

'True,' Dan agreed dryly. 'By the way, George, what did you want to see me about?'

'Just to let you know that James is coming to the Savoy on Saturday.'

'Then we had better sort this out right now. If James finds out we've upset her, he'll give us hell!'

George pulled a face. 'I'll have to see if I can return to active duty as well. It could be safer there!'

Both officers smiled grimly as they marched out of the office.

Dan drove straight to Grace's home, and when he knocked on the door, it was opened by her father.

'Good evening, Ted. We're sorry to bother you, but we would like to see Grace. May I introduce Colonel Askew.'

'Pleased to meet you, sir. I'm afraid she isn't here, Dan.' Ted turned and called, 'Where did Grace say she was going, Jean?'

'To the pictures. The Odeon, I think she said.'

'Ah, in that case she will be quite a while. You are both welcome to come in and wait.'

'Thank you.' Dan smiled. 'We are in a hurry, so we'll see if we can find her.'

'We can't wait around all evening,' George said, as Dan pulled up near the cinema.

'I don't intend to. We'll get the manager to put a message on the screen, asking her to come outside.'

George looked at his nephew in disbelief. 'And you think that will put her in a receptive mood, do you? She's already angry enough, Dan!'

'I am not leaving it until tomorrow.'

George shrugged, knowing that when Dan was set on an action, nothing would change his mind. 'All right. I'll stand behind you.'

Dan laughed, and his uncle scowled. 'You've been nothing but trouble ever since you were born.'

'Stop grumbling. Let's find the manager.'

The two officers were an impressive sight as they marched into the cinema foyer.

Grace was startled and alarmed when her name came up on the screen asking for her to come outside immediately. Fortunately she was only six seats in from the aisle and didn't have to disturb too many people as she left. Her heart was thumping as she hurried out. When she saw the two officers waiting for her, she was even more worried.

'What's happened?' she asked, rushing up to them.

'We need to talk to you about this afternoon,' George told her.

For a moment she couldn't quite grasp what he was saying. Then it registered, and she looked from one officer to the other in astonishment. 'Are you telling me you had my name put up on the screen, just because you want to talk to me?'

'Sorry about that, Grace. It was Dan's idea.'

Her gaze fixed on the major. This was unbelievable!

'You frightened me. I thought the invasion must have begun – or there had been some disaster.'

'It is a disaster,' Dan told her. 'We've never had to explain ourselves before – let alone apologise.'

The sight of these two powerful army officers standing

in front of her, and looking slightly uneasy, was too much for Grace. She fought to hold on to her emotions.

'The need to apologise is a disaster?'

'Absolutely. We've never been in this position before, have we, George?'

'Damned uncomfortable thing to have to do without practice.'

Grace could contain herself no longer, and burst into laughter. They were working as a double act!

'This is ridiculous!'

'Yes, isn't it?' Dan grinned, seeing her sense of humour taking over from anger. 'Nevertheless, it must be done. Don't you agree, George?'

'Oh, absolutely. We can't have our girl misunderstanding our motives. So, I think we should go to the pub across the road and have a drink.'

'But you can't go in a pub,' Grace declared. 'It will probably be full of soldiers, and having two officers walk in will spoil their evening.'

'Why?' Dan asked, innocently.

There was a huge mirror in the foyer and Grace made them turn round to face it. 'You have to ask why? Take a good look at yourselves. In full uniform you would intimidate anyone.'

'Do you know what she's talking about, George?'

'Not a clue, dear chap.'

They were enjoying themselves now. Grace was laughing so much she had to find a chair to sit on. 'Heaven help this country with you two in charge. You are impossible!'

'That's the nicest compliment you have ever given me.'

Dan came and sat beside her. 'So, will you come and have a drink with us? After we've finished grovelling we can be friends again.'

'How can I refuse such an invitation? And I must admit to being curious to see how you manage such an unfamiliar task.'

Grace walked between the two men as they crossed the road to the pub, and reflected on what the major had said about them being friends again. Was that what had grown between them over the last few weeks? Certainly, she would never have spoken to James the way she did with Dan. Although having respect and liking for each other, Grace had never crossed the boundary between boss and secretary. That divide had never really been there with this difficult man. How could it, when he had dragged her round muddy fields, made her hide in ditches, and had even thrown her round a monster of an assault course. Perhaps they had become friends.

When they reached the pub, Dan held open a door marked Saloon Bar, and winked at her. Yes, friends, she thought. She liked that.

They could hear the noise coming from the Public Bar, but it was quieter in here.

'What are you going to have?' Dan asked, ushering her towards a table in the corner.

'A gin with lots of tonic, please.'

'Double whisky for me. If they've got it, of course,' George said.

Dan soon returned with two drinks each. 'Saves keeping going to the bar,' he explained.

There was silence between them for a moment as they all savoured their drinks, and then Dan asked, 'Why were you angry when you heard what we were saying, Grace?'

'You were having a row about me, as if I was some burden you didn't know what to do with. I was offended, and hurt. I am not some helpless female who can't make her own decisions, and it was insulting to hear you in a heated argument about me.'

'I apologise for that. It was entirely my fault,' Dan explained. 'I am returning to my regiment this Sunday, and George told me I must tell you today. I knew that, and had been putting it off. I suppose guilt made me explode. We have become fond of you in the short time you have been with us, and our only desire was to help you. We see now, though, that we had no right to make enquiries about another job without your permission. And for that, we both apologise, and ask for your forgiveness.'

Grace glanced across at the colonel who was staring at his nephew as if he couldn't believe what he had just heard.

'He's good, isn't he,' Grace remarked.

'Good gracious!' The colonel took a swig of whisky. 'I've never heard him be so humble!'

'Ah, but was I convincing enough?' Dan gave Grace a questioning look.

'You were very eloquent, and I believed you meant every word. Now it's my turn. I knew the job with you was at an end, and I was feeling sad about it. It has been an adventure, and I have enjoyed working with you. I will have happy memories to take away with me. That is why when I found you arguing about what to do with me I was very hurt, and I reacted badly. I hope you will also accept my apology for speaking so disrespectfully to both of you? I was wrong, and I'm sorry.'

'That's very generous of you, Grace, but you don't need to apologise to us.' The colonel raised his glass. 'Here's to friendship.'

'Friends,' Dan said, clinking his glass against Grace's.

Chapter Nine

'You look lovely, dear. I've always liked you in that deep blue frock. The colour suits you so well.'

'I'm glad it looks all right, because it's the only suitable frock I've got. I've lost a bit of weight since I last wore it, though.'

'Well, that is hardly surprising.' Jean studied her daughter with concern. 'You've been through a lot, and Dan has had you running around the country.'

Grace laughed. That was true enough!

'Will you be the only girl there?' her mother asked.

'I really don't know, but I expect so. I won't stay long if I am, but I must put in an appearance. Dan's rejoining his regiment tomorrow, so I won't see him again.'

'It's a shame you are out of work again so soon. Have you decided what you're going to do?'

'I'm not going to rush in to anything.' Grace sighed. 'I wish Helen was here.'

There was a knock on the front door, and Grace picked up her bag. 'That will be the taxi Dan has arranged for me.'

'Give Dan our best wishes, Grace. He's such a nice boy. We really liked him.'

'I will.' Grace hurried out, smiling. Her mother insisted on calling Dan a boy, and she wondered what he would think about that?

When Grace arrived at the Savoy Hotel, she was shown to a private room. There was already quite a crowd there, and she was pleased to see she wasn't the only woman. They were smartly dressed, and all the men were in uniform. It seemed as if almost everyone was in a uniform of some kind now.

Dan came to her immediately. 'You look lovely. I've only ever seen you wearing office clothes or army fatigues. Let me introduce you to everyone. You already know quite a few.'

'My goodness!' she exclaimed. 'This is quite a gathering. I thought there were only going to be a few of us.'

'I told them to bring their wives or girlfriends, and I invited a few others.' He took two glasses of champagne from a passing waiter and handed one to Grace. 'Let's forget the war for a few hours, and enjoy our celebration.'

She nodded, raised her glass to him. 'Thank you for an interesting few weeks, and I wish you all the best, and especially safety as you move into the future. Mum and Dad also send their best wishes on your return to active duty.'

'That's kind of them. Thank them for me, and tell them that I enjoyed meeting them.'

Dan introduced her to a few she didn't know, and then left to greet more guests just arriving. Grace had been well trained during her years at the lawyers, and moved confidently round the room, talking to different people. Bob was there, and the soldiers from the assault course, and she spent time with them talking and laughing about that day.

The colonel came up to her with a broad smile on his face. 'Someone you know has just arrived, Grace.'

She faced the door, but Dan was blocking her view as he greeted the new arrival enthusiastically, slapping him on the back. When he moved aside, she gasped. The airman standing there was James. He was laughing as the colonel strode towards him. The affection between the three of them was obvious, and Grace felt a lump in her throat as she watched. Her Brian had been killed, and she shuddered to think what the chances of survival were for these men. She pushed the thoughts aside. All any of them had was this moment, and they could be happy tonight.

'Who is that?' Bob asked.

'James Meredith. I used to work for him before he joined the air force.'

'He's wearing wings. What does he fly?'

'A Spitfire, I believe. He had a pilot's licence before he joined up.'

'Those poor buggers are having a rough time,' one of the other soldiers remarked. 'They take to the air every day, not knowing if it might be their last time. It's a desperate fight, and if they can't hold off the Luftwaffe, then we will really be in trouble.'

'They won't fail,' Grace said with confidence. 'And before this war is over, we are all going to have to show the same courage as the airmen, soldiers and sailors.' She smiled. 'This isn't the time for such serious talk, so let's all celebrate together, shall we?'

'Too right! Where's that champagne?' Bob called a waiter over, and everyone was smiling again.

Grace waited until James saw her, and then she walked towards him, smiling with pleasure.

He grasped her hands. 'It's good to see you, Grace. How are you?'

'I'm fine, and it's lovely to see you. I didn't know you would be here. How is the air force treating you?'

'Oh, it's lively. I'm getting in plenty of flying.' He laughed, and changed the subject. 'How did you get on working with Dan?'

'It was different – and lively!' she added, making them both laugh.

'I'll bet it was! He told me he's returning to his regiment tomorrow, so what are your plans now?'

'I haven't decided yet, but I might consider joining one of the forces.' Grace was surprised when she heard herself say that, as it wasn't high on her list of jobs. Perhaps being surrounded by all these uniforms had prompted the idea. And really, what else could she do? Everyone was being called upon to do something for the war effort.

'James,' Dan had just arrived, 'what would you like to drink?'

'No alcohol for me. I'm flying again in the morning.'

'Right. I'll get you an orange juice.' Dan smiled at them, and said jokingly, 'As you can see, Grace hasn't come to any harm working with me.'

James watched his friend stride away. 'I didn't think I would ever see him walking freely like that again.'

'He's worked hard to get fit, and I'm pleased for him. He isn't the kind of man you can give a desk job to.'

'Lord, no! It would have driven him mad. He's got to get back in the fight again.'

Grace nodded. 'Yes, he's got a score to settle.'

'Did he tell you that?' James asked, giving her a startled look.

'He didn't have to. I've watched him fighting frustration and anger. I don't know exactly what happened to him and his men in France, but it won't let him rest. Revenge is a strong word, but I would use it in this case.'

'I've always known you are good at discerning a person's character, but you've summed up that complex man very accurately. Do you like him?'

'Yes, I do,' she admitted.

'For all his faults, he's easy to like, isn't he?'

'We've all got faults. Some are appealing – some are not.'

'That's very true. Grace, will you keep in touch with George, so he can tell me how you are getting on?'

'I'll do that.'

'Now, if you will excuse me, there are a few people I must say hello to. Then I must head back. You take care, Grace.'

'You do the same.' She watched him walk away. On the surface he looked the same, but he had changed. It was hard to pin down because it was well hidden. It didn't take a genius, though, to know that fighting daily to keep the Luftwaffe from dominating our skies was taking its toll on the pilots. They knew, and so did everyone, that if they failed, Hitler would invade.

'Grace, come and have something to eat,' Bob urged. 'I've never seen so much grub.'

'I am hungry.' She walked with Bob towards the tables laden with food, not allowing her disturbing thoughts to show.

Without being obvious, Dan was watching Grace as she moved around the room.

'James has trained her well,' George said, coming to stand beside his nephew. 'See the way she goes to anyone standing on their own, or looking slightly ill at ease?'

Dan nodded. 'They often had nervous or difficult people at the law firm. She's used to putting people at their ease. That was part of her job, and she's still doing it. That efficient business woman is always on show, but I've seen that mask slip once or twice. She's got a stubborn streak a mile wide.'

'That's probably what has been holding her together after the death of her husband. Nevertheless, she could be an asset. How is her German?'

'Much improved. Keep an eye on her, George. I want to know where she is, and what she's doing.'

'I will, of course. I like the girl, and James has already

asked her to stay in touch with me. What are you planning, Dan? And don't give me that innocent look. I know you too well.'

'I want her to join the army. I took her regularly to an army camp, so she could see what it was like. The idea of enlisting was put to her when she took the driving test, and I made her run the assault course with me. With luck, that might have been enough to plant the seed in her mind.'

'I wouldn't hold out much hope of her doing that. She doesn't like being told what to do with her life, however subtly it's done. She doesn't have to join the forces. With her qualifications, she can find a job anywhere.'

'I know all that, George, but after losing her husband, she wants to do something worthwhile. Her friend, Helen, has already taken that step, and if James hadn't sent her to us, she would already have joined the forces.'

'Maybe.' George sounded doubtful. 'She could join another service, though. And you still haven't told me why this matters to you. And I know it does. Is this more than liking on your part for the girl?'

'Don't be ridiculous, Uncle! There's no point me telling you what is on my mind, because if I don't survive this war, then none of this will matter.'

'What are you two discussing so seriously?' James wandered up to them, eating a sausage roll.

'We were just wondering when you are going to marry that girl of yours?' Dan lied. 'How long have you been courting her? Three years?'

'Two, actually. Getting attached is not a good idea.'

James looked across the room at Grace. 'There are too many widows around already.'

'Will you both stop this?' George scolded. 'You two are going to come through this – we all are! And that's an order!'

'Yes, sir!' Dan and James said in true military style as they snapped to attention.

'We never disobey orders, sir,' James said, laughing. 'Would you mind asking the Germans to stop shooting at us?'

'I'll send an official message first thing in the morning. Now, Dan, isn't there anything stronger than this fizzy stuff?'

'Tell the waiter what you want and he'll get it for you.'

James checked his watch. 'I'm afraid I must leave. Sorry I couldn't stay longer.'

'We understand. It was great to see you, and thanks for taking the time to come. We must try to get some leave at the same time.'

'I'll look forward to that. Cheers, and congratulations on your return to full health, Dan.'

After a few quick goodbyes to a few people, including Grace, James left.

'He's a good pilot, George,' Dan said, when he saw his uncle's worried expression. 'He'll come through this.'

'Of course he will.' George studied his empty glass. 'I need a whisky.'

It was nearly midnight and the party was showing no sign of breaking up. Grace had stayed longer than she had meant to, and decided it was time to leave. After making sure her taxi was outside, she went over to Dan.

'Thank you for a lovely evening. I have enjoyed it very much, but it is time I was on my way. I've said goodbye to everyone, except you and Colonel Askew.'

'It's been a pleasure, Grace.' George smiled. 'And I hope you are going to keep in touch with me? You know where to find me.'

'I'll do that, sir.'

Dan took her arm. 'I'll walk out to the taxi with you.'

It was quite cool after the heat of the room, and Grace felt as if she'd had a bit too much champagne. 'Thank you for the driving lessons – and the fun.'

Dan smiled down at her. 'Yes, it was fun, wasn't it?'

She nodded, suddenly needing to get this goodbye over. It was harder than she had imagined it would be. She held out her hand. 'Goodbye, Dan. You take care of yourself.'

He bent and kissed her cheek. 'Thank you for looking after me so well. You look after yourself, as well, no matter what you do. Goodbye, Grace.'

When she got in the taxi and it drove away from the hotel, she felt like crying. *You've certainly had too much to drink*, she told herself sternly. She rested her head back and closed her eyes. What a strange few weeks it had been.

Chapter Ten

'Wake up you lazy thing! It's ten o'clock, Grace.'

Someone was shaking her. 'Go away!'

'Not a chance. I've only got forty-eight hours.'

The familiar voice began to penetrate Grace's sleepy mind. She opened one eye, and then shot upright.

'Helen! When did you arrive?'

'An hour ago. That must have been some night out. I've never known you to sleep past seven.'

'I drank a bit too much champagne.' She reached for the cup of tea on her bedside table, and grimaced. 'I'm so thirsty.'

'Serves you right. You shouldn't have let the soldiers get you drunk.'

'I wasn't drunk!' she declared indignantly. 'A bit light-headed, that's all. Have you come home to lecture me?'

'Would I dare?' Helen told her, grinning.

'Oh, I'm so pleased to see you. I'm not sure what to do next, and I want to talk about it with you. It always helps to clear my mind. How much leave have you got?'

'I've already told you. Forty-eight hours, so stop wasting it and get out of bed. I'll go and talk to your mum and dad while you get dressed.'

'I'll be ready in no time.' Grace swung her legs out of the bed. 'Ask Mum to make a big pot of tea.'

'Ah, here she is at last,' Ted said as his daughter walked in to the kitchen half an hour later. 'I think she would have slept all morning if you hadn't arrived, Helen. Dan must have thrown a lively party.'

'It was very good, and he'd invited a lot of guests. The champagne kept coming, and you should have seen the food there. Goodness knows what an evening like that must have cost.'

'I don't think he is short of money, dear.' Her mother handed her a steaming cup of tea. 'He has the air of a man used to wealth.'

'Has he? I really don't know anything about him. He never talked about his life outside of the army. Anyway, it was a splendid party, and I was so pleased when James arrived. He only stayed for a short time, but it was good to see him again.'

Jean shook her head sadly. 'How was he, Grace? Those poor boys are fighting for their lives – and ours. Did he say anything about that?'

'He was fine, Mum and, no, he never mentioned

anything to do with the war. He spent most of his time with Dan and the colonel.'

'We met Dan, you know, Helen,' Jean told her. 'He brought Grace home one evening, and they were both covered in mud. He came in and had supper with us. Such a nice boy.'

Grace shook her head and grinned at her friend. 'He must be around thirty.'

Helen stood up. 'Come on, we're going out. I want to hear how you got covered in mud.'

'We'd been hiding in ditches.'

'What?' Helen stared at Grace, and then pushed her out of the door. 'You've got some explaining to do!'

It was Grace's turn to stare aghast at the military car parked outside her house. 'How did that get here?'

'I drove it here.'

'You can drive? I've passed a test, as well. Can I have a go?'

'Only if you promise not to dent it. I had to bring an officer to London, and I've got to collect him in two days. I can keep the car until then, but we can't go far. I must be careful with the petrol.'

Grace was eagerly inspecting the car. 'This is nearly the same as the one I learnt in. You didn't tell me you'd had driving lessons.'

'I'm learning all kinds of things.'

'Such as?'

'Now, now,' Helen chided, 'you know you mustn't ask questions.'

'I've signed the Secrets Act.'

'Doesn't make any difference. You might be a spy, for all I know.'

'Damn! You've guessed, and I thought I was being so clever about it.'

'Get in the car,' Helen laughed. 'Drive to Hyde Park, and we'll go for a walk. You can then tell me what on earth you have been up to with this major of yours.'

'He isn't mine, Helen. I probably won't ever see him again.'

Helen gazed into space for a moment, and then said, 'This war is going to be like that. We meet people, wave them goodbye, and they're gone. We've got to accept that, haven't we?'

'It's a sad fact of life now, I'm sorry to say.' Grace started the car and concentrated on driving, thrilled to have the chance.

After parking the car, they walked slowly, enjoying the peace and beauty of the park. It was a lovely August day, and a lot of people were about.

'You drive well, Grace.'

'Thanks. I was taught by the best. So how are you getting on with whatever it is you're doing?'

'I'm enjoying it, and meeting a lot of interesting people.'

'French?'

'Some. You said you wanted to talk.'

Grace nodded, knowing the subject of what her friend was doing had been firmly closed. They could no longer share details of their lives, and that was another result of this war.

'I'm thinking about joining the forces and I wondered

if you have any regrets about what you're doing.'

'None whatsoever.' The reply was instant. 'I wanted to do something that would make a difference, and I think I have found it. I feel useful, Grace, and that means a great deal to me. If you stay a civilian you could end up in a dead-end job. Is that what you want?'

'You know it isn't. Dan tried to get me another job at the War Office, but I'm glad he didn't succeed because I would have turned it down. I am concerned, though, that I could find myself doing the same work in the forces.'

'But it's what you're good at! You have a real talent for looking after people. Do you think you made his life easier by being at his side whenever he needed you?'

'Well, yes, I suppose I helped him get through a job he hated.'

'Of course you did. Don't waste your talent, Grace. All you can do is to take that step and see where it leads. If you are given something you don't like, then you can always put in for a transfer. It's time to move forward.'

'I never thought of that.' Grace smiled. 'I'm so glad you came home today. I'll go for it!'

'That's the spirit! Which service are you considering?'

'The ATS.'

Helen laughed. 'That sounded positive. Got used to working with army officers, did you?'

'As a matter of fact, I did.'

'In that case don't settle for anything less than a general,' Helen joked. 'Now that's decided, I want to know how you are really coping with losing Brian. You're very good at hiding your emotions, but tell me what you are really feeling.'

They found a bench and sat down before Grace spoke.

'I was devastated, and it still hurts so badly. Keeping going is helping, though, and while I was working for Dan, there wasn't much time to dwell on it. It was one crazy day after another, and as I watched him fighting to get fit again, I understood his pain, frustration and anger. They were the emotions I was struggling with and, in a strange way, it helped me. The few weeks we worked together were difficult for both of us. Do you know, though, at the end we laughed with each other, and it felt liberating. When he was ready to leave, he declared us friends, and that was how it felt.'

'I wish I'd met him.'

'You would have liked him.' Grace smiled wistfully. 'I needed those few weeks. Now I'm ready to move on.'

The two days spent with Helen had been fun. It had been wonderful to be together again, to talk and joke like old times. Those old, carefree days were gone, unfortunately. The battle raging in the sky day after day was desperate, and the threat of invasion was still hanging over them. With the enemy now occupying France, it was easy for them to attack shipping. Being an island it was vital the convoys got through, but the losses were awful. Grace's heart went out to all those merchant and Royal Navy sailors. The army was building up to strength again after Dunkirk, and the factories were working day and night to turn out the needed armaments. Everyone was doing so much, whatever the cost to themselves, and so must she.

Brian would have wanted her to do what she could.

The recruitment office was crowded when Grace reached it, and she had to wait an hour for her turn to talk to one of the officers.

'Sit down,' he said, without looking up from the files on his desk.

She watched him shuffling through papers, and smiled to herself. Here was another soldier who didn't want a desk job. Boredom and irritation practically radiated from him.

'Right, miss,' he said sharply, pushing a form towards her. 'Fill that in and sign it.'

She pushed it back. 'I don't sign anything without knowing what it entails.'

He looked up, eyes narrowed. 'Then don't waste my time. You came to join the ATS, didn't you?'

'I came to discuss it, but if you are not prepared to do your job properly, then you are wasting my time. I'll see someone who is more civil.' She stood up and started to walk away.

'Wait!' He was suddenly in front of her. 'I apologise for my rudeness. I am not having a good day, but that is no excuse. I've been at this for three weeks without a break, and my temper is frayed. Can we start again?'

'We'll give it a try.' She sat down again.

'What would you like to know, Miss—?'

'Mrs Lincoln.'

'Ah, well, if you're married . . .'

'My husband was killed in France,' she said, not giving him a chance to finish what he was saying.

106

He inclined his head in acknowledgement. 'And how do you feel about that?'

'Angry. If you are going to ask me daft questions, then we have nothing else to discuss.'

'Humour me, Mrs Lincoln.'

'All right, but you are only allowed one more stupid question.'

He laughed, showing interest for the first time. 'Do you believe we should be fighting this war?'

'Fighting is the only way we are going to win it – and we must win.' She held his gaze as he studied her intently.

'Tell me about yourself.'

Grace gave him a brief outline of her work at the lawyers and her qualifications. Before leaving, Dan had given her a sealed envelope to give to any prospective employer. She handed it to the officer.

'This is a reference from my last job.'

'And why did you leave that job?'

'Major Chester had recovered enough from his injuries to be able to rejoin his regiment, so my services were no longer required.'

His head shot up. 'You worked for an officer?'

She nodded. 'At the War Office.'

He quickly slit open the envelope and read the contents. 'Major Chester states that you speak fluent French and good German. You can also drive, having received instruction to army standards.'

'That's correct.' Grace was surprised that Dan had included German, but he had made her work at it, and if he thought it was good enough, then she wasn't going to deny it.

He stood up. 'Please wait here, Mrs Lincoln. I won't be long.'

Lieutenant Greaves knocked smartly on the door at the end of the passage, and stepped inside.

'I've got a present for you, Captain,' he said, a smile on his face. 'You've chosen the right day to come here, sir, and check up on us.'

Captain Norris sat back and studied the man in front of him. They had met on the beaches at Dunkirk, and had been firm friends ever since. 'You look pleased with yourself.'

'I'm hoping this find will be enough to release me from this detail – sir.'

'Cut out the "sir", Jack, there's no one else here. Tell me what this is about. If it's as good as you obviously think, I'll see what I can do about releasing you from interviewing young women. Though it's a duty most men would enjoy.'

'Then give it to one of them. I've had enough!'

'All right.' The captain laughed. 'I'll get you back to your beloved tanks. Now, what have you got for me?'

'Read that.' Jack handed over the letter and waited, watching the captain's expression carefully.

After reading it through twice, he looked up. 'I met Major Chester briefly once. He was in a bad way, and I'm pleased to know he survived. What is this girl like?'

'Bright, speaks her mind when she needs to, and appears to be strong-minded. I have the feeling she would take responsibility and act on her own initiative.'

'You've deduced all of that in one short interview?'

'Ah, well, I wasn't as polite as I should have been, and she told me off very firmly.'

'Did she?' The captain was on his feet. 'Take me to her.'

To pass the time while she waited, Grace gazed around the busy room. There were several tables, and the women in the queue went to an empty one when their turn came. Most of the recruitment officers appeared to be polite, making the girls feel welcome. It had been her misfortune to get one who would rather be somewhere else.

Her interviewer was returning, and he wasn't alone. She wished she knew what Dan had said in that letter, because it had certainly caused a reaction. She wasn't quite sure if that was good or bad.

'Mrs Lincoln, I'm Captain Norris.' He sat down at the table. 'I understand you want to join the ATS.'

'I'm thinking about it.'

He smiled. 'Your qualifications are excellent. Major Chester regarded you highly, and I am sure the service would be pleased to have you – should you decide to join.'

'Could you tell me what kind of work I would be asked to do?'

'That would be decided after you have completed the basic training. I can't make any promises at this point, you understand, but your chances of obtaining a responsible position are good.'

Grace nodded. She would have liked to know before joining, but that obviously wasn't the way it worked.

He smiled again. 'What is your decision, Mrs Lincoln?'

Her hesitation was only a second or two. 'Where do I sign?'

Both officers smiled now, and the captain stood up to shake her hand.

'Lieutenant Greaves will deal with the necessary paperwork.' He nodded to the other officer. 'Bring the papers to me when they are signed. I will attach Major Chester's reference to them and add a few comments of my own.'

'Yes, sir.'

'It's been a pleasure to meet you, Mrs Lincoln.'

Grace watched him walk away, and then sat down again, ready to take this next step. 'What happens now?' she asked, handing the signed form over to the officer.

'You will receive an official letter telling you where to report. Then, as already mentioned, there will be the basic training. After that it will be decided what kind of job you will be doing.'

'Do I have any say in the matter?'

His smile was wry. 'Not a lot, as a rule, but your chances could be better than a lot of the new recruits. The reference from Major Chester will carry weight. I'm sure you will be all right.'

'We'll see, won't we?' She smiled and stood up. 'And I hope you soon get an assignment more to your liking, Lieutenant. Major Chester hated being tied to a desk, as well.'

The officer laughed. 'You recognised the signs, but you have made my day more interesting. I have enjoyed meeting you, Mrs Lincoln, and wish you all the best for the future.'

'Thank you, Lieutenant.' Grace headed out of the building feeling relieved to have finally made the decision. A smile hovered on her lips as she thought about the interview. That was the last time she would be able to speak her mind to an officer.

She saw a cafe across the road, and headed for it. She needed a strong cup of tea!

Chapter Eleven

A week or so later the letter arrived telling her to report to a camp in Northamptonshire on the 7th of September.

'They haven't given you much time,' her mother complained. 'That's tomorrow!'

'I'm glad I haven't had to wait too long. Don't look so worried, Mum. I'll be all right, and I've got to do this.'

'I know, dear, but we'll miss you. I know you and Brian would have moved into a place of your own eventually, but this is different. You will be alone.'

'No, I won't. There will be lots of other girls there, and we'll soon get to know each other.'

'Don't fuss, Jean.' Ted walked in to the kitchen. 'Grace is more than capable of looking after herself. Anyway, it will be an adventure, won't it, Grace?'

'It will,' she laughed. 'Don't forget, Mum, that Dan

112

took me to an army camp quite a few times, so I have some idea what to expect.'

'Of course. And talking of Dan, don't forget you promised to let Colonel Askew know what you're doing.'

'I haven't forgotten, Mum. I'll do that today.'

As soon as breakfast was cleared away, Grace went to the War Office. She no longer had her pass, so she had to wait while they checked to see if the colonel could see her. She would leave a message for him if he wasn't there.

He soon came striding towards her, a wide smile on his face. 'Grace, how lovely to see you. I'm afraid I can only spare ten minutes. Phone next time, and we can meet when I am free.'

'I won't be able to come again. I'm going away. I've come to tell you that I've joined the ATS, and will be going to a camp in Northamptonshire tomorrow.'

'Ah, that's splendid. Thank you for letting me know. Perhaps you could find the time to drop me a line now and again? I'd like to know how you get on.'

'I'll do that, sir.'

He nodded. 'I miss having you and Dan here. It seems so quiet.'

'I imagine it is,' she laughed. 'May I ask how he is getting on?'

'He's delighted to be back in the fray, you know. He's fit and happy again, thank goodness.'

'I'm pleased to hear it. I mustn't keep you any longer. Thank you for seeing me, Colonel Askew.'

'All the best for the future, my dear.'

* * *

The next day Grace caught the train, excited, but also apprehensive, and sad at the same time. She was leaving behind everything that was familiar, and heading for a life that was full of uncertainties. Her mother had been tearful at the station, and Grace had tried to explain that this was the right thing for her to do. The house held so many memories of Brian, and the large bed felt empty knowing he would never be there again. It had been hard to leave her parents, though, but her dad had remained cheerful and positive. That had been a great help.

The train was crowded, but after much searching, Grace managed to find a seat. She settled back and gazed out of the window at the passing countryside, not really seeing it. Her mind was now on what awaited her at the end of the journey.

That time seemed to come all too soon, and as Grace walked into the camp, she was reminded of the times she had spent with Dan when he'd been training to get fit again. About twenty girls had arrived on the same train, and most of them were looking worried.

'What do we do now?' one of the girls whispered to Grace.

'We'll soon find out. Our instructions are on the way.'

'Oh, help!' the girl exclaimed when she saw the soldier marching towards them. 'Now this is actually happening, I'm scared!'

'You'll be all right.' Grace smiled. 'What's your name?'
'Peggy.'
'Pleased to meet you, Peggy. I'm Grace.'

'You don't look scared.'

'I'm sure there isn't anything to worry about. If we follow orders we'll be all right.'

'Can I stay with you?'

'Of course.' There wasn't time to say anything else, as the procedure of checking them in began. They were issued with uniforms, had a medical, and given a string of instructions. After a long day they were finally taken to their sleeping quarters.

'Oh, no!' Peggy cried in dismay. 'This is just a hut, and there are twelve beds in here!'

Grace couldn't help laughing at the dismay on some of the faces. 'Did you expect single rooms?'

'I didn't know what to expect.' Peggy suddenly grabbed Grace's arm and pulled her towards two beds at the far end. 'Quick! Let's bag these. They are away from the door, and it won't be so draughty. This place will be freezing when the weather gets colder.'

'Good thinking.'

They made a dive for the beds and sat on them, laughing. This propelled the other girls into action, and there was chaos for a while until everyone was settled.

Grace stood up and raised her voice above the noise. 'We haven't had time to get acquainted, so we should all introduce ourselves. I'm Grace Lincoln from Ealing, in London.'

Each girl introduced herself in the same way, and they were soon talking and laughing with each other. They had survived the first day, and there was relief all round.

'Quiet!'

The chatter stopped abruptly, and all eyes turned to the female officer standing in the doorway.

'We have just received news that London has been bombed. As many of you come from there, I thought you should know.'

Grace went cold. They had been expecting this, of course, but for it to happen on the day she left . . . She stood up. 'Thank you for letting us know, ma'am. Do you know which areas have been attacked?'

'What's your name?'

'Grace Lincoln, ma'am.'

'Well, Lincoln, we believe the main attack has been on the docks. The information coming in isn't detailed yet. I'll let you know when the situation is clearer.'

'Thank you, ma'am.'

'Get some rest. Tomorrow will be busy as we try to turn you into soldiers.'

There was silence until the officer left, and then one girl said, 'I hope my folks are all right.' There were worried murmurs of agreement.

'Grace!' another girl called. 'You sounded as if you know what you're doing when you spoke to that officer.'

'I worked for an army major before coming here. I picked up a few tips.'

Sleep wasn't easy that night as Grace tossed and turned. She had to find a way to get in touch with her parents quickly. She wouldn't rest until she knew if they were all right. George immediately came to mind. She'd phone him if she could. He wouldn't mind, she was sure.

*　*　*

116

Colonel Askew was so busy he hadn't had any spare time for a couple of weeks after the first raid on the 7th September. Somehow, Grace had managed to get hold of a phone the next day and contact him. He had already checked to see if her parents were all right, and had been able to put her mind at rest straight away. This was the first opportunity he'd had to see Dan.

The moment he walked in to the officer's mess at Winchester, he saw him. His height made him easy to spot in a crowd.

'Hello, George.' Dan strode up to him. 'What brings you here?'

'Thought I'd have a break from London and bombs. I'll have a double whisky.'

'I ordered it the minute you walked in the door.'

'Initiative, that's what I like to see.'

An orderly brought the drinks from the bar and they sat down.

'You're looking well,' George said, after taking a good sip of his drink. 'How is the leg holding up?'

'Good as new.' Dan waited. His uncle didn't just turn up without a good reason. 'So, Hitler hasn't been able to destroy our air force, he's started bombing London.'

'In retaliation to our raid on Berlin, I expect. I was going to phone you, but decided to come instead. I miss you and Grace at the War Office.' He took another sip of his whisky. 'As I told Grace.'

Dan's expression didn't change. 'And what did she say?'

'She laughed. I would have liked to spend more time with her, but I had a meeting to attend. I won't have the chance to see her again, though, because she's gone away.'

'Oh, to get away from the raids?'

'No, of course not. She left before that started.'

Dan frowned. 'And you've waited this long before telling me? Where has she gone?'

'Northamptonshire.' George looked at his nephew, but couldn't read anything from his expression. 'How the hell did you know what she would do?'

'George! What are you talking about? Get to the point.'

'Grace has joined the ATS.'

A slow smile appeared on Dan's face. 'Good for her. And the answer to your question is, I didn't know. I was hoping she would, though.'

'Why?'

'Because it's right for her. She needed to make a fresh start – somewhere away from her normal home life with all its memories. Did she give you any details?'

'I only had ten minutes with her, and all she told me was her destination.'

'Hmm. I know the camp.'

'Dan! I know that look. Don't interfere. Grace won't thank you if you do. Leave her to make her own way.'

'What makes you think I'd interfere?' Dan gave his uncle an incredulous look. 'I'm just curious to know where she will be assigned after basic training.'

'She has promised to write and let me know how she is getting on. I'll tell you, but you make sure you leave it at that. You are taking too much interest in her, however much you deny it. She's a nice girl, Dan, but she isn't for you.'

'You're letting your imagination run away with you again, George. I'm taking an interest in her because she's a plucky girl, and she helped me through a rocky time. Is it wrong to be grateful for that?'

'No, of course not, but remember, your regiment will probably be among the first to be sent to fight. Don't get involved. She has suffered enough.'

Dan's eyes narrowed. 'Do you know something?'

'No, but there's no harm in being prepared. Just remember what I've said. Keep away from that camp. If you go striding in there, you could make life difficult for Grace.'

'You are acting as if Grace is your daughter.'

'If she was, you wouldn't get anywhere near her. You never keep a girlfriend more than a couple of weeks before you move onto the next one. You should be married by now – or at least thinking about it.'

'I haven't found anyone who would put up with my lifestyle yet. I'm a career soldier, George, and a wife would have to be prepared to move around, never having a permanent home, and be capable of mixing with all ranks right to the top. You were lucky, you found one, but there aren't many around. And if you've come here to lecture me, then you can stop right now. Why the devil do you think I've asked you to keep in touch with Grace? You've misinterpreted my motives towards her completely.' Dan picked up their empty glasses. 'And if you're hinting that I could cause grief by not surviving, I can tell you now that I'm not going to die in this bloody war! Same again?'

George nodded and grinned as he watched his nephew

order more drinks. He had done what he came here to do. It was a mystery how the two of them could have become so fond of that girl in such a short time, but she was still coping with the grief and loss of her husband. He wasn't absolutely sure what Dan's feelings were towards Grace, but alarm bells were ringing in his head. He could be completely wrong, of course, but a little warning wouldn't go amiss. And he felt very protective towards her.

'There you are.' Dan put the drinks on the table. 'I hope you're not driving?'

'I'm staying overnight.'

'That gives us plenty of time to catch up on the rest of the news, then. Do you know how James is?'

George took a deep breath. 'Two days ago, on 15th September, I paid a visit to Kenley. It was the most harrowing day I have spent since Dunkirk. As soon as the planes came in to refuel, they were off again. Everything they had was flying, and there were losses each time they returned. My heart was thumping until I saw James get out of his Spitfire at the end of the day. It's bad, Dan. Those men are so tired they fall asleep anywhere. I never got a chance to say more than a few words to James. When I said I didn't think they could keep that up, James slapped me on the back, and said of course they could. Then he was asleep. I left him, knowing he would start all over again at first light.'

'They are doing a valiant job, and giving the rest of us the time needed to recover to full strength. The Luftwaffe are suffering high losses, and the daylight raids they are making on London are madness.'

'I agree. Göring wanted to wipe our planes from the skies, but he hasn't been able to do that. Intelligence says Hitler has abandoned his plans to invade – for the time being, anyway.'

'He didn't have any choice. If he'd attempted it immediately after Dunkirk, we would have been hard pushed. We're building up our strength again, but we still need more time.'

George nodded. 'And those weary pilots are giving us the time; it mustn't be wasted. I would say he's decided to break the will of the people with these raids.'

'It's going to take time, but Hitler will be defeated eventually. He has to be! The alternative is unacceptable.'

'Agreed. Many believe that this little island, standing alone and facing the might of the enemy, can't possibly survive. They are wrong, and in that conviction we will never waver, no matter how rough it becomes.'

Dan lifted his glass. 'Let's drink to that. With Grace now in the army, Hitler doesn't stand a chance,' he said, a slow smile appearing. 'I expect her to rise steadily up the ranks.'

'Without any help from you!'

'She won't need my help, George. There's natural leader there, just waiting to be revealed.'

That wasn't how Grace was feeling at that moment. She was worried about being away from home with the raids going on – and the basic training. If she wasn't so tired she would laugh. The first few days on the parade ground had been a shambles. Some didn't know their left from their right, and kept marching when the rest had stopped, causing chaos and much milling around. The look on the sergeant major's face had been something to see. Grace thought that picture would always remain with her. Two weeks of hard slog and they were beginning to march without too many mistakes. Two more weeks to go.

'We didn't do too badly today, did we, Grace?' Peggy dropped onto her bed and stretched out with a sigh of relief. 'We marched like professionals. I even saw the sergeant major almost smile today.'

'Almost?'

'Yes, well, that poor man has been sorely tried. I expect he's forgotten how to smile.'

'Don't you believe it,' Grace said. 'They've probably been laughing at our antics in their bar every night.'

'I'd love to know what they've been saying,' Peggy laughed. 'We'll show them, though. In another two weeks we'll be as good as the men. Then we'll find out what job we'll be doing. What are you hoping for, Grace?'

'I really don't know. I suppose it will be clerical work of some kind. What about you?'

'I'd like to be assigned to the Transport Division, if I can. I've always been fascinated by mechanical things.'

'Let's hope you're lucky.' Grace smiled at Peggy. The frightened girl she had met on the first day had disappeared. She had grown in confidence and was thoroughly enjoying life in the army. A couple of the other girls were not faring so well. The rest of them had gathered round to encourage and support those struggling. The comradeship between them had grown over the two weeks, and Grace felt it was helping to strengthen the whole squad. She wondered if this was one of the things Dan had missed while at the War Office. He had certainly fought hard to get back to his regiment.

Remembering those times brought her thoughts back to those she was separated from. Letters from her parents were cheerful; assuring her they were perfectly all right. She had also heard from George, and he'd told her, proudly, that James was now a squadron leader. Like her parents, he had made light of the bombing. In two weeks she would be able to see for herself exactly how bad it was.

And in two weeks, this group of girls who had melded together so well would be assigned to different postings. They would be saying goodbye to each other, probably never to meet again.

Chapter Twelve

The camp gates were a welcome sight, and Dan could hear the groans of relief behind him. It had been a tough run with heavy packs, but if the men were to endure the rigours of battle they had to be very fit. Many of them were new recruits and had to be toughened up quickly.

When he reached the parade ground he stopped. There were still five men with him, and the others weren't far behind. Not one of them had dropped out, and that was an improvement.

'Well done, men,' he said, easing the pack off his back and dropping it on the ground.

'Good run today, sir,' the sergeant stated, watching as each man arrived, and calculating their condition.

Dan studied one of the soldiers who had stayed with him all the way. He was a new recruit, and had only been with them for a week.

'You managed that well, Johnson.'

'Thank you, sir. I reckoned if you could do it, then so could I. I watched you all the way and never let you get more than six paces in front of me.' He grinned. 'I was told you were impossible to beat, so I wanted to get through the gate before you. Couldn't quite manage it, though, but I'll have you next time, sir.'

Cheeky sod, Dan thought, highly amused. 'I can see I'll have to watch you, Private.'

Johnson grinned again, and then hurried to take his place in the ranks of men now lined up in order.

'He's a bit sure of himself, sir,' the sergeant muttered. 'I'll discipline him for talking to you like that.'

'No, let it go. We'll sort him out over the next few weeks.'

The sergeant's mouth twitched at the corners. He had been one of the men with Major Chester on that harrowing trek to reach Dunkirk, and had come to know and respect him. It was good to have him back.

'I'll look forward to that, sir.'

They gave each other an amused look, and then Dan said, 'You can dismiss the men now.'

'Yes, sir!'

When the men had left the parade ground, Dan lifted his pack and swung it on to his back.

'Hello, Dan.'

He spun round and smiled with pleasure at the major general standing there. 'Stan! What a surprise. Are you going to be stationed here?'

'No. I'm still at Aldershot. I came to see you.'

'That sounds ominous. What does the Intelligence Service want with me?'

Stan Haydon laughed. 'You know we'd like you to join us, but you're a fighting man, and it's useless trying to pry you away from your regiment. I need to discuss something with you – in private.'

'Right. Come to my quarters. I need to clean up, and then you can tell me what this is about.'

Showered and in a clean uniform, Dan made a pot of coffee, Stan's favourite beverage, and sat down. 'How can I help you, Stan?'

'I've been sent files of possible recruits for the Intelligence Service. Normally, I wouldn't have even bothered to consider this one. You know I'm always doubtful about having women in my section, but there was a letter from you attached to her file. Her name is Grace Lincoln. The report from Northamptonshire and your letter told me what her qualifications are, but I'd like you to tell me what she is like as a person. Her husband was killed in France, and that worries me. Is she mentally stable and able to cope with disturbing situations without becoming emotional?'

'I can say without hesitation or doubt that she can.' Dan then gave Stan a detailed account of the few weeks Grace had worked for him. By the time he had finished, Stan was smiling.

'She sounds as if she might be worth considering.'

'I'm sure you would find her very useful.' Dan didn't elaborate further. He had been careful not to say anything to influence Stan's decision in any way.

'I'll ask to interview her first, then, but if I have any doubts about her I won't take her. There are others to choose from.'

'Of course. The final decision is yours. Will you let me know how things turn out?'

'Yes, as soon as I've seen her.' Stan looked at his watch. 'Let's have dinner, and then I'll buy you a drink. I want to hear how you managed to get so fit again. I was told you were finished as a soldier.'

'You don't want to believe everything you hear.'

That was an interesting visit, Dan thought, as he watched Stan drive away. Several attempts in the past had been made to move him to Intelligence, but that wasn't for him. He had a strong feeling that the major general hadn't come just to talk about Grace. He'd used that as an excuse. Stan had watched him carefully all the time he had been here, and if he had shown the slightest sign of not having recovered completely from his injury, he would have been transferred – like it or not. He continued to watch the car disappear through the gates, and blessed those weeks he'd pushed himself to the limit to regain full mobility again. That sergeant had certainly known what he was doing, and Grace had brought some fun and quiet support. He really did wish her the very best for the future. The Intelligence Service might be just the thing for her. He hoped it worked out, but that would be up to Stan.

'Sir.'

Dan turned. 'Yes, Sergeant.'

'I thought you would like to know that Johnson is

bragging he'll beat you next time, and they've started a book on it.'

'Really? We are definitely going to have to do something about that man.' Dan kept a perfectly straight face, and asked, 'How much have you bet?'

'A pound on you to win, sir.'

Dan removed his wallet and handed over two pound notes. 'Put that on for me to win – in your name, of course.'

'Be a pleasure, sir.'

Both men looked at each other and burst into laughter.

'Johnson's new and doesn't know you. He doesn't realise you let some of us stay with you today. And he's cocky enough to want to get one over on an officer.'

'I've watched him and he believes he's better than everyone else. We've got to make him see that he is part of a team, or he could be trouble when we're in action. That could endanger other lives. I won't have someone who is a risk under my command. If we can't calm him down, then he will have to go elsewhere.'

'I've also come to the same conclusion, and that's why I didn't put a stop to it. I knew you would find a way to deal with him.'

Dan nodded. 'We'll let him swagger for a couple of days, and then we'll run his race. This might be the best way to deal with him. Don't let anyone know I'm aware of this though.'

'Not a word, sir. I'm relieved to see you made a complete recovery after France.'

'I was lucky. The bullet didn't damage anything vital. Infection and loss of blood caused the problems.'

'And walking on it for miles. It didn't have a chance to heal.'

'There wasn't any choice, was there? I certainly wasn't going to risk getting captured again.'

'Not likely, sir! When you said "run", I was off as fast as I could. I still can't believe we came out of that alive.'

'But we did, and one day we will go back.' Dan's expression showed his determination. 'And it will be a different story next time. In the meantime, we've got to get this lot fighting fit. Arrange a training run for three days' time – early morning. Without packs. We'll see what kind of speed everyone has.'

'Yes, sir!'

There was a suppressed air of excitement as the men lined up. Betting had been brisk, Dan had been told, involving a lot of the camp. Those loyal to Dan had laid money on him, but others had believed Johnson's boasts. Dan wasn't happy about letting this go ahead, but felt it was the best way to deal with the situation. Putting Johnson on a charge or transferring him would only make him worse. This had to be settled today, once and for all.

'We are going to take a nice ten mile run today without packs, so you can enjoy the scenery.' There was a ripple of amusement through the ranks. 'It's quite warm, so remember to drink plenty of water along the way. Same route as last time. Off you go.'

Dan started behind everyone else with the sergeant beside him.

'What are your tactics, sir?'

'I'll take it easy for the first few miles, and then gradually move forward.'

'Right. I'll keep the pace steady until they start to spread out. Watch Johnson, he might make a sprint for it early, hoping to leave you behind.'

The sergeant then went to the front to urge the men on, and Dan jogged along. He loved to run, and from a youngster he had competed regularly. Not only did he have stamina, but could muster a good turn of speed in a sprint. He might need that ability today. Johnson was good, but he was too sure of himself, and that was a mistake. Dan also suspected that he had a low opinion of officers, and if he could outrun one it would make him feel a big man. With that kind of attitude he would be a liability to the regiment.

After five miles Dan was in the middle of the group which was now widely spread. There were a few who really struggled to finish a run, but all Dan asked was that they do their best, and showed a determination to finish.

Johnson was in the front, running easily, and Dan knew he mustn't let him get too far in front of him or he wouldn't stand a chance. He began to close in on him to keep within sprinting distance.

The gates were in sight before Dan made his move, remembering all the races he had competed in. Johnson gasped in surprise as he passed him. It was close, but with a final spurt, Dan managed to reach the parade ground ten yards ahead. Much to Dan's delight, the sergeant also passed Johnson at the last minute. They were just recovering their breath when a dozen more men arrived.

They immediately went up to Johnson, who just shook his head, speechless.

'I think that settles it, sir,' the sergeant said under his breath.

'I hope so.' Dan took a swig from his water bottle. 'I wouldn't like to try that again. I'm not as young as I used to be!'

'You'd never know it, sir. That was damned hard though.' He began to count the men on the parade ground. 'Still four to come, sir.'

'We'll wait. I want to say a few words before the men are dismissed.'

Ten minutes later the stragglers arrived. One young boy was really struggling, and the other experienced men were encouraging him on. He could hardly stand when he stopped by the sergeant.

'Sorry I'm last, sir,' he gasped. 'I ain't no runner.'

Dan strode over. 'Don't apologise. You have shown courage and determination to keep going even though you were suffering. Those are the qualities I look for in my men. You will make a good soldier. Well done!'

The young recruit straightened up, a look of surprise on his face. 'Thank you, sir.'

Dan turned to the men who were all listening intently, even Johnson. 'You will all have different talents and skills, and every one is needed to make up an effective fighting unit. I don't give a damn who comes first or last. What I want to see is you all working together for the good of all. Like the three men who stayed behind to help someone who was in trouble. It's qualities like that that make a regiment strong – and I mean us to be one of the best.'

When he saw the nods of approval from some of the men, he turned to the sergeant. 'You can dismiss the men now.'

Later that afternoon, Dan was doing what he most disliked, paperwork, and wished he had Grace there. She would have dealt with it in no time at all, but he didn't have that luxury now.

There was a sharp rap on the door and the sergeant marched in. He held out a wad of pound notes. 'Your winnings, sir.'

He waved it away. 'Arrange for the men who took part in the run today to have a beer with their evening meal. If it comes to any more, have it put on my bar bill.'

'I'll do that, sir. What shall I tell the men?'

'Just say it's from you, out of your winnings.'

The sergeant grinned. 'They will never believe that!'

'Really? Do you make their lives that much of a misery?'

'I try, sir.'

Dan laughed, remembering a sergeant or two he had encountered when he had been starting out. 'All right, then, tell them it's from my winnings, and if any of them try to pull a stunt like that again, I will have the whole squad on latrine duty for a month.'

'That should do nicely, sir.'

Dan pushed the paperwork aside and sat back. 'How is Johnson taking defeat?'

'The men are ribbing him a lot, but he seems to be taking it well and joining in the laughter. He did say he thought all officers just stood around giving orders. A couple of men who were with us in France put him right on that point. I think he'll be all right now, but I'll keep an eye on him.'

'The next few weeks will tell us if he is going to fit in. Thank you, Sergeant.'

He saluted and marched out, leaving Dan to his paperwork.

Chapter Thirteen

The parade had gone off without any mistakes, and they were all feeling rather proud of themselves. Grace had loved the feeling of everyone marching in perfect time. There had been a rhythm to it and she had found this particularly enjoyable, making all the hard work over the last four weeks worth every blister. Their time at this camp was now over, and seven days of leave lay ahead. First, though, they were each being seen and given their new postings.

When Grace's name was called, she marched smartly into the interview room.

'Sit down,' the female officer ordered. 'You've done well while you've been here. How do you feel about army life?'

'I like it, ma'am.'

She nodded and handed Grace some papers. 'At the end

of your leave you are to report to Major General Haydon at Aldershot barracks. He already has your details, but give him the sealed envelope as well.'

'What will be my assignment?'

'That will be explained when you get there, but this is only an interview. If the major general doesn't think you are suitable for his outfit, you are to immediately return here. You will then be given a new posting.'

This wasn't at all what Grace had expected, and it was most unsatisfactory. The other girls had been given definite postings.

The officer looked up and actually smiled. 'Don't look so perplexed. We wouldn't be sending you if we didn't consider you very suitable for Major General Haydon. He is a stickler for punctuality so make sure you arrive on time. All the information telling you where to go when you get there and the time of your appointment is in the folder. Good luck. You may go and enjoy your leave.'

'Thank you, ma'am.' Grace stood up and marched out of the room, to find Peggy waiting for her.

'What did you get?'

'Nothing yet. I've got an interview at Aldershot after my leave.'

'Doing what?'

'I don't know. All I was told was that the major general will explain when I get there.'

'Ah.' Peggy nodded. 'They're gonna give you something special 'cos you're clever.'

Grace pulled a face. 'The major I worked for gave me

a reference. I don't know what was in it, but I have the feeling it might be causing them trouble in deciding what to do with me. I wish they'd given me some idea, though, because now it will be on my mind while I'm on leave. How did you get on?'

Peggy beamed. 'Transport! Isn't that terrific?'

'I'm so pleased you got what you wanted.'

'So am I! And as this is our last night together we've arranged a big party to celebrate surviving the basic training.'

'Good. Let's forget everything and just enjoy ourselves tonight, shall we?'

'Absolutely!'

The next morning there were tearful goodbyes as they all prepared to go their different ways. As the train chugged along, Grace reflected on the last four weeks. It had been hard, but there had also been a lot of laughter. Even the aching muscles and blistered feet hadn't dampened her enjoyment. She had liked being with so many girls. It had made her realise that she had led a quiet life until then. Helen had been her friend from childhood, but apart from that she had worked for men, and never mixed socially with the other girls at work. The last weeks were now over, and there was something new ahead of her. Though what that could be was a mystery. She was hoping for something more than being a secretary, but that was probably all they would give her. Still, as Helen had said, it was something she was good at, so she mustn't be too disappointed.

She sighed, and told herself to stop worrying about it. Take each day as it comes – and today she was going home! It would be lovely to see her parents again. This was the first time she had ever been away for any length of time, and she had missed them. She wished Helen could be there as well, but that was too much to ask.

Grace had listened intently to the news reports about the bombing, but was still shocked when she saw the extent of the damage. It was a relief to see that their area was relatively unharmed, and when she turned in to her road it was lovely to see their house still standing.

The moment she put her key in the front door it was pulled open by her smiling parents. Her mother was in slacks, which was something she had never seen before. It took her by surprise, but she didn't remark on it.

'We saw you arrive!' her father said as he hugged her.

'Oh, it's so good to see you.' Her mother held her at arm's length to study her. 'You're looking well. The army obviously suits you. You must be hungry after your journey.'

'I am,' Grace agreed. 'All I've had is a sandwich and a cup of tea on the way home.'

'Come on, then. We've delayed dinner in the hope you would soon arrive. We can talk while we eat, and get some food inside us before the raids start.'

'How bad are they?' she asked, glancing at the tin hat in the hall with ARP stamped on it.

'They're coming over at night now.' Her father looked at his watch. 'They'll be here around nine o'clock.'

'I hope you are both going to the shelters.' Grace sat

at the table, the smell of her mother's cooking making her realise just how hungry she was.

'We do – sometimes.'

'What do you mean "sometimes", Mum?' Grace demanded.

'It depends how close it is,' her father explained. 'Don't worry, we've got an Anderson shelter in the garden now, but we don't use it unless we have to. It's rather damp, and we need our wellington boots on if we go down there. There's too much underground water here.'

'Waste of precious ground, if you ask me,' her mother said. 'We could be growing vegetables on that plot.'

'Your safety is more important,' Grace pointed out.

'You're right, of course.' Her mother put a plate of steaming food in front of her. 'It's only a veg pie, but it is filling.'

'It smells and looks delicious.'

'Eat up, then,' her father told her. 'You'll need that inside you tonight. Once the worst of the raid is over we go and help the rescue services. Your mother has joined the WVS, and they go out with a tea van.'

So that was why her mother was dressed like that. They hadn't mentioned any of this in their letters. 'You've been keeping things from me!'

'Don't look so shocked, darling.' Her mother smiled sadly. 'People need help. The Women's Voluntary Service is there to give a hot drink to rescuers, firemen and those made homeless or in shock. A cup of strong tea is always a comfort.'

'I see.' Grace shook her head. 'I came home intending to persuade you to move out of London, but I'd be wasting my time, wouldn't I?'

'We're not leaving. We'll take our chance, like everyone else. Now, eat up before the sirens go. If the bombs start to fall we'll dive under the table.'

Grace stopped with her fork halfway towards her mouth and stared at her mother in disbelief. 'You're not serious?'

Her mother shrugged. 'It will protect us from flying glass.'

'But not if the bloody house comes down!'

'Language, dear. I hope you haven't picked up bad habits at that camp?'

'Mum! You're incredible, do you know that?'

'Yes, dear. Your father has always told me I am.'

Ted was grinning, and when Grace caught him winking at her, she burst into laughter. 'All right, I'll watch my language. So, do you think there will be a raid tonight?'

'They've been coming every night. A lot of families sleep down the underground stations, especially if they've got young children.' Her father finished the last of his meal and sat back with a sigh.

'I expect many parents are wishing they'd left their children in the country. It must have been hard to send their youngsters away to live with strangers, though.'

'It was, Grace. Some children settled in the homes they were evacuated to, but others wanted to come back. There didn't seem to be any danger then.' Jean shook her head sadly. 'It was the wrong thing to do, but it's easy to be wise with hindsight.'

Suddenly the eerie wailing of the sirens filled the air.

'Here they come!' Ted said, grimly. 'Grace, you go to the shelter if you want to.'

'Not without you,' she told them firmly.

'If I were you, darling, I'd change out of that smart uniform. Slacks would be better.'

'All right, Mum. I've got my army slacks with me. They will be more comfortable.' Grace grabbed her bag and dashed upstairs to change as quickly as she could. The drone of bombers approaching could already be heard.

It only took a couple of minutes and she was back with her parents. They were sitting at the kitchen table and Ted was shuffling a pack of cards.

'What now?' she asked, sitting down.

'We wait and play pontoon.' Ted began to deal the cards. 'Quite often a plane comes in first and drops markers over the target. I've been out and had a look, and it looks like it might be the East End again.'

'Poor devils.' Jean picked up her cards.

Grace did the same. There was a feeling of unreality to be sitting here like this as the guns opened fire on the raiders. If the majority of people were showing the same fortitude, then there was no way Hitler was going to force this country into submission.

She lost track of time as the bombs whistled down, and a couple of times the house shook and they dived under the table. Then they crawled out and continued their game of cards. It was the most frightening and extraordinary experience she had ever encountered.

When at last the all-clear sounded, they went outside and Grace gasped in horror. The sky was red, like a sunrise. London was burning.

'I've got to go, Grace,' Ted told her, already moving towards the door. 'The rescue services are going to need all the help they can get.'

'I'm coming with you.' She fell into step with her father as he collected his tin hat and hurried out of the front door. 'What's Mum going to do?'

'She'll be with the WVS on the tea van.'

'You didn't tell me any of this in your letters,' she complained.

'What would you have done if we had told you?'

'Worry!'

'Exactly. That's why we didn't say anything. We can't sit back and do nothing, any more than you can.'

'No, of course you can't,' she admitted, as they reached a group of men at the end of the road. Many were in uniforms of the various rescue services, some were neighbours she knew well, including Helen's father, and there were men obviously on leave like herself. It was a mixture, but one thing was clear; they all wanted to help.

An old bus trundled up and they all managed to squeeze in, and it wasn't long before they reached a roadblock. They walked the rest of the way, clambering over and round smouldering debris. The next two hours were spent searching for anyone who might be buried under the rubble.

It was light when Grace's father tapped her on the shoulder. 'That's all we can do here. Time to call it a night.'

She straightened up, numb with fatigue. 'Did you find anyone?'

'Two. Dead, I'm afraid.' He took her arm. 'Come on, the bus is waiting.'

'I haven't seen Mum.'

'She'll be down at the docks, I expect.'

That first night set the pattern of the rest of Grace's leave – air raids at night, and sleeping when they could. She worried about leaving her parents to that hell, but knew that no amount of pleading would make them leave London. It hadn't been a restful leave, but at least she knew what the Blitz was really like, and how involved her parents were. It was worrying, but she was proud of them, and everyone was labouring to keep everything going. No one was getting much sleep, but after each raid, the people were making their way to work, determined to get there any way they could, despite the destruction. Life went on a day at a time.

Grace finished packing her bag and sat on the bed, running her hands over the cover. She hadn't spent much time in this room, which was just as well. She was moving on, as Brian would have wanted, but she missed him so much. They had been childhood sweethearts, and there had never been anyone else for Grace. Would the pain ever go?

She wiped away a single tear, and stood up. The things

she had seen and done over the last week had made her emotional – and that would not do.

Dawn was lighting the sky. Her next day was here, and she had orders to follow.

Chapter Fourteen

Grace hadn't given a thought to what awaited her at Aldershot, but she would soon find out, she thought, as she was escorted to a waiting room. There were three others waiting to be interviewed, and Grace was the only woman. Whatever this was about, she didn't think her chances were good. The men waiting didn't look like secretaries. They were all late twenties to early thirties with upper-class accents, and not a private among them.

Each interview lasted at least half an hour, and she studied the faces as they returned and sat down again. They all looked confident.

It had been a long wait as she was the last to be called. The major general was a distinguished man, around six feet, greying slightly at the temples, with piercing blue eyes. She felt his scrutiny, and knew he would remember every detail about her.

'In the next room, Private Lincoln, there is a German pilot who was shot down over London. I want you to talk to him and see if you can get any useful information out of him. He doesn't speak English.' He handed her a pen and pad. 'Make a note of everything he tells you.'

This was the last thing she had expected, and for a moment the shock paralysed her. A mental picture of the destruction and suffering she had just seen filled her thoughts.

The major general was still studying her. 'Say if you are not up to it.'

He had spoken sharply, and that snapped her back. With a touch of anger in her voice, she said, 'I relish the chance to meet him, sir.'

She opened the door, stepped inside and closed it softly behind her. First she took in the room, noting where everything was, and then turned her attention to the man sitting at the table. He was handsome, with fine, chiselled features, sandy-coloured hair and hazel eyes.

Grace smiled and sat opposite him, not saying a word. Something was nagging at her, but she couldn't see what it was. She made a few notes in shorthand on the pad, and then looked up, smiling again. For about ten minutes she talked to him, making detailed notes of their conversation.

And then it hit her. She was furious with herself for not spotting it sooner. 'You have had a long day,' she said sweetly. 'Would you like a cup of tea?'

When he nodded, she stood up. 'I'll have one sent in to you.' With her hand on the door she switched to English. 'Don't ever take up acting as a profession. You would starve.'

145

The astonished look on his face made her day worthwhile.

'How did you get on?' the officer asked.

'It's all here.' Grace handed him the pad and watched him frown. 'Don't worry if you can't read shorthand, sir. Apart from my assessment of the situation there isn't anything there you don't already know. The officer in there would like a cup of tea. He's had a tiring few hours, and I'm sure he would like to change into his own uniform. Oh, and it would be wise to remove that wristwatch before doing this again. It's English.'

The frown disappeared and was replaced by surprise. 'Did that give him away?'

'It was a series of small things. I was suspicious straight away by the absence of a guard in the room. I hardly think you would send a woman in with a prisoner without some protection. In my work for a lawyer I met all types – guilty, innocent, liars, violent men and even killers. Your German fooled me for a while, but not for long. Do I have your permission to leave now, sir?'

'No, you do not! Go and wait outside.'

The three men smiled rather smugly when Grace stormed out, clearly annoyed.

'It looks as if that didn't go well,' one remarked.

'Oh, it went very well. I just don't like being taken for a fool. That charade was unnecessary!'

They all looked puzzled, but didn't pursue the subject.

'Where's that tea I was promised?'

'I'm not so sure you deserve one. What the hell happened in there, Bill?'

146

The man leaning casually against the open door gave an amused chuckle. 'I put on my best performance for her, but she saw through my deception. She even had the cheek to tell me not to take up acting as a profession. You'd think having spent some of my childhood in Germany I'd be able to convince her I was really a German pilot. And don't be fooled, behind that lovely face there is a sharp analytical mind. And her German is good, by the way.'

Stan nodded. 'She worked with Dan Chester for a while, and I suspect he's been coaching her. He speaks it like a native.'

'She's the only one who realised I wasn't German. What are you going to do?' Bill asked, walking over to the desk and picking up the notebook. As he read he began to laugh.

'I'd forgotten you can read shorthand. What does it say?'

'Believe me, Stan, you don't want to know. She does not have a very high opinion of our method of interviewing a prospective secretary. I like her, and would say she is the right person for intelligence work.'

'I know, damn it!' Stan gazed out of the window for long moments. 'It's going to cause complication if we take her. There will be some situations we can't send her into.'

'Agreed, but she could still be more useful than the other candidates we saw. She can be my secretary while we see what she is capable of.'

'No, she bloody well can't! You can forget that idea, Captain Reid.'

Bill tried to look hurt. 'Anyone would think you don't trust me.'

'I don't. If she was a plain, unattractive woman, it would be different – but she isn't.'

'Take one of the men, then.'

Stan shook his head. 'Not one of them spotted the deception, so that leaves us with the most suitable candidate – a woman. And get out of that blasted uniform. If you wander around in that you'll get arrested or shot.'

'Don't take your bad mood out on me, Major General. This exercise was your idea. If you are dead against working with a woman, why did you agree to see her?'

'I was curious. Here, read this letter from Chester.'

There was silence while Bill read through the letter, and then he lifted his head. 'Is this the Major Chester you keep trying to have transferred to us?'

Stan nodded. 'As I've said, she worked for him while he was at the War Office.'

Bill whistled through his teeth. 'She speaks fluent French, as well, and is a qualified driver. Take her, Stan. If she doesn't work out you can always have her transferred. I don't think you have a choice.'

'You're right.' Stan called the duty corporal in. 'Tell the three men they can go, and bring the woman in here.'

'Yes, sir.'

This was taking a long time. If they didn't dismiss her soon she wouldn't be able to get back to Northamptonshire today. Perhaps they would let her stay here overnight. It was a shame because Aldershot wasn't too far from London, and she might have been able to get home more often. Any hope of a posting here had gone the moment she had seen through their bit of theatre. She had been cross, and had shown it, unfortunately. If they had wanted to find out how good her German was, all they'd needed to do was give her a proper test. And why was that so important? What section of the army was this? The uniform badges were unfamiliar to her.

The duty corporal came over and told them they could go, and Grace stood up, intent on leaving.

'You are not dismissed,' the soldier told her. 'You are to come with me.'

She was escorted back to the office. When she walked in, the pretend German stepped forward and bowed gracefully. 'Captain William Reid at your service, Private Lincoln.'

There was such an air of devilment about him, and her irritation instantly disappeared. Captain Reid didn't look as if he took anything seriously, though that was probably an act, she suspected. She couldn't help laughing and joining in his game. 'It's a pleasure to meet the real you, sir.'

'The pleasure is all mine.' He grinned, showing a row of perfect white teeth. 'Now, if you will excuse me. I have to change out of this uniform. The major general thinks I will get shot if seen wandering around in it. Though I suspect he would like to shoot me himself for failing to convince you that I was a German.'

'If you don't get out of here now, that is a distinct possibility, Captain!'

'Yes, sir!' Bill opened the door, turned and winked at Grace, then disappeared.

When she turned back to the major general there was a smile on his face. *Ah*, she thought, *he has a sense of humour. Thank goodness.*

'That is the first time anyone has caught him out.'

'You do this often, then, do you, sir?'

'We've found it the most effective way to find out, quickly, if a person is suitable for this kind of work.'

'And what work is that, sir?' Grace was sure she was going to be reprimanded and sent away, so she wanted to know why she was here. There would be a black mark on her record after this, anyway.

He didn't answer the question, instead he asked, 'Did you like working for Major Chester?'

'It was interesting, sir.'

His mouth twitched at the corners. 'No doubt.'

There was a rap on the door and the corporal came in carrying a tray of tea.

'Would you like a cup of tea?' he asked when the soldier had left.

'No, thank you, sir. I can get one on the train.' Now she was puzzled. Why was this officer offering her tea?

He looked up sharply. 'Where do you think you are going?'

'I've been told to report back to Northamptonshire for another posting.'

'Why do you need another posting?'

'Because I've messed this one up,' she told him bluntly.

'What makes you think that?'

'I didn't do what I was supposed to, and I spoke my mind when I discovered the German was a fake, sir.'

150

'I admit that in most units that would have immediately disqualified you, but not in this case. We are looking for different qualities. Pour the tea for us and sit down. Whether you like the way we do things, or not, you have your posting. A decision I could live to regret, and if you mess up you'll be out of here very quickly.'

Grace, stunned by this announcement, set about pouring the tea without commenting. What could she say? He obviously didn't want her, so what on earth was going on here?

The captain swept in. 'Ah, the tea I was promised. Any biscuits?'

He sounded just like Dan and she smiled at the captain. 'Digestive or custard creams, sir?'

'Both please. I see he has you working already.'

'Private Lincoln was under the impression she had failed our little test, Bill.'

The smile was there when he took the tea from her. 'Not a chance!'

After serving both the officers, she took her own tea and sat down as ordered.

'You obviously don't have any idea why you have been sent to us, or what branch of the service we are.' The major general sat back, watching her carefully.

'I wasn't told anything, sir. I assumed it was for secretarial work.'

'You will officially be classed as my secretary, of course. Our main task, though, is to gain information – anything that will tell us what the enemy is planning, or an insight into his strengths and weaknesses. We are a part of the

Intelligence Service, and we need people who can sift the wheat from the chaff – so to speak. You have shown that ability, and your other languages could be useful.'

Now she understood what that test had been about, but it still seemed a strange way to decide on someone's suitability for this unit. She was surprised that she was being given such an opportunity.

'I am taking you against my better judgement, but as of this moment you are attached to the Intelligence Service. If you are not happy and will apply for a transfer, I want to know – now.'

'I will not do that, sir.'

He nodded. 'As far as anyone is concerned you are the secretary of an officer. You have already signed the Secrets Act, so I don't need to remind you never to talk about the work we do here.'

'I understand perfectly, sir.'

'As you will be the only female in this outfit you will be given quarters in a house on the edge of the camp. You will be on call day or night, and if you are sent for I expect you to come immediately. Keep a small kitbag packed should we have to travel.'

'Yes, sir.'

'I wouldn't normally take a woman with us as that could present problems.' He paused, studying her reaction with his usual scrutiny, as if he was reading her mind. 'I am taking a chance with you, however. I made extensive enquiries regarding the time you worked for Major Chester, and I understand he dragged you through mock battles with the Home Guard, hiding in muddy ditches and getting filthy. On one occasion he even manhandled you over an army assault course, and I was told that you did all this without complaint.'

'That is correct, sir.' Grace fought to keep a straight face when she noticed the captain's amused expression. 'The assault course was a celebration. I had just passed my driving test, and Major Chester was once again fully fit.'

'A celebration for which one of you?' the captain laughed.

'Both of us, sir. And as this was the end of our time of working together we wanted to finish with laughter.'

'Remarkable! I would really like to meet this major, Stan.'

'I'll introduce you if we come across him.' He turned his attention back to Grace. 'Do you still see Chester?'

'No, sir. Our association ended when he returned to his regiment.'

The major general nodded, and then stood up. 'The soldier on duty outside will show you to your quarters. Dump your gear, have a meal, and then return here. You have two hours.'

Grace stood up and saluted smartly. 'Two hours. Understood, sir.'

Chapter Fifteen

It had been five months since Grace had been able to get home, and her parents were overjoyed to see her.

'I'm sorry I couldn't get leave over Christmas and the New Year,' she told them. 'I would have loved to welcome in 1941 with you, but we did have a celebration at the base. We survived 1940 without an invasion, thanks to our pilots, and that's a relief to everyone.'

'It certainly is, and we missed you, darling, but you must be very busy working for such a high-ranking officer. He relies on you a lot, I expect.'

Grace nodded and smiled at her mother, being careful not to show her frustration. She had anticipated unusual and even exciting work after what had been said at the interview, but that hadn't happened. She had been kept in the background, and much of her duty had been routine. The men had disappeared from time to time, and never took her with them. If this continued she would have to put in for a transfer, but she was really reluctant to do so. It would have been admitting defeat, and she didn't like doing that.

'You didn't tell us you had been promoted,' her father said, with a touch of pride in his voice. 'Two stripes!'

Grace pulled a face. 'I've only just been given the stripes, and I haven't done anything to deserve them.'

'You are too modest, darling. I'm sure you are invaluable. The general must think so, or he wouldn't have promoted you.'

'Major general, Mother,' she corrected.

'Whatever you say, dear.' Her mother smiled broadly. 'We've got some good news for you. Can you guess what it is?'

'Er . . . the war is over?'

Her parents laughed, and Ted said, 'Helen's coming home on leave in two days' time.'

'That's wonderful! I'll be able to see her because I've got seven days.'

That news cheered her up. It had been ages since they had seen each other, and she happily spent the rest of the day with her parents catching up on all the news.

The raids weren't every night now, and everyone was grateful for the respite, however short it might be.

Helen arrived a day earlier than expected, and once they were together they couldn't stop talking. It was as if they hadn't been apart for many months.

'What shall we do tonight?' Helen asked.

'Don't you want to spend it with your family? You haven't seen them for ages.'

Helen shook her head. 'They've told me to go off and enjoy myself. I've only got three days and I want to have some fun!'

'Don't you have any fun where you're stationed?' Grace asked.

'It's all pretty serious most of the time. What about you? Do you get a lot of laughs in your job?'

Grace pulled a face. 'You're right. We both need a light-hearted night of fun. So what can we do?'

'There's someone here to see you, Grace,' her mother called up the stairs.

'Oh dear, I hope I'm not being ordered back. Come on; let's see what this is about.'

Jean was standing at the bottom of the stairs, smiling happily. 'I've put them in the front room.'

'Oh, oh, officers!' Helen whispered.

'Well, it can't be Dan or George, because Mum would have taken them straight to the kitchen.'

When Grace opened the door and stepped in she stared in amazement at the two men standing there. One she had never seen before, but the other she knew very well.

'Squadron Leader Meredith!' she exclaimed. 'How lovely to see you.'

He laughed, stepping forward to take her hands in his. 'And it's lovely to see you, Grace. The other one standing there with a big grin on his face is Tim. I hope you don't mind us descending upon you like this?'

'You are both very welcome.' She pulled Helen forward. 'This is my friend, Helen.'

With the introductions over, Jean came in with a tray of

tea and home-made cake and then left them alone again.

'Would you girls like to come dancing with two lonely pilots tonight?' Tim asked.

'Lonely! Now that is hard to believe,' Helen said, laughing.

'Sad, but true. We expected to have to share one beautiful girl, but it's terrific to find two of you. Absolute stunners, as well.' Tim grinned. 'We'd better do something classy tonight, James.'

'They haven't said they'll come with us yet.'

Tim stepped forward and bowed low gracefully. 'Please!'

'Where did you find such a charmer?' Helen wanted to know.

'On my wing, and once on the ground I can't seem to get rid of him.' James smiled at Tim, making the strong bond between them obvious. 'But we are serious about wanting you to come dancing with us. What do you say?'

'Well, we were just wondering what to do to have some fun tonight, weren't we, Helen?'

'We were, and dancing with two dishy pilots sounds like fun to me!'

'Great. We'll pick you up at seven.'

'We'll be ready. Now, please sit down and finish the tea and cake, or my mother will be offended.'

'Can't have that!' Tim dived for the cake. 'I'm starving and this looks delicious.'

'Well, well,' Helen said, when they had gone. 'You never told me your boss looked like that! I always thought he was a boring middle-aged man.'

'Really?' Grace laughed at her friend's rapt expression. 'Tim is rather attractive as well, isn't he?'

Helen did a little jig. 'Pity we haven't got fancy evening dresses, but I guess uniforms will have to do.'

'Everyone will be in uniform. We'd look out of place in ballgowns.'

'We've got two hours so I'm off to wash my hair. See you at seven!'

Grace watched her friend run out of the room, showing the exuberance of carefree days before the war came and changed all their lives. Tonight two hard-pressed pilots needed to relax and enjoy themselves, and so did two troubled army girls. And there was no denying it. Whatever Helen was doing she wasn't finding it easy, no matter how she tried to hide it. As for herself? Well, she had been excited at the chance to work for the Intelligence Service, but it had been day after day of frustration. The major general had pushed her into the background, and was keeping her there. She felt useless.

'Grace!' Her mother looked in the room. 'They told me they had come to ask you out, so there's hot water if you want to get ready. I knew you'd be pleased to see James again.'

'I was, and thanks, Mum.'

'Did you know he was on leave?'

'No, I haven't seen or heard from him since the party at the Savoy last year. I was surprised to see him. We were only ever boss and secretary. We never mixed socially. I wonder how he knew I was on leave.'

'He said Colonel Askew told him.'

'Ah, I see.'

'You girls go out and enjoy yourselves, and let's hope we have a quiet night.'

They were ready and waiting when the men arrived in a powerful sports car.

'Where did you get this?' Helen wanted to know as Tim held the door open for them.

'We borrowed it.'

'Does the owner know?' Grace asked as she settled in the front seat with James.

Both pilots laughed but didn't answer the question.

They were taken to a club in Piccadilly, and when Grace saw it, she said, 'They won't let us in here. It looks like a private club.'

'Yes, they will,' Tim told them confidently, guiding them towards the entrance.

The doorman took one look at the wings on their uniforms and opened the door at once.

'Good evening, sirs. See the manager and he will give you one of the best tables.'

The place had appeared quite small from the outside, but that was deceptive – it was huge, and packed.

A man hurried up to them and led them to a table near the band and on the edge of the dance floor. A bottle of champagne arrived immediately, and the waitress smiled.

'Good evening, sirs. The manager said your first drink is on the house.'

'What service,' Helen laughed. 'You must have been here before.'

'First time,' James told her.

Grace looked at the pilots with fresh eyes. They were being shown respect and gratitude for what they had done – and were still doing in saving this country from invasion. They took to the air time after time, not knowing if they would come back.

After enjoying their first drink they took to the dance floor. Grace partnered James, and it seemed strange to be dancing with the man who had been her boss. This battle-hardened pilot was nothing like the lawyer she had worked for, though. He had changed, and that wasn't surprising. None of them were going to come out of this the same.

'Have you seen Dan?' James asked, breaking her train of thought.

'Not since we left the War Office. Why?'

'I just wondered. From what I've heard you got on well together.'

'We did. Just as you and I got on well together as boss and secretary.'

'Ah.' He smiled. 'He hasn't tried to get in touch with you, then?'

'No, why should he? What are you getting at, James? Is he all right?'

'He's fine. I was curious, that's all.'

Grace shook her head, remembering that the major general had asked the same question.

'If you are thinking there might have been more than work between us, then I can soon put that right. Dan was injured, angry and frustrated; I had lost the husband I loved. We helped each other through a difficult time, and then we went our separate ways. End of story. As you are so curious about my private life, where is your steady girlfriend tonight?'

'She was furious about me joining the air force, so she went off and married someone else.'

'Oh, I'm so sorry, James!'

'Don't be – I'm not.' He smiled down at her. 'Now we've got that out of the way, let's forget everything and enjoy ourselves. It looks as if Tim has really taken to Helen.'

The evening was the most relaxed and enjoyable Grace had spent since the death of Brian almost a year ago. Tim and James kept them laughing with jokes and stories. The war was put to one side for a few hours, and this was something they all needed. There wasn't even an air raid that night to spoil their fun.

It was two o'clock in the morning when they finally arrived back home. The pilots hugged and thanked Grace and Helen for making the evening so enjoyable, and then drove away, heading for their base in Kenley.

Brian had been killed in May, 1940, and when that month arrived Grace was feeling particularly low in spirit. There had not been any improvement in the job and she was feeling useless. She was trying to take each day as it came in the hope she would be given something more responsible to do, but she was beginning to despair that would ever happen. Surely the major general trusted her by now? She didn't want to spend the rest of the war like this. There wasn't even enough work to keep her occupied during the day. While she had been at the War Office there hadn't been a moment to spare, and that was the way she liked it.

Grace smiled, remembering the days she had followed that dynamic man through muddy fields, getting filthy, and loving every minute. It had been just what she'd needed at that time as she had struggled with the pain of loss.

With a sigh, she picked up the book she was reading. An early night was the thing to do.

'Wake up!'

Grace was being shaken and she sat bolt upright, still fuzzy from sleep. The woman in charge of the house was standing by the bed.

'You are to report to your office immediately, and take your bag with you.'

'What time is it?' Grace shook her head, trying to clear it.

'Five in the morning. Hurry, the summons sounded urgent. They've sent transport for you.'

Springing into action, Grace tumbled out of bed, dressed with speed, ran a hand through her hair, grabbed her bag and rushed out to the waiting car.

'That was quick,' Captain Reid remarked when she arrived.

'I was told it was urgent.'

'Let's move, then,' the major general ordered. 'We have a long journey ahead of us. You sit in the front, Lincoln.'

'Yes, sir.' Grace did as ordered, assuming that the two officers needed to talk during the journey. They hadn't told her where they were going, and she knew better than to ask.

They were dropped off at a railway station Grace had never been to before, and as all the signs had been removed in case of invasion, she wasn't sure where they were. At a guess she would have said it was Kings Cross. Even this early in the morning it was busy.

When the train arrived she followed the officers to a private compartment. Once in, the captain closed the door, and even though the train was crowded, they had it to themselves. The men looked edgy and excited. Grace was curious to know what this was all about, but they weren't volunteering any information, and she didn't ask.

It was, indeed, a long journey, and Grace occupied her time by watching the passing countryside, trying to guess where they were.

One of the bags the men had brought with them contained flasks of tea and packets of sandwiches. This was very welcome as there hadn't been time for breakfast.

When they finally arrived at their destination there was an army car waiting at the station for them. As soon as they drove out of the station and into the countryside, Grace knew where she was – Scotland.

It was late in the day when they reached their destination. It was a large building bristling with activity.

'You won't be needed tonight. I will send for you in the morning,' the major general told her. 'You will be shown to your room.'

Grace watched the officers walk away, and gave a slight shake of her head. She wasn't going to be given even a hint of what they were doing there, or what was expected of her. Ah, well, that was nothing unusual in this job.

A woman, in civilian clothes, came up to her, smiling. 'Welcome. If you will come with me I'll show you to your room. Dinner will be at eight.'

'Thank you. I'm very hungry after such a long journey. Where is the dining room?'

'It's the first room on our right. Don't go to the next one along – that's for the officers.'

They walked up the winding staircase and Grace took in every detail of the place. It was old, but very elegant. 'Is this a hotel?' she asked.

'It was until the army took it over. I was offered the job of staying on and running the place.'

'You worked here, then?'

'No.' The middle-aged woman gave a grim smile. 'My family have owned it for several generations. It has been our business and our home. We will get it back when the army no longer need it.'

'This must be very hard for you.'

'Sacrifices have to be made in this war. And at least this has been commandeered for officers.'

'Yes, indeed.' Grace knew only too well what it was like to make sacrifices.

'Here we are. You will be sharing because we haven't enough rooms.'

When Grace stepped inside the room she stopped in amazement when she saw the girl already there. They stared at each other for a moment, not able to believe their eyes.

'Grace!' Peggy leapt to her feet and threw her arms around Grace. 'How wonderful! What are you doing here?'

'I really don't know,' she laughed. 'It's good to see you again. How are you getting on?'

'Terrific! I'm driving the top brass around. This place is heaving with them. Do you know what's going on?'

'Sorry, I haven't been told a thing.'

'Never mind.' Peggy did a little jig of pleasure. 'Let them get on with whatever it is they are doing. We've got a lot of catching up to do.'

After a good wash and change of clothes, Grace felt a whole lot better. Meeting Peggy again had lifted her spirits.

They were the only two women there so they had the dining room to themselves. They talked non-stop right through the meal and in their room until the early hours.

Although she hadn't been told what time she would be needed, Grace was downstairs early. When they decided they needed her she would be waiting and ready.

It was ten o'clock before the officers arrived – by the front door, shaking rain off their hats.

The captain smiled in a distracted way when he saw her. 'It's pouring out there.'

'Good morning, sirs. I didn't know what time you might need me, so I stayed down here where you could find me. What are your orders for the rest of the day, sir?'

'Collect your bag and be back here in thirty minutes. We are going back to Aldershot.'

'Yes, sir.' She spun round and walked up the stairs.

Whatever they had been doing it obviously hadn't been successful. The major general was in a bad mood and had spoken sharply, showing his irritation. It was a shame they were leaving so soon, she thought, as she hastily packed her bag. This was the first time she had been to Scotland and would have liked to see a little of the countryside. She had also hoped to have more time with Peggy.

Peggy was out, so Grace left a note for her, picked up her bag and went downstairs where the officers were already waiting.

The captain smiled apologetically at her. 'This has been a waste of time for you, hasn't it?'

'No, it hasn't, sir. A girl I met at training camp is the driver to one of the officers here. It was good to see her again, and we've had a lovely time.'

'I'm glad someone has!' Stan muttered, still clearly not a happy man.

The journey back was long and tedious. Although it was late when the driver dropped them off at the office, Grace made a much needed cup of tea. Sensing they weren't going to discuss anything in front of her, she asked, 'Do you need me any more tonight, sir? If you have notes, I would be happy to type them up for you now?'

'There isn't anything urgent. You may go.'

'Very well. Goodnight, sirs.'

As Grace walked back to her digs she puzzled over the officer's obvious dislike of her. He had made it clear that he didn't want a woman working with him, but if he had felt so strongly, then why did he accept her instead of one of the men? She had been careful to always be cheerful and helpful; never complaining or being insubordinate. She usually got on well with anyone she had worked for in the past. So what was wrong? Was he trying to make her put in for a transfer? She shook her head. That didn't make sense, but, if by some chance that was his intention, then he was wasting his time. She was staying.

'That was disappointing.' Stan ran hand over his eyes. 'A mad dash to get there and we got nothing. There had been no need to call us there in such a hurry. What did Rudolf Hess really think he would accomplish with that ridiculous peace offer?'

'It's crazy, and Hitler will be furious, because I can't imagine he would sanction Hess coming here.'

Stan smiled for the first time that day. 'There is that to be grateful for, I suppose.'

'You are treating that girl very badly,' Bill said, changing the subject. 'If you are hoping she will go of her own accord, then you are going to be disappointed. I don't believe she is the type to run from a challenge. With her qualifications any other officer would snap her up. We're lucky to have her, Stan.'

'You're right.' Stan gave a wry smile. 'I thought I was being so clever. When I saw that letter from Dan Chester and paid him a visit, I was intrigued. He was careful not to influence my decision in any way and gave me only the facts concerning her abilities. It was only when I spoke to others I discovered that their relationship might be closer, and I thought it might be a way to entice him over to us. I was wrong on all counts.'

Bill stared at Stan in astonishment. 'I know you've always wanted him here, but that was never going to happen. When Grace went to work for him her husband had been killed in France only a few weeks previously. She would have been coping with her grief, so anything more than liking and friendship between them would have been impossible.'

'I didn't know that at the time. Chester never mentioned it and neither did anyone else.'

Bill was shaking his head. 'You obviously didn't look into her background enough, and it's not like you to make such a blunder. Now you've got to accept that she was the best candidate for this job and give her a chance.'

'I know.' Stan sighed, and changed the subject. 'Now I have another matter to discuss with you. Do you think you could pass yourself off as a German pilot?'

'As long as Grace isn't around,' he joked. 'What do you want me to do?'

'Go into a prisoner-of-war camp as a downed pilot. They might talk freely to one of their own.' When Bill began to speak, Stan held up his hand to stop him. 'Before you answer, let me finish. I know you've mingled with prisoners before, but that was only for a day. We are asking you to stay there, and only the commander will know who you really are. We think there are one or two Nazis in the camp who are causing problems, but no one is talking and we don't know who they are. It could be dangerous – very dangerous.'

'Where is this place?'

'Somerset.'

'Nice part of the country. When do I get captured?'

'After the next big raid. Once in the camp you will be on your own, Bill. This isn't an order. You are quite at liberty to refuse.'

'If it isn't an order, then I volunteer for the mission.'

Chapter Sixteen

His damned phone never stopping ringing, Dan thought as he strode into the office and grabbed the offending instrument. 'Chester! Ah, hello, George. I'm busy at the moment; can I call you back?'

'I've got some bad news, Dan. James has been shot down over the Channel, and we don't know if he's dead or alive.'

'Oh, hell!' Dan sat on the edge of the desk and bowed his head in shock. 'Are they searching for him? He might still be alive. Have his parents been told?'

'Not yet. James evidently left instructions that I was to be notified first. I don't want to tell his family until I have some definite news.'

'No, you're right.' Dan was having trouble grasping the fact that he might never see his lifelong friend again, and he could hear that his uncle was very upset. People were being killed all the time but somehow you never thought it was going to happen to you. 'Let me know the moment you hear anything.'

'I will.'

He put the phone down, and when he looked up his sergeant was standing in the doorway. He beckoned him in.

'What is it, Sergeant?'

'I've got news you must hear, sir.' He was excited enough to make him drop his military bearing. 'Hitler's invaded Russia! It's all round the camp and the officers are coming from all directions. They're gathering in the strategy room for a meeting. I've been sent to tell you, sir. What a damned foolish thing to do!'

'If that's true then it is absolute madness on Hitler's part!' Dan declared, heading for the door. 'Oh, Sergeant, get someone to listen for my phone. If Colonel Askew phones they are to come and get me immediately – no matter where I am.'

'Yes, sir. I'll come myself.'

As Dan marched through the camp his mind was assessing the implications of this astonishing news. To hear about this on top of being told that James was missing had come like body blows. *James*, he thought angrily, *you had better still be alive and in once piece, or I swear I'll kill you myself. You bloody fool! You had to go and fly planes, when you could have stayed in the comfort of your office with Grace. And you needn't think I'm going to tell her!* He shook his head to clear it of such daft thoughts and swung into the meeting room.

* * *

Later that evening while he was having a drink in the officers' bar he was called to the phone. He was dreading the news his uncle might have.

'Have they found James, George?'

'Yes, and apart from a couple of broken ribs, a dislocated shoulder and a prolonged dip in the sea, he's in reasonable condition.'

'Thank God!' Dan exclaimed with relief. 'Where have they taken him?'

'The military hospital in Aldershot. Grace is stationed there so I'll try and see her while I'm there. It will only be a quick visit because this place is in uproar after today's news.'

'I'm not surprised. Everyone is dumbfounded at the lunacy of this move by Hitler. We'll talk about it later, George. You get off to see James, and tell him I'll come tomorrow.'

'I'll do that, Dan.'

Dan put the phone down and took a deep breath before ordering another drink. What a day! The non-aggression pact between Germany and Russia hadn't meant a thing to Hitler. In his opinion the German leader had made a monumental blunder, but only time would show what kind of an impact this would have on the war. The best news he'd had today was that James had been found alive. He would sleep tonight after all.

'That was a damned stupid thing to do, James,' Dan declared as he walked up to his friend's bed.

James turned his head and glared at the tall man

standing beside him. 'You're a fine one to talk! And what are you still doing here? I thought they would have sent you to where the fighting is by now.'

Dan grinned, pulled up a chair and sat down. He recognised the symptoms of anger and grief smouldering under the surface, and knew just what to do.

'So, what happened?'

'If you've come here to ask stupid questions then I'm going to sleep!'

When James closed his eyes and turned his head away, Dan watched him for a moment, and then said quietly, 'I'm not going away, James, so you might as well tell me what's troubling you.'

'That damned fool had to go and chase him!' James didn't open his eyes. 'He swooped down when I was in the water, and then took off in hot pursuit of the one who shot me down.'

'Who was this idiot?' Dan asked, prompting to keep his friend talking.

He opened his eyes then, showing his anguish. 'Tim! He was heading straight for the French coast, and he hasn't returned. He didn't have enough petrol to pull a stunt like that!'

'Did he have enough to reach the coast?'

'Just.'

'What's his full name?'

'Timothy Sheldon. He shouldn't have risked his life like that, Dan.'

'Perhaps not, but it was his choice, James. In the heat of battle you sometimes have to make a snap decision, regardless of the risks. You might have done the same thing if he'd been the one in the sea instead of you.'

'You're right, of course.' James sighed. 'Thanks, Dan. Your usual clear thinking has helped. I've been feeling so bloody angry.'

'I know exactly what it's like. When I got back from France and they gave me a desk job, I was ready to explode. Then this girl arrived who organised the office with calm efficiency. She didn't fuss or ask questions, she just got on with whatever I asked her to do. When I found out that her husband had been killed only a few weeks previously, I marvelled at her composure and courage. It made me realise that riling against what had happened was a waste of energy and would accomplish nothing. "Take each day as it comes", she told me.'

'Ah.' James smiled for the first time. 'Grace.'

Dan nodded.

'She's stationed here, you know. George was going to let her know I'm here. Why don't you go and see her, Dan.'

'No. We parted friends, and that's the end of it. I have no intention of seeing her again.'

James gave his friend a speculative glance. 'No ties, eh? Thinking you might get killed, are you?'

'After France I'm not so certain of my immortality.'

'I know what you mean. I've had a few near shaves, but I really thought I was a goner this time.' James gave a quiet chuckle. 'Grace always said that lightening doesn't strike twice. If that's true then she won't be made a widow a second time in this war, so perhaps I should increase my chances of surviving by marrying her.'

Dan stretched out his long legs and grinned, pleased to see his friend more relaxed. 'Do you think she would have you?'

'Not a chance. She's far too sensible to marry again so soon – if she ever will. I met her husband a couple of times and they were very much in love. They had been childhood sweethearts and I don't think, in her mind, that anyone else could replace him.'

'That's the impression I got,' Dan agreed. 'Anyway, we both made it through this time, so what do you think about Hitler invading Russia?'

For the next hour they talked until James was having a job to keep his eyes open. Dan stood up just as a nurse appeared.

'You must leave now, Major. Squadron Leader Meredith must rest.'

'I'm going, Nurse.' He smiled down at his friend. 'I'll see if I can find out what happened to Tim, James.'

'Thanks, Dan. Come again when you can.'

'I will. Sleep well and get your strength back. You're strong and the bones should heal quickly.'

Although it was late when Dan arrived back at camp, he phoned his uncle to tell him that James was fretting over his lost pilot friend, Tim.

'Well done for finding that out about him, Dan. He wouldn't talk to me about it. I'm tied up with meetings at the moment so could you phone the commander of Kenley to find out if there is any news about Tim. I know Peter Harrison well, so mention my name when you speak to him.'

'I'll do that first thing in the morning. Get some rest, George. You sound tired.'

'I am. Let me know how you get on. Goodnight, Dan.'

'Night, George.'

Tim followed the two men as they moved stealthily through the darkened village. They made faster progress after reaching the open countryside and soon reached an isolated farm. They pushed him through the door of the building, shut the door and bolted it securely. When the lamps were turned up it took Tim a moment or two to adjust to the sudden light. There were five other people in the room – an elderly husband and wife, and two young men who were probably their sons. When Tim's gaze rested on the other person he gasped, not being able to believe his eyes.

'Helen?'

'Hello, Tim. Are you hurt at all?'

'A few bruises, that's all. What are you doing here?'

'I'm working with the resistance. We are going to try and get you back to England. You must never tell anyone you saw me here. Do you understand that?'

'I won't say a word. I promise.'

'No one knows what I'm doing – not even my family and friends. They receive letters from me so as far as they are concerned I am still in England. Everything is arranged to keep it that way. If I'd known it was you arriving tonight I would have disappeared until you had been moved on. The damage is done now and I have to trust you never to speak about this meeting.'

'I understand perfectly just how dangerous this is for you. I will never breathe a word of this.'

She nodded, said something he couldn't understand to the others, and he saw them relax. He was now wishing he had paid more attention to French lessons at school. His limited knowledge was not enough to cope with this.

'Are you hungry?'

'Starving.'

The entire group sat around the large, scrubbed wooden table, and the woman served them with bowls of stew and chunks of home-made bread.

Tim was so hungry it tasted like the best meal he had ever had in his life, and the woman smiled when he tucked into a second bowl. He was then taken to a derelict looking barn where there was a concealed cubbyhole filled with straw and items for his need while in there. Helen told him he was to stay there and not come out until someone came for him.

'How are you going to get me back home, Helen?'

'We have several routes in operation, but I'm going to see if I can get you back by the quickest way possible. We have to contact London first. Be patient and don't go wandering around. If the Germans discover this family are hiding you they will be shot.'

'I won't do anything to jeopardise their safety.'

'I'm sure you won't.' Helen smiled. 'I had to warn you, though. Get some rest.'

'And you take care,' he told her as she climbed through the small entrance.

For the next two days he was cooped up in the small

room. He was fed at irregular times, and often heard people, sometimes German voices, but he kept very quiet. He was worried about Helen. He had liked her from the moment he had set eyes on her, and to find her here had really shaken him. This was damned dangerous.

When Helen did finally arrive the relief was immense.

'Come on, Tim. There is a Lysander due to arrive tonight with another agent. They will take you back. We must hurry!'

He was stiff after being confined to that small space and he was glad to get out and stretch his legs. The field was about a mile away and they reached it without mishap. Then they settled down in some trees to wait. No one spoke and Tim could feel the tension radiating through the group.

After what seemed like an age, Tim heard the sound of a small plane, and watched as the men ran out to put lights to mark the landing spot. He was jumpy, expecting Germans to arrive at any minute. He would rather be up in the air than on the ground like this! At least he had some control up there; down here he felt too vulnerable.

When the plane landed one of the men grabbed hold of Tim and rushed him towards the Lysander. He was on the plane before he had a chance to thank his rescuers or say goodbye to Helen. The plane was back in the air in what seemed a matter of seconds.

Tim suddenly felt absolutely drained and ran a hand over his eyes.

'You all right, chum?' the pilot said as they climbed and headed for the coast.

'Yes, thanks. This is a blasted dangerous game you are all playing.'

The pilot chuckled. 'You can relax now. We will be landing at Tempsford, Cambridge. Sleep if you want to.'

Tim closed his eyes. He'd become an expert at snatching sleep whenever he could during the height of the battle. They all had.

'We've landed, sir!'

'What?' Tim sat up quickly. 'Have I slept all the way?'

'You went out like a light as soon as we were over the Channel.'

A cheer went up from the ground staff when Tim clambered out of the Lysander, and calls of 'Well done, sir. Welcome back'. He was quite touched by their obvious delight.

A squadron leader stepped forward and shook his hand.

'You look as if you've had a rough time. I expect the first thing you need is a shower, shave and change of clothes.'

Tim grimaced, conscious for the first time about his dishevelled state. His uniform was torn and dirty, and he had several days' growth of beard. But that could wait.

'I must phone Kenley first, sir. My squadron leader was shot down over the Channel and I need to know if he survived.'

'Kenley were informed that you might be arriving tonight, and they sent a message for you. Squadron Leader Meredith was found and is in Aldershot Military Hospital with relatively minor injuries, and suffering from a prolonged dip in the sea.'

'Oh, thank God!' The relief sweeping over Tim made him sway slightly after days of worrying about his friend.

'Come on. Let's get you cleaned up and a good meal inside you. Then the MO must check you over. You look exhausted. The debriefing can wait until tomorrow.'

That was going to be tricky, Tim thought, as they walked towards the building. He had made a promise to Helen that he would never talk about the people who had helped him, and nothing on this earth would make him break that promise. Without them he would either be a prisoner – or dead.

An hour later he was feeling much better, but he was surprised at just how much the last few days had taken out of him. After the relief of hearing that James was all right, everything had seemed to sweep in on him, making him realise fully the danger he had been in. Thanks to Helen and her friends, though, he had come through and would be able to carry on the fight.

'You've come out of this well,' the medical officer told him when the examination was finished. 'All you need is rest. You are wound up like a spring. There's a bed in the next room, so get some sleep.'

'I've got to get back to Kenley.' Tim stood up and headed for the door. 'Must see if I can borrow transport of some kind.'

'Oh, no you don't, young man.' The MO stopped him. 'You are not going to drive or fly anything tonight. Sleep!'

'I can't sleep, Doc, and it isn't worth going to bed. It's three in the morning. Anyway, I slept on the plane.'

'As soon as it's light you can return to your base, but I'm not letting you go before then.'

'All right.' Tim gave in and walked into the other room.

The next thing he knew the sun was streaming through the window.

Chapter Seventeen

The debriefing had taken a long time, but thankfully they had accepted that Tim couldn't give the names or places of his rescuers in France, as lives depended upon his silence. After that he had spoken to Colonel Askew and Major Chester to ask that James not be told he was back. He wanted to surprise him.

He strode into the ward and saw his friend at once. He was sitting in a chair reading a book. When Tim reached him James saw his feet first, and then his gaze shot straight up to his face. He reached out and prodded him.

'I am real!' Tim laughed.

'Good grief! I thought I was hallucinating. Where the hell did you come from?'

'I wouldn't call it hell, but that's a close description.' Tim sat on the edge of the bed. 'I got back last night and came as soon as they would let me. I've been worried sick in case they hadn't found you.'

'It took a while. You gave me a fright when I saw you disappearing towards France. I knew you didn't have enough petrol to get back, you blasted fool. I ought to put you on a charge for pulling a stunt like that.'

'Will it help my case if I told you I thought he was ready to dive on you while you were in the sea and I dumped him in the water as well?' Tim asked, smiling broadly.

James laughed then. 'Oh, it's good to see you. Tell me what happened after that.'

'After shooting him down I made for the nearest land. I was running dry when I crossed the coast, so before bailing out I turned the Spitfire towards the sea, and jumped. I didn't want the plane to come down on land and alert the Germans that I was there.'

'Good thinking. What happened then?'

'I had a rough landing in some trees, but got away with only bruises. Some locals found me and took me to a safe place. I stayed there until a Lysander arrived and brought me back.'

'You were lucky.'

Tim nodded. 'So, how long are you going to be in here? I've got some leave now.'

'Another couple of days, they think. I'll be grounded for a while and so will you. Perhaps we can get together with Grace and Helen again. Grace is stationed here and has been in a couple of times to see me. Why don't you find her and ask if there's any chance of them getting leave together again?'

'Good idea. I'll do that.' Tim knew that would be impossible, but he had to go along with it. There was no way he would give even a hint of what he knew.

He stayed with James until the nursing sister came and threw him out. 'I'll see if I can get hold of a car, James. That will make it easier for you to get around.'

'You've disturbed my patient long enough,' the sister said, trying to give Tim a stern look. 'Time to leave.'

'I'm on my way, sister.' He strode out with a smile on his face. Oh, it was good to be home!

The door connecting the offices was open and Grace heard someone come in and the major general shake hands with him, but she couldn't see who it was.

'There's someone to see you, Grace.'

She looked up, startled to hear him use her Christian name. When she saw the smiling man behind him she leapt to her feet. 'Tim! Oh, it's so good to see you!'

'Hello, Grace.' Tim hugged her in a fierce embrace. 'You're even more beautiful than the last time I saw you.'

She laughed, so relieved to see he was alive. 'And you're still the master of flattery. Where have you been? And does James know you are all right?'

'I've just seen him. I took an unscheduled trip to France.'

'How did you get back?'

'By Lysander.'

Major General Haydon was still standing there, watching and listening intently.

'Make a pot of tea, Grace. I'm sure Tim would like to stay a while and talk to you.'

He'd said it again! 'If that's all right with you, sir?'

'Of course.' He smiled at Tim. 'Good to have one of our precious pilots snatched back from under the noses of the Germans. Well done, young man.'

'Thank you, sir. It's good to be home.'

'Enjoy your tea, and don't feel you have to rush away.' He turned towards his office, and then stopped, looking back over his shoulder. 'If you have a spare moment later, I would enjoy hearing about your experiences in France.'

Grace knew exactly what he was doing. All the friendliness was because he wanted information, and by the expression on Tim's face, he knew as well.

As the door closed, Grace put her fingers to her lips and nodded towards an intercom on her desk. The red light was showing to indicate it was on.

Tim nodded and began to talk about the night in London they had all enjoyed.

When a call came through for her boss, Grace connected it and then flicked the switch to turn off the intercom. This was the only time she was allowed to disconnect it. 'Now we can't be overheard, Tim. He's an intelligence officer, and you know he will squeeze you for any information he can get.'

'I realise that, but I've already been through a vigorous debriefing by my own people. I can't talk to anyone else about what happened, and he knows that.'

'It won't stop him trying, though.'

Grace's door surged open and a German pilot walked in accompanied by two guards.

'What the . . . ?' Tim was immediately on his feet, and

stepped towards the German. He had lost too many good friends to feel kindly towards any of them.

Grabbing his arm, Grace stopped him. 'It's all right, Tim,' she laughed. 'This is Captain Reid. He likes dressing up as the enemy.'

Bill grinned and bowed gracefully towards them. The two guards were obviously in on the charade and having difficulty in keeping straight faces. 'I've just been arrested. Is his lordship in, Grace?'

Still laughing, she checked that he had finished his phone call. 'He's free now. You can go in.'

'Ask the guards to wait outside your door, Grace. They won't take orders from me.'

'I should think not. You are their prisoner, Captain!'

He saluted Tim. 'Sorry I can't stay and compare notes on tactics with you, sir.'

'Oh, for heaven's sake!' Grace pushed Bill towards the door.

There was a look of utter disbelief on Tim's face as he watched Bill disappear into the other office. As soon as the guards had stepped outside, he turned to Grace. 'What kind of a madhouse do you work in?'

'I really do wonder at times,' she admitted. Then she told him about her interview here and had him roaring with laughter.

'The captain didn't fool you then.'

'Not for long. He's very good, but James taught me to look past the outward appearances for small details. He was a master at reading body language, and there will often be something in gestures that will give a sign that they are hiding something. The eyes can tell you so much as well. I've heard it said that they are the windows to the soul.' She gave a small smile. 'That's another one of my mother's sayings; she's full of them. Anyway, I have only ever met one person who could mask his feelings completely when he wanted to, and that was Major Chester.'

'Really? I'm intrigued. What do you see in me?'

'Are you sure you want to know?'

He laughed. 'Come on, Grace. Let me see if you really can do this.'

'All right. I would say that you are guarding something you don't want to talk about, and it's very important to you. And considering what you have just been through it isn't hard to guess it is something that happened in France.' She laughed at his expression. 'Don't worry, Tim. There isn't anything clever about that. I could say the same thing to hundreds of men who have had traumatic experiences. There is always a reluctance to talk about it.'

'Don't believe her when she dismisses that ability so easily,' said a quiet voice from the doorway. 'She is very perceptive.'

'I'm sure you are right, Captain,' Tim said. 'It also makes me see why James was such a successful lawyer. The ability to sum people up accurately also makes him an excellent squadron leader.'

'Call the guards back, Grace,' her boss ordered. 'Then you can both help us.'

Once everyone was there, he said, 'Tim, your experiences will make your advice invaluable. I want both of you to take a good look at the German pilot. He's been shot down

187

over London and bailed out, landing in a garden. What's wrong with him?'

'He's too clean,' Tim said immediately. 'Jumping from a stricken plane wouldn't be easy, and after landing in a garden, he would be a mess. His uniform would probably be torn – mine was, and I was filthy by the time I extracted myself from the parachute.'

'Good. Grace?'

She studied him intently for a few moments. 'Shoes.'

'I left my flying boots behind when I jumped. These were given to me.'

'You might get away with that, Captain. And for goodness' sake take that wristwatch off; it's far too expensive for you to have been given that.'

'How do you know I'm wearing it?'

'By the amused look in your eyes. You are testing me, Captain. If you really were a downed German pilot who had been captured, you would be afraid, not knowing what was going to happen to you. Even angry. What happened to the rest of your crew?'

'They didn't survive.'

'Then you would be sad and very angry.'

'And another small thing,' Tim said, smiling wryly. 'I ended up with quite a few bruises as well.'

Grace had an uncomfortable feeling that this wasn't a joke. Her boss was definitely on edge. 'I don't know what you are wearing underneath, Captain, but for the deception to be complete it mustn't be English underwear.'

'All German, expect for the shoes and watch.'

Tim reached into his pocket and held out a watch.

'You'd better take this, Captain; it's a genuine German pilot's watch.'

'My word, that's good of you.' Bill removed his own watch and handed it to Tim. 'We'll swap, and I promise to return this to you.'

They shook hands, and Grace could see respect in their eyes for each other – and perhaps the beginning of a friendship.

'Anything else?' Stan demanded. When Grace and Tim shook their heads, he turned to the guards. 'You know what to do. You've heard what has been said, so mess him up a bit.'

Bill grimaced. 'Thank you for your good advice, Grace and Tim. I think!' Then he saluted and turned towards the door.

'Be careful, Bill,' Stan said quietly. 'We won't be far away.'

He nodded, spun round and said to the guards, 'Right men, let's get this show on the road.'

Stan stared at the door for a few moments, and then looked at Tim. 'I could do with a strong drink. Will you join me, young man?'

'My pleasure, sir.'

Tim hugged Grace. 'James and I will be grounded for a while so let us know if you have any time off.'

'I will. I had a letter from Helen and she said she is hoping to have leave at Christmas.'

'That would be marvellous if we could all meet up again.' He kissed her cheek, and left with the officer.

Grace found it hard to settle down to work. Her mind

was focused on what had just happened. The wonderful part was that Tim was alive and well, and that was a huge relief, and must be especially so to James. He had been distressed about his missing friend. The thing playing on her mind, though, was what Bill was playing at. At first she had assumed it was one of his games with new recruits, but it had soon become clear that this was not a game. She fervently wished they would take her into their confidence. It was worrying not knowing what was going on.

It was over an hour later when her boss returned, and instead of going straight to his office as he usually did, he sat by her desk.

'Tim's a fine young man.'

'Yes, sir, he is.'

'Is he your boyfriend?'

'No, sir. He's interested in my friend, Helen.' Where was this leading? Why was he suddenly so friendly?

'Ah. And is your friend in the forces?'

'The FANY, sir. She's an interpreter for the Free French.'

'Speaks the language well, does she?'

'Her grandmother is French, and I learnt the language from them. They live next door to us.'

'That was useful.' He smiled and nodded. 'Why don't you pop along and see James? I understand he could be discharged in a day or two.'

For a moment she was lost for words. He was acting quite out of character. 'Um, I can go this evening, sir.'

'You won't be able to. We are leaving at six o'clock. We might be away for a while.'

'Where are we going, sir?'

'Somerset.' He stood up and smiled again. 'Off you go, then, Grace. Be back before six with your bag.'

'Yes, sir.'

The day was full of surprises, Grace thought, as they sped along in a comfortable car, with a driver and a lieutenant in the front. The car had a privacy screen raised so anyone in the front couldn't hear what was being said in the back. Grace had expected to go by train again, but it looked as if it was going to be luxury all the way.

'I expect you are wondering what this is all about,' Major General Haydon said.

'Yes, sir. Where is the captain?'

'He's already there. Bill is posing as a German pilot and has been taken to a prisoner-of-war camp. He is there on an intelligence mission. That was why we were so intent on making him look genuine. We won't see him for a couple of days, but I want to be close at hand. I didn't like this idea, but it came from high up and orders are orders. I don't believe that these men will talk, and the risk of putting someone in there with them is too great. I have brought you along in case we need your skill with German, though I hope that won't be necessary.'

Grace caught her breath. 'That's dangerous, sir.'

'I know. In your opinion is he good enough?'

She had never seen her boss worried, but he was now. 'His German is excellent, and he has enough acting flair to pull it off. Actually living among them, though, means he mustn't let his guard drop for a moment.'

Stan nodded. 'I might have to ask you to step in as

interpreter if things go wrong. My German isn't good enough. Do you think you could do that?'

'Yes, sir,' she told him confidently. 'I won't let you down if I'm needed.'

'Thank you, Grace.'

Chapter Eighteen

It had been past midnight when they had arrived at their destination and Grace hadn't taken much notice of her surroundings. The sound of birds singing woke her, and the early morning sun was streaming into the room. She jumped out of bed and ran to the window, and the sight that met her eyes brought a smile of pleasure to her face. They were on a farm.

There was a knock on the door and a middle-aged woman looked in. 'Ah, you're awake. I thought you might like a cup of tea.'

'I would love one. Thank you. We didn't have much time to get acquainted last night. My name is Grace.'

'I'm Enid. I hope you slept well.'

'I did. The bed was so comfortable and it was quiet after London. Is this your farm?'

'It's been in my husband's family for three generations.

Drink your tea before it gets cold. Your officer is already up and about.'

'Is he!' Grace quickly drank the tea. 'Then I must hurry.'

'No need to rush. He's gone riding with our son, and they won't be back for a while. Come down when you're ready and I'll cook you a nice breakfast.'

There was such a tempting smell coming from the kitchen and it only took Grace thirty minutes to find out what was for breakfast. She couldn't believe the amount of food put in front of her – two eggs, bacon, sausage and mushrooms.

'You can't give me all this,' she gasped. 'It's taking all your rations!'

Enid laughed. 'It's all from the farm, dear, and with an important officer staying with us we are expected to feed you well. You eat up and enjoy it.'

'Do you take in guests regularly?' Grace asked, already tackling the sumptuous breakfast.

'We are quite remote and it's often convenient for military officers to stay here. The prisoner-of-war camp is only a few miles away, and my husband, Dave, was told you needed to be near. We are happy to help in any way we can.'

'That is kind of you,' Grace said, clearing her plate. 'Do you mind if I have a wander round until my officer returns?'

'Not at all, dear. You go where you like.'

It was a lovely morning and Grace stopped by a field of golden corn almost ready for harvest. It was such a beautiful and tranquil sight after the noise and destruction

194

of London. She sighed, Brian would have loved this. It had always been his dream to live in the country.

She continued walking, deep in thought, and then she heard her name being called. Lieutenant Grover was striding towards her and she saluted when he reached her.

'Do you know where Major General Haydon is?'

'He's gone riding, sir.'

'We'll have to find him, we are needed at the camp.'

On hearing that, Grace's tranquil mood evaporated and was replaced with worry.

'I'll see if anyone knows where he might be.'

She was just about to return to the house when horses appeared from behind a barn.

The lieutenant made his way over to them, and after a short discussion Stan Haydon came to Grace and told her to come with them.

Nothing was said when they got into the waiting car and drove to the camp, where the commander was waiting for them.

'What's the problem?' Stan looked worried.

'Not sure how serious it is, but you might need to get your man out of there. I can't pull him out because it will look suspicious. The best way would be to interview several of the prisoners, including the captain. That way he can let us know if his identity has been discovered without anyone else knowing. I'll choose them.'

'Right. Go ahead.' Stan turned to Grace. 'Come with us.'

The commander looked at Grace and shook his head. 'You can't bring a woman in here. It will be too unsettling for men locked up without female company.'

'They won't be interested in me, sir,' she pointed out, disappointed that she was going to be sidelined again. 'I'm English.'

The camp commander grinned. 'Where did you find her, Stan?'

'She was recommended by several people, so I sent for her thinking she could easily be dismissed.' He laughed softly. 'I was wrong. You are right, though. Stay in the car, Grace, and I'll send for you if I need you. I'm not sure my German will be up to this.'

'They all speak passable English, Stan.'

'Ah, that's all right, then.'

Grace watched them walk away and disappear in to the camp. Just when she thought they might give her something important to do, she had been told to wait – again! She had never been overly ambitious, always content to be a good secretary, but after her lovely husband had been taken from her so cruelly she burnt to be useful. She wouldn't call it revenge; not the same emotion that Dan struggled with, but it was close. The way things were going she was going to have to rethink her contribution to this war, and settle for what she had been trained for. If she could make an officer's life easier by taking care of all the details in his day, then that would be of help, surely.

The driver put his head in the car. 'This might take some time. Would you like me to see if I can get you a cup of tea?'

'That would be lovely, thank you. White, no sugar, please.'

'I'll see what I can do.'

The tea was welcome and Grace spent the time talking to John, the driver. It was two hours before Stan and the lieutenant appeared.

'Is everything all right, sir?' Grace asked as they drove back to the farm.

'For the moment. There was a fight last night and Bill stepped in to stop it, earning himself a cut lip for his trouble. I wanted to take him out, but he insists on staying. I've told him to keep out of trouble.' Stan sighed wearily. 'Not much hope of that. The daft sod!'

'I'm sure he is well aware of the dangers, sir, and will be careful.'

'Hmm.' He didn't sound as if he quite believed that as he handed her a small exercise book. 'Can you read that?'

The pages were filled with shorthand, and after a quick glance she nodded. 'He obviously wrote this in a hurry, but I should be able to make sense of it.'

'Bill said you would. I want you to decipher that and make me a copy when we get back to the farm. We've got a typewriter in the boot of the car.'

'Yes, sir.' Grace had continued reading and gave a quiet laugh at one of Bill's descriptions.

Stan sighed noisily. 'You can leave out the swear words and any irrelevant remarks. I only want the facts, Grace.'

'His language is quite moderate, sir, but he does have an amusing way of describing things.'

'Don't I know it! If he wasn't so darned clever I wouldn't put up with him.'

'No, sir.' Grace looked at the man beside her and they

197

both laughed. 'He's also very charismatic and I even liked him when, for a brief period, I thought he was a German pilot.'

'That's the effect he has on all the women. He reminds me of Dan Chester. They are both too clever for their own good, don't you think?'

'Both are intelligent, I agree, but I wouldn't say they are similar in character.'

'I suppose you're right, but they are both damned difficult men to handle.'

Grace nodded, and they smiled knowingly at each other. This was the most relaxed they had ever been with each other, and it was a good feeling.

She worked all afternoon on the captain's notes. Some of it had clearly been rushed and was difficult to decipher, but this didn't worry her. She was enjoying the challenge, something that had been lacking in this job so far, and as the notes took shape she could see there was important information there. Bill was obviously good at his job and she was sure that Major General Haydon would be pleased.

They had been given a room downstairs to use as an office, and as soon as the notes were typed she took them down there.

'Good – you've finished.' Stan held out his hand for the document. 'What have we got, Grace?'

'I think you'll find some of it useful, sir.' She handed over the papers and went to leave, but he told her to stay. She waited while he read, frowning the way he always did when concentrating.

'We'll have to get some of this checked out, but if true, Bill will have gleaned some information. I'm not sure if it's important enough to put his life at risk in this way, though,' he remarked, looking up. 'I'll give him two more days in there and then I'm getting him out.'

'Is there anything else I can do for you, sir?'

'No, that's all for today. You've done a good job on this. We will just be playing a waiting game for the next day or so.' He smiled. 'Why don't you take this opportunity to learn to ride?'

'A horse?' she asked, horrified.

He laughed at her expression. 'You'll love it. Meet us by the stables at seven in the morning.'

'Is that an order, sir?'

'If that is what it takes to get you on a horse – then it is. I don't believe you are afraid of horses or anything after the tales I've heard about you and Dan.'

'Yes, well . . .' her mouth twitched in amusement at the memories.

'So you might as well add horse riding to your skills.'

'Yes, sir.' As she left the room she could hear him laughing. She was beginning to like this job – at last.

Horses were not for her, Grace vowed as she slid out of the saddle, relieved to feel solid ground under her feet. That had been the most uncomfortable two hours she had ever spent.

'There, that wasn't so bad, was it?' Stan said as he dismounted.

Grace glared at him. 'I would rather tackle an army assault course than get on another horse!'

'You did well considering it was your first time.' He grinned. 'What could be more enjoyable than an early morning ride in beautiful countryside?'

'Would you like a list, sir?'

'You're not a country girl, are you?' he laughed. 'Come on, let's get breakfast. I'm starving.'

Fortunately she didn't have to repeat the morning ride again. The next day she was kept busy until the evening when Bill arrived at the farm still wearing his German uniform.

'What are you doing here?' Stan exclaimed the moment he walked in the door. 'We had arranged to collect you in the morning.'

'I escaped.' Bill winked at Grace.

'Be serious, damn you! What happened?'

'I'd done as much as I could there without arousing too much suspicion, so I decided to come and visit you. Nice place. Is there any food?'

Stan gazed up at the ceiling in exasperation. 'Don't tell me you broke through the fence.'

'I walked out, but I did bring two guards with me for appearances' sake. I told the men they were taking me to another camp. What about that food?'

'Grace, for heaven's sake arrange that for him. We won't get any sense out of him until he's had something to eat.'

'What would you like, Captain?'

'Anything, Grace. I missed dinner.'

There was plenty of a delicious mutton stew left from dinner and they watched as Bill devoured two helpings, and then sit back with a sigh of satisfaction.

'Didn't they feed you in the camp?' Grace asked.

He nodded. 'It wasn't as special as that, though. You can't beat fresh farm food. I hope we're staying here for a couple of days, Stan?'

'We will be leaving first thing in the morning, but I'll let you have breakfast first. If you've quite finished eating I want your report.'

'Tonight?'

Stan nodded. 'Bring your notebook, Grace.'

Grace followed the officers, and took her seat, ready to record what was said at the meeting. She had assumed they would want to talk in private, but she was being included – again. There was now hope that she was trusted at last.

The debriefing went on for two hours and Grace had pages and pages of notes. 'Would you like this typed up tonight, sir?'

'Good Lord, no. It's midnight. Leave that until we get back to Aldershot.'

They had only been away for a few days, but there was a pile of correspondence waiting for them. Grace began to sort through it, putting the urgent ones out for immediate attention and the two personal letters to one side for later. There was an enormous amount of work to get through before thinking of anything else.

It wasn't until lunchtime the next day that she had time to read her letters. The first one was from James saying they would be in London on Saturday and could she meet them at the Savoy. The thought of an evening out with James and Tim made her smile in anticipation. The smile quickly faded as she read the second letter. It was from Helen's parents asking her if she knew where their daughter was. They hadn't heard from her for a couple of weeks and that was unusual, so they had taken a trip to the New Forest where they thought she was stationed, but she wasn't there. No one would give them any information and they were worried.

Grace immediately wrote to them explaining that secrecy was necessary, and because Helen's work as an interpreter was probably sensitive it wasn't surprising they weren't given any information about her. She could have been sent anywhere in the country and finding time to write wasn't always easy. Grace sealed the letter, hoping it would help to put their minds at rest. It had planted a seed of doubt in her mind, though. Their letters to each other had been irregular with lengthy gaps in between, but Grace understood the situation they were both in, and it hadn't worried her.

'Ah, Grace, you're here.' Bill came in and sat down. 'I want to give Tim back his watch. How do I get in touch with him? Is he still at Kenley?'

'As a matter of fact I'm meeting him and James in London on Saturday evening.'

'Marvellous! Would you mind if I came along? I'd like to see him again.'

'I'm sure you would be very welcome. They will be there around six o'clock.'

'Terrific! I'll commandeer a car.' He stood up, smiling broadly and then bent to kiss her cheek. 'Thanks, Grace.'

'Keep your hands off my staff!' said sharp voice from the doorway. 'Try your amorous advances on women of your own rank.'

Bill grinned boyishly, not at all put out by the reprimand.

'I was just thanking Grace. We're going to meet James and Tim on Saturday. Want to come?'

Stan laughed softly. 'You're lucky – I've got another appointment or else I might have accepted.'

Grace watched the two men. They always spoke to each other like this but the respect they held for each other was evident.

Laughing, Bill kissed her cheek again and marched out of the office.

Stan was shaking his head. 'Don't get attached to that man, Grace. He will end up in serious trouble before this war is over. Like Dan Chester he's a risk-taker.'

'I don't intend to become fond of anyone, sir. I don't want to suffer the pain of loss again.'

'Of course not. Sensible girl.'

It was lovely to see James and Tim again. They were both fully recovered from their crashes and back to flying again, which was the only thing they wanted to do. Grace introduced Bill to them and they were soon all laughing at Tim's account of seeing a German pilot in Grace's office.

'I've gatecrashed your evening to return your watch, Tim.'

'Oh, thanks. We can swap back.' He removed Bill's watch from his wrist. 'I've been wearing it all the time to keep it safe.'

Bill gave the young pilot an incredulous look. 'You take to the air every day, being shot at, and you think that was keeping it safe?'

Both pilots grinned, and James said, 'He's safer in the air than driving a car. Did it help with your masquerade?'

'Perfect.'

'You'll join us for the rest of the evening, Bill?' Tim suggested.

'I'd like that.'

They found a comfortable corner to sit and talk, enjoying a quiet, relaxing evening together. It amused Grace to see the looks being cast her way and could almost hear their thoughts — what was a girl of low rank doing with three officers?

'It's a shame Helen isn't home as well,' James remarked.

At the mention of her friend the worry came back and Grace wished she knew what Helen was doing. She seemed to have disappeared. That wasn't unusual in this war, of course, when secrecy was so tight and you often didn't know where your friends and relatives were.

'I'm hoping she will be able to come home for Christmas. It is ages since I've seen her.'

'When you write next time, tell her we're expecting her.'

'I will, James.' Grace smiled at Tim. 'It would be fun to go dancing again, wouldn't it?'

'It certainly would.'

The tone of his voice made her study him intently. Tim had answered as if he doubted that would happen. Bill and James were talking together so Grace leant forward and spoke quietly. 'What's the matter, Tim?'

'What makes you ask that?'

'Just a feeling, and it has something to do with Helen. Don't you want to see her again? If that is so, please say and we won't come out with you again.'

'I would love to see her again and I really hope she does make it home soon.'

There it was again. His demeanour had changed at the mention of Helen; he had become guarded. 'What aren't you telling me, Tim?'

'I don't know what you mean.' He sat back, smiling. 'Working with those intelligence boys is making you suspicious. I haven't seen Helen since we went dancing.'

That sounded like a lie, but why would he deny it? If they had been in contact with each other there was no need to hide the fact, surely? She shook her head, perhaps he was right and she was concerned about nothing. 'Sorry, Tim, but I had a letter from her parents and they are worried. They don't know where she is.'

'I'm afraid that's happening all the time. I have an older brother in the navy and we haven't a clue where he is. It's just the way things are, Grace.'

'You're right, and that's just what I told them.' Grace relaxed. 'That letter must have spooked me.'

'That's what it is.' He stood up. 'Another drink everyone?'

Chapter Nineteen

'I might have known I'd find you in the middle of a field in the freezing cold!' Stan stamped his feet and blew on his hands.

Dan spun round and saluted smartly for appearances' sake, pleased to see his uncle again. 'What brings you out here, George?'

'I've been trying to get hold of you for days.' He cast an expert eye over the scene. 'Are they battle ready, Dan?'

'That's a question none of us can answer until we're faced with it. The majority of them were raw recruits after Dunkirk, but I believe they will do well when the time comes.'

'You're working them hard so I would say you are expecting to be shipped out soon.'

'You would probably know before me.'

'You'll be here for Christmas and a while after that. I can't tell you what is being planned.'

'Of course not.'

'Can we go somewhere warmer to talk?'

'You're spending too much time in that cosy War Office. It's making you soft, George.'

'I'll only be there for a few more months and then I'm returning to active duty – at last. Every experienced officer is going to be needed in the field.'

'I agree. Let me transfer command and we can return to the camp.'

George watched his nephew with a touch of pride. He was a damned fine soldier and he prayed he would survive this conflict.

'In just one week this war has taken a completely different course,' George said as they drove back. 'The Japanese bombed Pearl Harbor on the 7th December, then we declared war on Japan, and the United States and Germany declared war on each other. What a week!'

'And totally unexpected.' Dan stopped by the officers' quarters. 'Let's get something to eat. Can you stay for a while?'

'Until tomorrow.'

'Good, that will give us the evening to talk.'

They walked towards the building and George looked pointedly at Dan. 'Putting that all aside for the moment, we've still got to do something about Rommel in North Africa. Warmer there.'

'In more ways than one.' Dan glanced at his uncle and they nodded to each other, understanding the hint.

They were surprised to see Stan and another officer waiting inside.

'Ah, Dan, I was hoping we'd see you.'

'If you've come with the same request the answer is still no.'

'Oh, I've given up on that hope.' Stan held out his hand. 'Good to see you again, George.'

Bill noted the way they greeted each other. They were all officers of different ranks but obviously knew each other well. Well enough to dispense with formalities when no one else was around.

'We were just going to get some lunch. Would you like to join us?' Dan suggested.

'Thank you. May I introduce Captain William Reid? Bill wanted to meet you, Dan, and I think you'll find you have a lot in common. Like you, he spent some years in Germany.'

During the meal they were soon comparing notes, interested in each other's experiences.

'How is Grace working out, Stan?' George asked.

'Quite well,' was the casual reply.

Bill stopped in mid-sentence and snorted in disgust. 'He still won't admit he's met his match. They've had a tussle of wills ever since Grace came to us. Stan wanted a man but none of those sent to us were suitable so he had to take Grace. He's done everything he could to make her put in for a transfer, but she wouldn't give in.'

A deep rumble of laughter came from Stan. 'She's stubborn; I'll give you that, and speaks her mind if pushed too hard.'

'She's also efficient.'

'I've never denied that, Bill, but what I was looking for

was someone to partner with you. I can't send a woman into a dangerous situation.'

'That's just what is happening with a certain organisation now.'

'We know what you are referring to, Bill. We both have the highest security clearance from working at the War Office,' George told him.

Stan nodded and looked round to make sure they were not being overheard. Even in a place like this they couldn't be too careful. 'I know the SOE have been recruiting women, and I also know that if given the chance they would take Grace as well. The fact remains that I couldn't put a woman with you, Bill. You love women far too much and if faced with a difficult decision you would put a woman first, and that just wouldn't work. I couldn't trust you to get the job done, regardless of the dangers.'

'See what I have to put up with, Dan?' Bill shook his head in exasperation. 'Not only is he underestimating me but he's also doing the same with Grace. Stan, you didn't see what she did to me in that interview. She wiped the floor with me! I'd say she's more than capable enough of looking after herself.'

'That's what I mean. My concern is for you, not Grace.'

Bill rested his head in his hands, muttering, 'I give up!'

A slow smile spread across Stan's face. 'She also told me exactly what she thought of our methods. I could have had her up on a charge of insubordination, and she has come close to it a few times since then.'

'That's my girl!' George declared. 'My godson, James, trained her well, so you watch your step, Stan. There are several of us with a keen interest in her welfare.'

'I've met James,' Bill told George. 'He's a fine man and interesting to talk to. While we were having a drink I heard Grace talking to Tim and she's concerned about her friend. Evidently she's part French and they seem to have lost track of her. I reckon there's a good chance she has been recruited to the Special Operations Executive, but I didn't say anything, of course.'

Dan was sitting back, listening but saying nothing.

'That's more than likely,' Stan agreed. 'I still wouldn't put a woman with you, Bill. I've always wanted you and Dan to work together.'

'Stan!'

'All right, Dan.' He held up his hands in surrender. 'I won't pursue the subject any longer. Bloody shame, though.'

'What do you think about America coming in to the war?' George asked, changing the subject.

'It's what Churchill has wanted but that was a terrible way for it to happen. When I heard the news I couldn't believe Japan would launch an attack like that. Then Hitler declared war on America. It was incredible and stupid. Hitler is already in trouble with the Russian winter, and those two countries could live to regret their decisions.'

Dan nodded. 'You're right. Hitler's making too many mistakes. Instead of invading immediately after Dunkirk when we were vulnerable, he's given us time to recover. We are once again strong and there won't be another Dunkirk!'

'This war has taken a surprising turn and Dan is right,' George agreed. 'Hitler did his best to destroy our air force and bomb us into submission, but that hasn't worked. Our day will come and we are not alone this time.'

Bill grinned. 'Boat loads of American troops will be arriving here next year. 1942 should be interesting.'

'I've got a whole two weeks!' Grace hugged her parents.

'That's wonderful!' her mother exclaimed. 'You and Helen will be able to relax and enjoy yourselves. You both look as if you need a rest.'

'She's home?'

'She arrived early this morning.' Ted took the heavy kitbag from his daughter and hoisted it onto his shoulder. 'I'll take this upstairs for you. What have you got in it for heaven's sake?'

Grace laughed. 'Presents and some tins of food. I'll have a cup of tea, Mum, and then I'll go and see Helen.'

'She sent a message to say she'll see you this evening. She's evidently been travelling a lot and needs to catch up on some sleep.'

'Sounds as if she's been busy and that's probably why we haven't heard from her very much lately.'

'I expect so. Anyway, there's another message for you. James called last week and asked if you would be home. When I told him you would be, he said they would call round on New Year's Eve in the hope you would be free to spend the evening with him and Tim.'

'That would be lovely, but would you mind me not spending the time with you and Dad?'

'Not at all!' Ted came into the kitchen. 'You girls go off and enjoy yourselves.'

'Thanks. Do you know how long Helen's got?'

'Three weeks.'

'What? Are you sure, Mum?' When Jean nodded, Grace said, 'Lucky devil. I wonder how she wangled that.'

'Well she hasn't had any leave for a long time so I expect they've given her extra this time.'

Grace shrugged and sat down. Perhaps they did things differently in the FANY. After taking a sip of tea she sighed with pleasure. 'There's nothing like your tea, Mum. You should taste some of the stuff we get. It's an insult to call it tea.'

The rest of the day was spent on catching up with all the local news, and in a quiet moment Grace wandered in to the front room. This was a very austere time with everything in short supply but her parents had made the room look festive. The paper chains were handmade and they had managed to get some holly and a small tree from somewhere.

Grace sat down and closed her eyes. It was at times like this the loss of Brian was the hardest. Coming home always made the memories come flooding back. *Damn the war*, she thought angrily, *and the man who had started it*.

'Are you asleep, Grace?'

Her eyes opened and she leapt to her feet. 'Helen! Oh it's so good to see you. Where have you been?'

Her friend grinned. 'Mind your own business. What have you been up to?'

'Mind your own business.' The friends laughed and

hugged each other. 'That's got the questions out of the way. Is that right you've got three weeks?'

'That's right. How much have you managed to get?'

'Two weeks, and we've got a date with James and Tim for New Year's Eve.'

'Lovely. It will be good to see them again.'

Instead of a sports car, James and Tim arrived in a smart officer's car. The girls watched it stop outside and grinned at each other.

'I wonder how they got hold of that,' Helen laughed.

'Goodness knows!' Grace shook her head. 'I suspect they are used to going after what they want in the air and on the ground.'

'I don't doubt that,' Helen agreed, putting her hand out to stop her friend from moving. 'Your mother's beaten you to the door.'

The moment the two men walked in, they stopped with wide smiles on their faces when they saw Helen was there as well.

'This is marvellous! We were hoping you would both be able to get home for the holidays. Good job we managed to get two, Tim.'

Grace was intrigued; it was hard to take in the fact that this was the same man she had worked for at the law firm. They each had one hand behind their backs and devilish grins on their faces. What had they been up to now?

'Ready?' James asked, and when Tim nodded they held out their gifts.

'Orchids!' Grace gasped. 'Where did you get those

from? No, no, forget I asked that. We really don't want to know! They are beautiful.'

'Glad you like them.' Tim stepped towards Helen. 'We've even brought pins with us.'

The girls stood patiently while the exotic blooms were pinned to their uniforms. Then the two pilots stepped back and saluted smartly. 'Here's to 1942.'

Grace and Helen joined in by returning the salutes, and then it was hugs all round with the two sets of parents joining in.

'Off you go and enjoy yourselves,' Helen's father said. 'You take good care of our girls, though.'

'We will, sir.' Tim had his arm resting across Helen's shoulder. 'No harm will come to them while they are with us.'

'Where are we going?' Grace asked James as they made their way to the car.

'Somewhere big and noisy,' was all he said.

James hadn't been joking. The Hammersmith dance hall was packed with people intent on forgetting the war for a few hours and having a good time.

The men led them straight to the dance floor and when James began to spin Grace around, she asked, 'What dance is this?'

'It's what the Americans call a "jitterbug" or "jive". Come on, I'll show you how to do it.'

At the end of the dance she was laughing with pleasure. 'Where did you learn that?'

'From a couple of American pilots.'

'But they aren't here yet. I thought the first troops would be arriving in January.'

'A few qualified pilots came over early and joined the RAF.'

'Really? I didn't know that.'

'There are quite a few different nationalities with us now.' James grinned. 'Tim is learning French from a French Canadian. I think he wants to be able to speak the language in case he ever finds himself in France again.'

'That would be useful.' Grace looked across the room where Tim and Helen were talking to another man in RAF uniform. 'You've both recovered well from your crashes. Has Tim told you exactly what happened to him?'

James shook his head. 'All he will say is that he gave his word to protect the people who helped him.'

'I can understand that. Whoever it was, though, must have been in touch with London because they sent in a Lysander.'

'There are British agents with the underground, Grace. He must have been lucky enough to contact such a group and I expect that's why he won't say a word. Anyway, enough of this serious talk. You need more lessons in the jive.'

Chapter Twenty

Closing the office door firmly behind him, Stan watched Bill sit down before walking over to his desk. 'London's crowded these days.'

Bill laughed. 'I don't suppose many of those American boys have ever been outside their own country before. You can't blame them for wanting to see London in the spring.'

'Hmm.' Stan studied the man in front of him for a moment, and then said, 'Do you think this risky operation will work?'

'Not sure, but we won't know unless we try.'

'You'll need someone with you. Preferably a girl who can speak French like a native. We can contact the SOE. They will have someone who could do that.'

'I've already got someone in mind.'

'Oh.' Stan frowned. 'Who's that?'

'Grace.'

'No!'

'She's perfect for this mission, and her French is excellent.'

'No!'

'Stop saying "No".' Bill raised his voice in an unusual show of anger.

'You can't take Grace. Find someone else.'

'At least give her the chance to refuse. If you don't ask her then I will. I'm the one going on this mission and I want someone with me I can trust. We've got two months to train her. And stop shouting!'

Stan sat back and took a deep breath. 'Just because we are long time family friends, doesn't mean you can be insubordinate, so watch your tone. I don't know why I'm getting so angry anyway. She'll never agree to it.'

'She'll jump at the chance. Bet you a fiver.'

'Five pounds? You are sure of yourself.'

'I met Dan at the War Office yesterday. He was visiting his uncle. We had lunch together and I managed to get him to talk about Grace. His opinion was that she would handle any challenge she was faced with and still keep her composure. You're stifling her, Stan, and it is an indication of her self-control that she hasn't shown her frustration. After talking to Dan I was certain she would be right for this mission.' The corners of Bill's mouth turned up in amusement as he sensed victory. 'So, are you going to risk a fiver?'

'It will give me great pleasure to take your money. Ask Grace to come in here.'

Bill jumped to his feet and opened the door. 'Grace, we need you.'

She came in and sat down, notepad at the ready.

'Don't record this. We would like you to settle an argument,' Stan told her. 'Bill will tell you all about it.'

'There is a chateau in the south of France with extensive grounds. The Germans have sealed it off completely and it is heavily guarded. We need to know what they are doing there. The resistance have been unable to get anywhere near it, so I have agreed to see what I can do. I shall be posing as a German army officer with a French girlfriend who is showing me around her country.' Bill paused, watching Grace carefully, but her expression gave no indication of her reaction to this news. That was just what he needed to see. 'We have been arguing, as I expect you heard, about my choice of companion for this mission. Stan has bet five pounds that you will refuse.'

That bombshell did produce a reaction. Grace sat up straight, her gaze fixed on Bill, searching for any hint that this was a joke.

'This is a serious request, Grace,' Bill said quietly. 'Before you answer, this will be very dangerous. We could be captured or killed – and you will have to jump out of a plane.'

'Take your time, Grace,' Stan told her. 'No one will think any the worse of you if you refuse.'

'When do you go?' she asked Bill.

'Sometime in June. That will give you two months to prepare. You will have to go through an intensive training programme.' Bill sat back and waited. He was well aware how dangerous this was going to be, but he was so sure she was right for this job.

Grace remained silent while she looked out of the window. When she turned back to Stan there was a slight smile on her face. 'You have lost your bet, sir.'

He handed over the five-pound note to Bill, his expression serious. 'You will still be able to change your mind over the next couple of weeks. After that there will be no backing out, Grace. Bill must be given time to replace you.'

'I won't back out, sir. I want to do this.'

Stan nodded. 'Bill is no stranger to risky missions and I trust his judgement that you are the right person for this. I do have one concern, though, and that is your motive for accepting.'

Grace frowned. 'My motive?'

'Yes. It has crossed my mind that you might be taking this on to avenge your husband's death.'

'That is something I, personally, cannot do, sir. The only comfort for me, and thousands of others mourning the loss of loved ones, will be the defeat of Hitler and his regime. That will only come about by each one of us working together. My only motive is to play my part by using whatever talents I have. You need have no concerns that I will be a liability to the captain, sir.'

Stan nodded slowly. 'I believe Bill has chosen well. I will expect to see you both back here by the end of June. Godspeed to both of you.'

'Thank you, sir.' Grace stood up when Bill did and they both saluted.

Once in the outer office Bill told her that they would be leaving at once. 'There is no time to waste, Grace. Pack your bag and I will be waiting outside your billet in a car.'

Bill had only given her half an hour and Grace rushed around the room grabbing items and packing them in her kitbag, and she was glad he wasn't giving her much time to think about her decision. Well, she wasn't going to have second thoughts. After Brian had been killed she had wanted to try and find something useful to do – something that would make a difference. At last the opportunity had come.

After a final glance round the room to check she hadn't forgotten anything, she grabbed her bag and ran down the stairs.

The car was already there with Bill propped up against it, smoking a cigarette. No one would guess from his relaxed, casual attitude that they were planning to embark on a dangerous mission. There was a slightly different air about him, though, making her realise there was much more to this man than she had originally thought. That man always joking and full of tricks was just a mask. It was going to be interesting working with him.

He stubbed out his cigarette and held the door open for her while the driver put her kitbag on the boot of the car.

'Can we talk?' she asked quietly once they were on their way.

He nodded. 'We are going to a manor near Guildford to start your training. Time is short so we will only be there for a week before moving on to the next place. You are going to have to learn quickly, Grace, because you've got to be able to take care of yourself if anything happens to me. You are going to be pushed to your limits. There will be times when you are exhausted and wish you had never agreed to this. I will be with you all the time because I must be sure you won't panic whatever the situation you are faced with. If you do then both of our lives will be at risk. If there is the slightest hint that you might not be able to deal with this, you will be straight back in the office. Is that clear?'

'Perfectly. I won't let you down.'

'I'm confident you won't or I would never have chosen you.' He gave a wry smile. 'I will also be reading your letters to make sure you don't give anything away.'

'I'll have to be careful what I say, then,' she told him.

'Very careful, Grace.' He turned to face her. 'No one must know what we are doing at these training camps. If you do happen to see anyone you know and they ask what you're doing there, you are not to say a word.'

'I know how important that is, Captain.'

'Call me Bill at all times from now on, even if top brass are around. We've got to be relaxed and easy in each other's company. Forget my rank. I don't want you snapping to attention and saluting me. That could be awkward in two months' time. That's all you need to know at the moment, so relax and enjoy the journey.'

They arrived just in time for lunch and were shown straight to the dining room. Several men nodded to Bill when they walked in and Grace guessed this wasn't the first time Bill had been here. During the meal she hardly noticed what she was eating, far too interested in her surroundings, and she was surprised to see an empty plate in front of her. She would not consider herself to be the nervous type, but did admit to feeling apprehensive, not knowing what the following weeks were going to be like. There was only one way to deal with this and that was to remember one of her mother's favourite sayings and take each day as it came.

An officer was striding towards them and she made a quick assessment of him. He was not a young man, but he moved with all the ease of being very fit. Not sure how she should act in this unusual place, she remained seated and only stood up when Bill rose to his feet.

'Good to see you again, Bill.' He shook hands with Bill and then turned his full attention onto Grace, his pale grey eyes fixed firmly on her face. 'And you've brought Grace with you. Come and see me when you have finished your meal, Bill, and bring Grace with you.'

'We'll be there very soon, Henry.' Bill grinned. 'Just in time for coffee?'

'Of course,' the officer laughed.

'Henry makes the best coffee I've ever tasted,' Bill told her as the officer walked away and they sat down again.

Over the next week Grace didn't have a moment to herself. They were cramming three weeks' training into one, and at night she gratefully climbed in bed. Her mind was buzzing with all the things she was being taught, but she was still able to sleep, much to her relief. Bill had handed her over to the various instructors, taking no part in the training, but he was always there, watching and assessing her progress. She was very aware that if he saw the slightest hint she wasn't able to cope, he would call a halt. There were obviously women around who were fully trained and he wouldn't have any trouble replacing her. *That wasn't going to happen*, she decided, determination surging through her. There were still several weeks to go, but as each day passed, her desire to go on this mission increased. But she would have to prove she was good enough, and that wasn't going to be easy.

At the end of the week she had to face the instructors for a verdict. This was the most nerve-wracking part of the week; so much depended on their assessment of her abilities.

'It's been a tough week for you, trying to absorb everything is such a short time,' Henry said. 'When I received these orders I declared that it couldn't be done. Do you think you have proved me wrong?'

Grace was aware that Bill was standing behind her by the door and he wasn't going to hear doubt from her. She looked at each instructor and then back to Henry. She smiled and nodded. 'I have proved you wrong.'

'You have a quick mind and a determined nature, and, yes, in your case I was wrong. This has been the easy part, though. It is going to get tougher, but as far as we are concerned you have done *quite* well. We shall watch the rest of your training with interest.'

Grace breathed a silent sigh of relief. Their verdict was not as good as she had hoped, but at least it seemed as if she had done well enough to go on to the next stage. She was obviously going to have to do better or Bill would take her off this mission. As she left the room she glanced at him but there was nothing to show how he felt about her progress in his expression. Bill had stayed to have a word with the instructors and she waited patiently outside for him.

Twenty minutes later he came out. 'Time to move on, Grace. Meet me outside as soon as you can.'

'I'm already packed. I'll be with you in ten minutes.' She hurried to collect her bag, wondering what had been said in that room after she left. She would love to know, but knew better than to ask. Bill obviously wasn't going to say anything until he was sure she was going to make it through the training.

They were soon on their way in the car with the same driver, so she knew it was all right to talk.

'Where are we going?'

'There's a plane waiting for us at Northolt airfield to take us up to the Highlands of Scotland where you will receive commando training. You will only have three weeks so it's going to be rough.' He turned slightly to face her. 'I'm relying on you to be honest and tell me the moment you decide not to go on. I will also pull you out if it is apparent we are asking too much of you. If we had more time I have no doubt you would pass the training schedule, but we don't have that luxury.'

'I fully understand that you have to be able to rely on me in a crisis. All I can do at this stage is promise that I will do everything I can to prove myself capable of coping with whatever is needed of me.'

'I can't ask for more than that.' He smiled then. 'I made the mistake of underestimating you the first time we met. I've watched you carefully since then and have come to realise you were capable of more than sitting in an office. We are living in extraordinary times, Grace. Times that are demanding more of us than we thought we were capable of. That has to be faced and accepted because it is the only way we are going to win this war.'

'I am prepared to face any challenge. I wouldn't have agreed to this otherwise.'

'And I wouldn't have asked you if I'd thought you were content to sit out this war in an office. Have you flown before?'

'No.'

'Didn't James ever take you up in his plane?'

Grace laughed. 'No, but I often wished he would.'

'Well, you'll get your chance today, though it won't be as comfortable. It will get us to Scotland quickly and that is the main thing. There isn't any time to waste. This mission must go ahead on time even if I have to go alone.'

'You won't have to do that! I'm coming with you, Bill, even if I have to work myself to a standstill during the training.'

'I'm asking a great deal of you, but there are two reasons for the intensive training. I want you to be able to take care of yourself – and I need you to be fully aware of the dangers we might face while in France.'

When Dan had manhandled her over the army assault course it had been easy compared to this, Grace thought as she eased herself into a hot bath with a groan of relief. She was bruised, battered and ached from head to toe. Bill had said this training was because he wanted her to be able to take care of herself. Well, she certainly would be able to after this! It had been a tough physical three weeks, and many times she had thought it was not possible to endure another day. When at her lowest she would glance across at Bill watching her and she had gathered her strength together and carried on. A smile crossed her face. It had all been worth it, though, because today she had actually been able to throw a man flat onto his back.

Tomorrow they were off to Ringwood airfield, near Manchester, for parachute training. She only had one week to master that. Bill had jokingly said there was nothing to it; when the door opened you just threw yourself out. It was the landing you had to be careful about.

Grace climbed out of the bath, dried off and fell straight into bed. She needed to sleep so there was no point worrying now and keeping awake. It would be time enough to worry when she was facing the challenge. After the parachute training there was only one more stop and that was to learn Morse code, among other things. That should be interesting.

Grace watched the ground rushing towards her and braced for the landing, trying to remember everything she had been told. She mustn't injure herself now. Concentrating hard, she rolled as she hit the ground, then scrambled to her feet and began to gather up the parachute. Bill had landed in the same field, and as he walked towards her, she grinned.

'I did it!' Grace was almost dancing with excitement.

'And I do believe you enjoyed it,' Bill laughed.

'I really did. It was the most incredible feeling.'

'Don't forget that the next time you jump it will be in the dark. We will go when there is a bright moon, though, so we should be able to see where we're landing. Ah, here's the truck. I'll buy you a drink. You deserve it.'

'Where are we going next?' Grace asked when they were settled in a quiet corner of the bar. Bill had been very economical with his information so far, but now they were nearing the end of the training she was hoping to be told more about this operation.

'A place in the New Forest. I'm cutting that to only five days, so just do the best you can. It's the beginning of June now and the forecast is for favourable weather in about seven days.'

Her insides tightened at this news, but she smiled. 'Nearly there, then.'

Bill nodded. 'I have some final arrangements to make so I won't be with you this time. I'll settle you in and then pick you up after. Only when we are ready to go will I tell you the plan.'

Ah, that answered one of her questions, then. She wouldn't know exactly what she had let herself in for until the very last minute. 'I understand. When are we leaving for the next camp?'

'At eighteen hundred hours.'

Grace finished her drink quickly. 'I'd better go and pack at once.'

They arrived too late for dinner but, evidently, they were used to serving meals at odd times. Grace was starving by the time Bill took her to the dining room. He had left immediately, not even stopping for something to eat. He appeared to know his way around these places, she thought, as she sat down. She had seen a very different side to him over the last few weeks and there was no doubt he knew what he was doing with undercover work. She now understood why he disappeared from time to time. He had once told her, jokingly, that he was a spy, and she had a strong feeling that was exactly the kind of work he was involved in.

'Hello, Grace.'

The familiar voice had her leaping to her feet. 'Helen! How wonderful to see you. It did cross my mind that you might be here when I knew we were coming to this area.'

Her friend laughed. 'It's good to see you, as well – but I'm not sure I'm too happy to see you in this place.'

'I'm just here to learn Morse code. Sit down and talk to me while I eat. I'm ravenous. I didn't dare eat anything before—' She stopped abruptly, remembering Bill's warning about being careful what she said if she met anyone she knew. It was hard to keep secrets from her friend, though.

'Have you seen Tim and James lately?' Helen asked as she sat down.

Grace nodded and waited while a meal was put in front

of her. She talked about the two men for a while, and then said, 'I'll be here for a few days, Helen, so perhaps we could have a few meals together.'

'I won't be here. I heard you were coming and wanted to see you before I left.' Helen grasped Grace's hands tightly and whispered, 'You take care.'

'I will, and you do the same.'

The look they gave each other didn't need words. They knew both of them were involved in dangerous work.

Chapter Twenty-One

The sun was going down and Grace stood by the window watching the light fade. Would there by a full moon tonight? Everyone was confident there would be and they were already at the airfield ready to go at a moment's notice.

'Nervous?' Bill came and stood beside her, placing an arm across her shoulders.

'Yes.' There was no point in lying.

'Waiting is the worse part. You'll be all right once we are on our way.'

'How many times have you done this, Bill?'

'A few. Being able to speak German like a native is useful, and that is why Stan has tried so hard to recruit Dan. We'd have made a good team, but he's a fighting man, and a fine one from what I've heard. We all have different talents and they must be used to the best advantage.'

Grace smiled. 'It would be difficult for Dan to blend into a crowd with his height.'

'Oh, I think he could do anything he set his mind to.'

'Would you have taken him with you if he'd been available?'

'Not this time. I need a beautiful woman who speaks fluent French.'

An air force officer came towards them with papers in his hands and a distracted look on his face. 'Just received the final report, Captain; you're good to go tonight at twenty-three hundred hours.'

Bill drew in a deep breath. 'Thank you, sir.'

'Clear night forecast.' He nodded to them both and then turned and left the room.

As soon as they were alone again, Bill led Grace over to a couple of armchairs. 'Time to brief you. The Germans have taken over a chateau set in extensive grounds. It is heavily guarded. Photos have revealed nothing and the resistance have been unable to discover exactly what it is being used for. The only thing we know is that high-ranking officers are continually going in and out. The resistance have to remain hidden, but I don't. However, this time I can't do it alone, and that's where you come in. I am going to pass myself off as a German officer on leave with a French lover who is showing me some of her country. You visited the chateau as a child with your parents to buy wine, and you take me there to see if they still produce excellent wines. When we are denied entry you will need to show great disappointment, upset that you have brought me all this way from Paris for nothing. Speak rapidly in French, and while I am trying to calm you it will give me a chance to be friendly with the guards.'

'What kind of a girl do you want me to be? Do you want me to act common?'

'No. You are classy and elegant. The kind of woman an SS officer would be pleased to be seen with.'

Grace stared at Bill in astonishment. 'SS! That will be dangerous.'

'I've done this before, and yes, it is risky, but it could give me more chance of being invited to the chateau. We're fairly sure social functions are being held there, but it's what they are doing *in* the grounds we need to know. The security is too tight for it just to be a place for officers to relax. Any questions?'

She pursed her lips in thought. 'I have been given some French clothes, but nothing classy and elegant.'

'I have chosen a couple of outfits for you. All the things we will need, together with a wireless set, will be dropped with us. The resistance will be waiting to take us to a safe house.'

'If you are supposed to be on leave we won't be able to stay around too long. It will be suspicious.'

'Five days at the most. It will be essential not to arouse any doubts about us. I don't want you to give any indication that you understand German. We will have to put on a convincing show of being lovers, but be assured that I would never take advantage of you.' Bill paused and sighed deeply. 'I lie. If I thought I had the slightest chance with you I would certainly take advantage of the situation.

But you already have several men waiting patiently for the right time to step in.'

Grace stared at him in astonishment. 'What on earth are you talking about?'

'Nothing you need worry about yet. I'm going to sit back and watch to see who wins.'

'You're talking nonsense. Are you all right?'

'First class. So, do you think you will be able to convince everyone we are madly in love with each other?'

'I'll put on a winning performance; one that will even convince you.'

Bill tipped his head back and laughed. 'I look forward to that.'

They were both laughing when a man entered the room and walked towards them.

'Good to hear laughter,' he said, sitting next to them. 'People are usually tense and subdued at this point. I'm Joe, your pilot. The forecast is for perfect weather and we will leave in two hours' time.'

'We're ready. I'm Bill and my partner is Grace.'

'Pleased to meet you. We should have a smooth flight and we'll try to drop you in the right place,' Joe joked.

'That would be appreciated,' Bill replied dryly.

'See you in a couple of hours, then.'

'Time to get into our kit, sweetheart.' Bill held out his hand to pull her out of the chair. 'Just getting in a bit of practice.'

'Thank you, my love.' Grace laughed. It was then she realised what he was doing. All this light-hearted nonsense had been to put her at her ease while they waited. He knew how to handle these situations, and her confidence grew. If anyone could make this a successful mission and keep them alive, then it was Bill.

'I do have one more question.'

He stopped walking and turned to her. 'Now's the time to ask.'

'How do we get back?'

'That is what the wireless is for. They will, hopefully, send in a Lysander for us. It all depends on the situation, and if we are in trouble we might have to scramble a bit.' He cast her an amused glance. 'But I understand you are quite good at that.'

Her mouth twitched at the corners. She knew who he had been talking to. 'By scramble I take it you mean we might have to find our own way back.'

'Could happen.' He patted his pocket. 'I've got a compass with me.'

'Oh, good,' she replied, grimacing. 'That is a comfort.'

Too close to the trees! Grace braced herself, gasping in relief as she skimmed past them and landed with a crash. Her parachute had snagged on a branch but, fortunately, it had broken and come down with her. That had been too close to disaster. As she sat on the ground winded, a couple of men silently appeared and began to gather up her chute. Strong hands were pulling her up.

'Are you injured, Grace?'

'No, I'm all right, but I made a lot of noise,' she said, relieved to see Bill. 'Are we safe?'

'Think so, but we'd better not hang around.' Bill

began to help the two men roll up the parachutes and hide them.

They worked quickly and silently until there was no sign anyone had been there. Grace looked around anxiously and was relieved to see that the resistance men had found their precious wireless and other supplies. Bill hoisted the pack onto his back and took her arm as the men beckoned them to follow.

It was at least a mile long walk, Grace estimated, and she was pleased when a building came into sight. Although it was dark, there was no mistaking that they were on a farm because she could just see the outline of a couple of barns. They were ushered through a door, and when the lamps were relit they were in a large kitchen filled with people.

One man grinned. 'Hello, Bill. What the devil are you up to this time?'

'Harry! I thought you were back in England.'

'Got delayed.' Harry studied Grace for a moment, and then smiled. 'Welcome to France.'

'Thank you. My name is Grace, and I'm pleased to be here – I think.' A deep chuckle rumbled through Harry, and she couldn't help noticing what an attractive man he was. He was around six feet in height with black hair and deep blue eyes. She realised with a shock that she was finding this type of man very appealing. Men with physical and mental strength like Dan, James, Bill and Harry, and just the type whose chances of surviving this war were slim.

Harry turned his attention back to Bill. 'I guess you are

235

here to have a look at the chateau. We haven't been able to get anywhere near the place. I thought they might send you, but you usually work alone, so why have you brought Grace with you?'

'She's my French lover who is showing me the countryside of her childhood while I'm on leave. She used to visit as a child with her parents and it is one of her favourite places.'

Frowning deeply at that news, Harry asked, 'Are you intending to go in the front door?'

'It's the only way left. Everything else has been tried.'

'That's crazy and is going to be damned dangerous,' Harry said, looking straight at Grace.

'We know that, Harry,' she told him.

He nodded, and then turned his attention back to Bill. 'If you do gain entrance and your identities are discovered, we won't be able to help you.'

'We wouldn't want, or expect, any of you to put yourselves in danger because of us. When we leave here, we are on our own.'

'I don't like it, Bill. You could both be throwing away your lives for nothing. It might turn out to be just a glorified brothel for the officers.'

'The feeling is that it is too well guarded for that, but you could be right. If that is the case then we can forget it, but we have to know, Harry. Now, will you introduce us to our hosts?'

The sound of voices speaking softly woke Grace and she opened her eyes. In the early morning light she could see Bill and Harry leaning against a sturdy beam in the barn loft, deep in discussion. She remained quite still, listening to the various noises of the farm awakening at dawn, and savoured the smell of the fresh straw they had been sleeping on. She had spent the night with two very attractive men, and it had seemed a perfectly normal thing to do. Bill was right. They were living in extraordinary times. Never in their wildest dreams had she and Helen imagined they would be involved in anything like this. Her life with Brian had seemed so straightforward. They would both work until they had enough money to buy a small house, then there would be a couple of children, and they would grow old together. All those plans, hopes and dreams had been cruelly swept away. This was her life now – a life where there was no room for future plans or emotional attachments. The need to win this war was all that mattered, and she would do whatever was asked of her.

'Are you awake, Grace?' Bill asked softly.

'Just about.' She hauled herself up to a sitting position. 'What time is it?'

'Six o'clock. We'll go to the house now to wash and change into our other clothes. Harry is going to get us a car, and after breakfast we'll be on our way.'

'How are you going to get a car, Harry?' she asked.

He gave a lopsided grin. 'Don't ask. See you later.'

Harry eased through the hatch.

'Be careful,' she said.

His head reappeared. 'Always.'

After breakfast, Grace had a good wash in a rather

primitive outhouse, and then dressed in a plain navy blue frock. It fitted perfectly and its simplicity made it quite elegant. The grandmother of the family insisted on setting her hair in an appropriate style.

'Now you look French,' she said with satisfaction.

Suddenly the elderly woman threw her hands up in horror, making Grace spin round to see what had alarmed her. The man who had just come into the room made her gasp, and she had to look closely to reassure herself that it really was Bill. She had once accused him of being a terrible actor, but there would be no doubt that this man was a German SS officer.

'Oh, Bill, you gave us a fright!'

Harry returned at that moment, stopped when he saw Bill, and after a short pause he shook his head.

'Dammit man! You're so convincing I nearly shot you!'

'You hesitated too long! If I had been the real thing you would have lost your chance. Did you get the car?'

'Reprimand accepted,' Harry told him. 'We couldn't get you a German one, but it's a decent French car, and the tank is almost full of petrol. Be sparing with it because we can't get any more. We've changed the number plates and the appearance of it as much as we could. It's round the back of the barn. There is also a room booked for you at the only hotel in the village.' Harry eyed Bill up and down. 'Not good enough for an SS officer, of course, but you must have a base for your supposed leave.'

Bill inclined his head, and as Grace watched it was obvious he had completely switched to the character of

238

the officer. There was a ruthless look about him, and when he turned to examine her appearance she wasn't sure she liked this man with the cold eyes.

'Will I do, *mon amour*?' she asked, lifting her head and meeting his gaze while reminding herself that she had to act as if she was in love with him. She smiled. 'Or would you like me to change into something else?'

He walked round her, inspecting her from every angle, then came to stand in front of her to run his fingers down her cheek. 'Don't be intimidated by the role I'm playing, Grace. I just wanted to see if I am convincing enough. You look beautiful.'

Grace actually shivered. Although Bill had smiled, there hadn't been any warmth in his eyes.

'Oh, you're convincing, Bill, but you're still going to have to be damned careful and not let the role drop for a second, or they'll have you.' Harry looked concerned. 'I don't like this idea at all. It isn't just your life you're chancing this time.'

'This is something I can't do on my own, Harry. And it wasn't my idea.'

'No, I don't suppose it was. You take risks, but you always have an escape route. This time you haven't. I just hope it's going to be worth it.'

'We won't find out standing around here. Time to go,' Bill said, shaking hands with the family who had helped them.

The grandmother kissed Grace on the cheek, but said nothing.

'Be safe,' Harry told them as they walked out of the

door. 'And, Grace, be prepared to be scorned when the French see you on the arm of such a man. You will be looked upon as a traitor by many.'

'I understand, but thank you for the warning, Harry.'

'That family took a chance with us being there, and we don't even know their names,' Grace said as Bill drove the car out of the farm.

'They have been told that what we are doing is very risky, so what we don't know we can't reveal if we are caught. If you are questioned, you met me at a hotel in Paris where you work as a receptionist. It is used by high-ranking German officers so you can't give the name for security reasons. We have been lovers for almost a year, but I have never talked about myself or what I do. Whatever happens, don't let your guard drop for a second.'

'Understood. I'll be very careful. I'd like both of us to come out of this alive.'

'If I get into trouble you must try to get away. Don't wait for me. I'll meet up with you when I can. You are not to put yourself in danger by wondering what has happened to me. Harry is waiting at the farm, and he'll take you to safety.'

'Let's hope that won't be—' Grace stopped talking abruptly. 'There's a roadblock up ahead!'

'I've seen it. Smile nicely, and remember you can't understand German.'

They were waved down and Bill stopped. When he got out of the car the soldiers on guard snapped to attention, and while Bill was talking to one of them, the other walked towards the car. Grace smiled, pretending she didn't understand what he was saying. Bill strode over and told her, in appalling French, that she had to show her papers. It was routine.

Talking to Bill rapidly, she handed over her fake papers for inspection.

Bill distracted the guard by shaking his head and saying that he couldn't understand what she was saying when she gabbled like that, making the guard laugh. After giving her papers only a cursory glance, he handed them back.

The other guard had been on the field telephone and Bill went over to him. Grace couldn't hear what was being said, but when the soldiers saluted again and Bill came back to the car, relief flooded through her as the barrier was lifted to allow them to continue their journey.

Once they were well away, Bill said, 'The chateau is a mile away and someone will be there to meet us.'

Tall iron gates had been erected at the entrance and barbed wire was stretched around the perimeter as far as the eye could see. There was also a tower, and on top were guards with a mounted machine gun. Not surprising the resistance hadn't been able to get near, and the place had caught their interest back home. Her insides churned uncomfortably. Bill was taking an enormous risk, but he appeared quite relaxed about it.

'Stay in the car,' he murmured, as he got out and walked over to meet the two officers waiting for him.

They talked for about ten minutes but it seemed like

hours to Grace. When Bill looked across and beckoned to her she took a deep breath and got out of the car. When she reached them, one of the officers spoke good French and began to ask her about her visits to the chateau as a child. Fortunately, learning about the place had been the final part of her training so she had a clear picture of it in her mind. Smiling, she told him what she remembered and explained how she had so wanted to visit again.

'Disappointing for you, *ma cherie*,' Bill said, 'but it is now a military base.'

Grace nodded and sighed. 'I would have liked to sample the wines. Are the vineyards still here, sir?'

'They are, but wine is not being produced at the moment. There are ample supplies in the cellars, though. I cannot allow you in today, but there will be a social this evening.' He turned to Bill. 'Perhaps you would both like to join us?'

'We would be happy to come.'

'I will tell the guards to expect you, and they will escort you to the chateau.'

'We will look forward to tasting some of the wines,' Bill told him.

As they drove away Bill said, 'I can say you are unwell and come on my own.'

Grace looked at him in astonishment. 'No you won't! We are in this together, and you need me as a distraction.'

'It's going to be very dangerous. I will be slipping away from the party to see what I can discover, and our chances of getting out of there again are not high.'

'I'm coming with you, Bill! Don't start worrying about me. That's just what Stan was concerned about, and it's the worst thing you can do. I'll take my chances, just like you.'

He reached across and squeezed her hand, but said nothing. She took this as acceptance.

Chapter Twenty-Two

They spent the afternoon walking round the village like tourists. It was not a comfortable time. An SS officer was regarded with hostility and Grace had to ignore the looks of contempt thrown her way as she walked arm in arm with him. Even this was dangerous in case someone took the opportunity to get rid of a lone German, but he was supposed to be on leave and they had to act the part. It was a relief to get back to the hotel.

They had brought their luggage with them, including the wireless, not wanting to put the family at the farm at risk of it being discovered. They had hidden it in the only place available – under the bed. Grace pulled out the one evening frock and hung it up to let the creases fall out. Again it was a simple style, but elegant and a shade of blue that matched her eyes perfectly.

By seven o'clock they were on their way. While they

had been getting ready, Grace's nerves had been jangling, but when they arrived at the chateau a strange calm settled upon her. She smiled at Bill. 'Wonder what the wine is like?'

'We shall soon find out,' he said, laughing softly as he slipped her hand through his arm. 'Here we go! If all goes well we could be on our way home in a couple of days.'

Grace didn't need to ask what would happen if it all went wrong – she knew, and so did Bill.

The main hall was packed with soldiers of every rank and quite a few women among them. Grace scanned the crowd quickly and noted that Bill was the only SS officer present. In one way that was a relief because they could have asked too many questions, but the other thing was that this made him stand out from the crowd.

The officer they had met earlier that day came over as soon as they entered the room. 'Welcome to our little gathering. Please help yourself to the food and drink.' He smiled at Grace. 'Please allow me to let you sample the chateau wines. We have some excellent ones.'

'Thank you.' She smiled enthusiastically as he escorted her to the bar.

He gave orders to the barman who then lined up six bottles and small glasses. He poured from the first one and handed it to Grace, asking for her opinion.

She took only a tiny sip of each as they worked their way through the selection, knowing she had to keep a clear head. As they discussed the virtues of each wine, Grace blessed James who had taught her a lot about wines at their frequent business functions.

'You are very knowledgeable about wine,' he said, giving her an admiring glance.

'I like good things.'

'And your escort can give you those things?'

Grace glanced across the room and saw Bill talking to a group of men. 'He can – and does.'

'You are the only woman here not adorned with expensive jewels. They expect such gifts.'

'Trinkets mean nothing to me. I prefer a simple look.' This officer was probing her relationship with an SS officer, and Grace knew she must be very careful.

He smiled, moving closer. 'A woman as beautiful as you does not need gaudy embellishments.'

He was flirting with her! She bowed her head and smiled. 'A charming compliment, sir.'

'Do you think your escort would mind if I asked you to dance? Is he the jealous type?'

'I would be happy to dance with you, and no, he isn't jealous or possessive. He trusts me.'

'Lucky man to have found such a treasure,' he said, guiding her to the dance floor.

During the evening she danced with several of the officers, and often with Bill, but she avoided talking too much to the women in case they caught any hint that she was not quite what she seemed.

Around eleven o'clock she was dancing cheek to cheek with Bill who whispered in her ear, 'They've all been drinking heavily so I'm going to slip out. Quite a few of the women have been shipped in from the village for the men, and a bus is due to take them back at twelve o'clock.

If I don't appear, you are to get on that bus and get out. Don't hesitate.'

'I'll do as you say.'

He asked one of the waiters where the toilets were, then kissed her cheek and walked out.

There was no sign of Bill when the party began to break up, so Grace mingled with the other girls and got on the bus with them. They had all had a lot to drink and didn't take any notice of her. She was worried sick about Bill, but he had told her to leave and she must obey his instructions. They had just driven out of the gate when there was a huge explosion and alarms began ringing. She held her breath, expecting the bus to be stopped and searched, but it didn't happen. Something had gone wrong. And why had there been an explosion? *Oh, Bill, if you're still in there, how are you going to get out?*

When they reached the outskirts of the village the bus was stopped, a soldier got on and walked along, inspecting each of the women closely. The driver was explaining to another soldier where they had come from. The girls were lively with drink and joked with the soldiers, so Grace joined in, not wanting to stand out from the others. After every inch of the bus had been searched, they were allowed to continue.

Grace bit back a sigh of relief as the bus drove along, but her relief was short-lived. The village was swarming with soldiers searching every home, including the hotel. She was dismayed when she saw one was carrying the wireless set, and another all of their luggage. They were looking for her as well now!

The bus stopped in the middle of the village and they were ordered off and told to return to their homes immediately. They went in different directions and Grace stayed with four who were walking together, all the time looking for somewhere to hide. She couldn't go back to the hotel, and desperately needed somewhere safe where she could decide what to do.

Her chance came when she saw a place they had explored on their sightseeing trip. When they reached the narrow passage between two houses she glanced around to make sure they weren't being followed, and then she slipped away from the girls. Once in the passage she removed her shoes and ran as fast as she could for the trees at the back. The area was rough and overgrown and very dark, but she didn't stop until she was inside the dense forest of trees. The decision when to stop was made for her when she tripped and fell heavily. She stayed on the ground trying to control her ragged breathing, listening for any sign of pursuit.

All was quiet.

How long she stayed like that Grace didn't know, but she eventually sat up and began to assess her situation. It was dire. She was in an evening frock, battered and bruised from her flight through the undergrowth, and the Germans were searching for her. At least she was still free, and she desperately hoped Bill was also hiding somewhere. He had said Harry would be waiting for her if there was trouble, and the obvious place to make for was the farm. That wasn't going to be easy because the mess she was in meant she could only move at night.

She dragged herself to her feet, grimacing with pain, and trying to get her bearings. There was still some of the night left so she had better try to cover some ground before dawn. It was imperative that she got out of this area, so she set off, hoping she was going in the right direction.

Dawn was just beginning to lighten the sky when she found a small stream, but as it didn't look too clean she just moistened her mouth and spat it out. She had left the trees behind a while ago and there didn't appear to be anyone around so she took the chance to try and clean herself up as much as possible. Then she tore a few inches off the frock to make it shorter and draped that piece of material around the neckline to fill it in. From a distance it should now look more like a summer dress. It wouldn't pass close up, though.

Grace crept towards a nearby road, needing to find out exactly where she was. It was a huge relief to see that even in all the confusion she had been travelling towards the farm. There wasn't far to go but it was light now and too dangerous to continue. The only place to hide for the day was in a deep ditch by some thick bushes. She climbed into it, covered herself with whatever loose vegetation was available, and closed her eyes to wait out the day.

Exhaustion overcame her and she slept for a while until hunger and thirst woke her up. At last it was dark and Grace was able to make her way to the farm.

Two hours later she stumbled through the farm gates, hardly able to stand due to the damage she had done to her feet on the journey. It had been impossible to wear her flimsy evening shoes over such rough territory.

Not wanting to put the family in more danger by going to the house, she headed straight for the barn. Climbing up to the loft took the last of her strength, but she made it and collapsed onto a pile of straw.

There were voices. Someone was giving orders. Grace surfaced sluggishly. After all that effort she had been caught!

'Grace! Wake up!'

English! Her eyes snapped open and she saw Harry bending over her. When she tried to speak nothing came out.

One of the men from the farm held a bottle of water to her lips and began to give her a sip at a time.

'Easy,' Harry said when she tried to take the bottle. 'Have some bread as well.'

The two men watched her silently as she tore off lumps of bread and sipped the water. When she'd had enough she managed to say, 'Thank you.'

'Where's Bill?' Harry wanted to know.

'I think he was still at the chateau.' Her voice trembled. 'I left him behind, Harry. I shouldn't have done that no matter what he'd told me to do.'

'You did the right thing.'

She shook her head, the enormity of what had happened finally registering with her.

'There wasn't anything you could do.' Harry gripped her arms, making her focus on what he was saying. 'If you had been caught they could have used you to make him give them information. For his sake, and everyone involved, you had to get away. Do you understand?'

'I suppose so.'

'There's no suppose about it, Grace. You had to avoid capture. Bill knows what he's doing. He can look after himself, and being on his own will give him more chance of escaping.'

Of course she knew that, but it didn't make her feel any better. 'There was an explosion. Why would something have exploded?'

'Bill must have found something vital and decided to get rid of it there and then.'

'But he didn't have any explosives with him.'

'Bill, among many other things, is a demolition expert. If he wanted to destroy something, he would have found a way.'

'Good heavens, Harry! I'm beginning to realise that I don't know this man.'

'You're not the only one to feel that way,' he laughed. 'He's like a chameleon. Now tell me what happened.'

The story was soon told, and when she was finished, Harry cursed. 'The discovery of the wireless is a real problem. You did well to remain hidden because after quizzing the hotel owners about your appearance they'll be searching everywhere for you. We've got to get you away from this area. You'll need new papers and clothes. That will take a few days to arrange. The Germans have already been here so let's hope they don't come back. Stay here and rest. The family will take care of you. I'll be back as soon as possible.'

'Is there any chance of letting London know what has happened?'

'The area is in uproar, Grace, and we can't risk it. You'll have to tell them when you get back.'

'How am I going to do that?'

'Over the Pyrenees into Spain and then on to Gibraltar. It's going to be a long, tough journey, so eat, rest and let your feet heal.'

Grace looked down at her lacerated feet, grimaced and held up the shoes she had been careful not to leave behind. 'I couldn't run in high heels, but I'll make the journey, no matter how rough.'

'I know you will. Bill wouldn't have brought you if he hadn't been sure you were strong enough, mentally and physically. You were here to give Bill a believable reason to be looking around the chateau. You have played your part well and done exactly what was required of you. Don't feel upset or guilty about leaving Bill behind. What we've got to concentrate on now is getting you home.'

Chapter Twenty-Three

Stan Haydon threw the papers aside, stood up and walked over to the window. *Those poor devils on the parade ground must be sweltering in this heat*, he thought. *August, and still no news!* The fact that something had gone dreadfully wrong was now undeniable. There hadn't been a communication from either of them. *Dear Lord, not both of them!* Pain laced through him. If they were on the run they would have got a message through somehow, even if they had lost the wireless. If they had been caught they would probably have been tortured and then shot as spies. Stan knew that was always a possibility with missions like this, but it didn't make it any easier to bear. And the awful thing was they might never know exactly what had happened to them.

He ran a hand over his eyes. They should only have been in France for two weeks at the most. As the days and

253

weeks had passed, hope faded, and now it was clear they weren't coming back. That is what everyone was saying but Stan refused to let the last shred of hope die.

There was a rap on the door and his temporary assistance looked in. 'Colonel Askew asking to see you, sir.'

Hell, this was going to be awkward. From the way George had spoken about Grace he'd gathered he felt protective towards her. 'Send him in, Potter.'

'Yes, sir.'

'Hello, Stan.' George strode in. 'Thought I'd pop in to let you know I've been transferred here.'

'You've managed to get rid of that desk job at last,' he joked. 'Sit down for a moment. I'll ask Potter to make us some tea.'

'Thanks. I was hoping to see Grace.'

'She's in Scotland with Bill at the moment,' Stan lied.

'When do you expect her back?'

'I haven't any idea. It might be some time.'

George looked at him intently. 'From the tone of your voice I would say you are worried. Why would that be, Stan? Remember I have the highest security clearance so whatever you say to me will go no further.'

'You're imagining things. I've got a lot on my mind at the moment, and I'm missing Grace's organising skills, that's all.' Stan stood up. 'I'll see about that tea.'

Potter stood up the moment Stan came into the outer office.

'Make us a strong pot of tea.'

'Yes, sir.'

Stan stood for a moment, trying to wipe the worry from his face. He was going to have to be more careful around George. The fact that Grace and Bill were missing couldn't be hidden for much longer, but he didn't want to say anything until he had definite news – good or bad. He couldn't tell the families that he had no idea what had happened to them. He couldn't!

He returned to his office, a smile on his face. 'The tea is coming right up. Now, I guess you are back on active duty, so tell me how you managed that?'

They talked about many things over the next hour and Stan was able to avoid any conversation about Grace and Bill.

He hadn't quite got away with it, though, because as George left he said, 'When you're next in touch with Grace, ask her to write to her parents. They are getting worried.'

'Will do.' They shook hands and as George left, Stan knew his story about Scotland hadn't been believed. That had been awkward and would only get worse now George was stationed here. He had to do something.

There was only one thing he could think of, and that was a very long shot, but it would make him feel as if he was doing something useful. It was obvious now that either their wireless set wasn't working, or they had lost it, so it was a case of searching for any snippet of information they could find. Alex Stewart was a good man and would help if at all possible. Stan dialled a number and waited. Eventually Alex came to the phone and Stan explained the situation to him.

'Can your wireless operators help me, Alex? We've tried everything we can to get in touch with them, but you might be able to pick up something from that area.'

'It isn't very likely after all this time, but I'll ask them to try.'

'Thanks. Can I have your permission to come there?'

'Of course. When do you want to come?'

'Now!'

'Right, I'll alert security. Would you like to stay for a couple of days?'

'I'd appreciate that if at all possible.'

'No problem. Get here in time for dinner. Jane will be pleased to see you as well.'

Stan replaced the phone, sat for a moment to gather his thoughts, and then dialled another number. There were a few things he must deal with before he left.

An hour later he had a small bag packed and climbed into the waiting car.

'Where to, sir?'

'Chicksands Priory, Bedfordshire. Do you know where it is?'

'No, sir, but I'll find it.'

'I've been there once so I'll give you directions when we get close.'

'Nice place, sir.' His driver said as they drove towards the priory entrance. 'I didn't know this was here.'

'And you still don't know.'

'Understood, sir. Will you need me while you're here?'

'No, I'm staying for a couple of days. You can return and I'll contact you when I'm coming back.'

The driver nodded and held open the car door.

Alex met him as he entered the building. 'Good to see you again, Stan. I've got a couple of girls doing sweeps to see if they can pick up any news. Would you like to see the ops room?'

'Very much. I really appreciate this, Alex.'

'Don't thank me yet. It's most unlikely we shall discover anything of use to you, but we'll give it a try. Have you told their families they are missing?'

'No, I've been avoiding that but I can't put it off much longer.'

The wireless operators were all WAAF and concentrating on what they were doing. Not one looked up when they walked in.

'All women,' Stan remarked.

'Yes, they've replaced the men, releasing them for other work. They are very good. Their patience and concentration is excellent.' Stan walked over to one girl and touched her shoulder to gain her attention.

She removed her headphone and looked up. 'Sir?'

'Eileen, I want you to meet Major General Haydon. It's his operatives you are looking for. Anything yet?'

'No,' she stood up to face Stan. 'If there's anything out there we'll find it, sir.'

'I'm sure you will.'

Eileen sat down again and resumed her work.

Alex looked at his watch. 'There's still an hour to dinner. Would you like to stay and watch for a while?'

'That would be interesting.'

'Well, if you will excuse me I'll come back for you in

a while. They'll search through the night as well, Stan,' Alex said kindly, and then left the room.

Over the next two days Stan spent most of his time in the ops room, fascinated by the skill and diligence of the operators. Collecting information was a vital part of the war effort and no small detail was dismissed as insignificant. Every time something was picked up Stan's heart leapt in hope, only to be dashed time and time again. Of course, coming here had been a vain hope, but it was better than waiting in the office hoping for news.

'Anything?' Alex asked, coming to sit beside him.

He shook his head. 'Not a whisper of anything unusual. Thanks for trying, anyway, Alex. The SOE haven't been able to find them and you were my last hope. I'd better be getting back.'

'Sir!'

Both men surged to their feet when Eileen called. She was listening intently and shaking her head, frowning deeply. Then she sat back and removed the headphones. 'They've gone. I could hardly hear it and there was only a short burst of two words, repeated once. Do the words "Jesters lost" mean anything to you, sir?'

Stan felt as if he had been hit in the stomach. 'Did it say "Jesters" or "Jester"?'

'I couldn't be sure, sir. It wasn't very clear.'

'What does it mean?' Alex asked Stan.

'That either one or both have been captured or killed. Did the sender give his code?'

'It sounded like "Saturn", but whoever was sending it

was in a hurry and didn't want to transmit for long.'

'That isn't a call sign I know, and it certainly wasn't sent by Grace or Bill, so how the hell did they know about Jesters? They wouldn't have given that information to anyone else.'

'Unless they were forced to, Stan.'

That would be Stan's worst nightmare, but every angle had to be considered. Someone out there had information only known to the two Jesters.

'It's looking bad. That message should only have been sent by one if the other was lost, and then it should have stated Jester one or Jester two, so we would know which one it was.'

'See if you can pick that up again, Eileen. It might be clearer another time.' Alex placed a hand on Stan's shoulder. 'Stay for dinner and leave in the morning.'

'I would appreciate some company this evening, and I couldn't refuse another of Jane's excellent meals. Thanks, Alex. Now I need to get out of here.'

'Let's walk in the grounds. It's a lovely day.'

The warmth of the sun and the sound of birds singing were soothing. They walked in silence and Stan gathered his thoughts. That brief message had only told him that someone he didn't know had sent it. Someone who shouldn't have had knowledge of the Jesters, unless Bill or Grace had told them, which was highly unlikely. That pointed to the worst scenario possible. They could have been caught by the Gestapo. If that was the case he could only pray they died quickly.

'Are you all right?' Alex asked, breaking the silence.

Stan nodded and drew in a deep breath. 'Just thinking things through. I now have confirmation that their mission went terribly wrong, and I must accept they won't be coming back. I can't delay any longer. They must now be listed as missing, presumed dead, as soon as I return to Aldershot. I will tell the families personally.'

'I don't envy you that task.'

'It will be hard, but it's something I must do myself. I'll contact my driver and leave first thing in the morning.'

Breaking the news to Bill's family had been bad enough, but he was dreading this. He had left it until the evening to be sure both of Grace's parents would be at home. He knocked on the door.

As soon as Ted opened the door, he introduced himself. 'May I come in, please? I have something to tell you.'

Ted nodded and Stan followed him to the kitchen where Jean was preparing dinner.

'This is Major General Haydon, my dear.'

She wiped her hands, and smiling, shook his hand. 'Oh, Grace works for you. Would you like a cup of tea?'

'Jean.' Ted took his wife's arm and made her sit down. 'I don't think this is a social call. He has something to tell us.'

He's already guessed I'm bringing bad news, Stan thought, frowning.

'Oh?' She glanced from one man to the other, noting their sombre expression, and turned pale as the realisation hit her. 'Grace . . . ?'

'We've been worried because we haven't heard from

260

her for a while, and that is not like her. Tell it straight, sir.'

'Grace was asked to carry out a certain task and readily agreed. It is my painful duty to tell you that both Grace and a captain are officially missing, presumed dead.'

'That means you don't know for sure,' Ted said huskily, putting his arm around his shaking wife's shoulders.

'Correct. I have delayed bringing you this sad news in the hope they would be found. They should have returned by the end of June at the latest.'

'Returned from where?' Jean asked, tears rolling down her face. 'Where did she go?'

'I can't tell you that, but I can assure you we will continue trying to find out what has happened. The moment there is any news I will come and tell you. Grace has shown great courage and you can be proud of her. I know, at this time, such words are meaningless, but they are true.'

Stan left the grieving parents and got back into the waiting car. Wherever he went today he was leaving behind heartbreak, and there was still one more to go – George Askew. How he needed a drink!

He also needed to get this unpleasant task completed today and, as luck would have it, he saw George near his office when they arrived back at Aldershot. He got out of the car.

'Could you come to my office, George, I need to speak to you.'

'Ah, there you are. I have been looking for you. Good Lord, man, you look rough. Tough day?'

'Couldn't be worse!' Once in the office, Stan poured two generous glasses of whisky and took a good swig.

George watched, leaving his own drink untouched.

'Where is Grace?' he asked firmly.

'Bill and Grace are missing, presumed dead.' Stan drained his glass, not knowing what kind of reaction he would get from George.

'I see. Have her parents been told?'

'I've just come from there. I'm sure they'd appreciate a visit from you.'

'I'll do that.' He took a sip of the drink and then slammed the glass down. 'What the hell happened?'

'I can't give you details—'

'Don't give that security rubbish! Start talking.'

It didn't take Stan long to relate what little he knew. 'We'll keep looking, of course. Arrangements have been made to get another operative into that area to see what they can find out.'

'Wipe that "but" out of your voice, Stan, and don't give up just yet. I'm sure Bill is an expert at avoiding capture, and Grace is very resourceful. They won't give up easily.'

'I'm well aware of that, but you have to admit the signs are not good.'

'No, they are not! You find them, Stan, and keep me informed.' George stood up. 'I'll have to tell Dan.'

When George left the office, Stan poured himself another stiff whisky. Thank heavens he didn't have to tell Dan that he'd lost Grace!

Chapter Twenty-Four

'Hello, George.' Dan turned the wireless down so he could talk on the phone. 'How are things?'

'Not good. I have some bad news, Dan.'

'Oh, what's happened?' Dan listened, his mouth setting in a grim line. 'Why the hell has Stan waited all this time before letting us know?'

When he heard the rest of the story, Dan swore fluently under his breath. 'What a stupid, crazy scheme! They've lost two valuable people and gained nothing! Don't tell me to calm down, Uncle. Any fool can see that a mission like that had little chance of succeeding. I'm on embarkation leave now so I'm coming there in the morning. Stan can tell me what he's intending to do about this. To say they are missing is unacceptable . . . I know there's a bloody war on, but that's no reason to go throwing good lives away. I'm in the mood to shake some sense into a few people!'

'That's how I feel.' George's voice betrayed how upset he was. 'I'll warn Stan you're coming, and then we can both go and see Grace's parents.'

'Yes, we must,' Dan agreed, his fury draining away and leaving him feel empty. 'They lost a son-in-law, and now they might have lost their daughter. They must be devastated.'

'And confused. They thought she was safe in an office. When are you shipping out, by the way?'

'Seven days.'

'Let's hope we get some news before you leave. See you tomorrow, and thanks for coming.'

George watched Dan striding towards him across the parade ground. For such a big man he moved with fluid grace without a trace of the injury he'd had.

'You're early. Have you had breakfast?'

'Not yet.'

'Good, we can eat together. Can't face this day on an empty stomach.'

Dan nodded and followed his uncle to the officers' mess.

'Do you know where you're going yet?' George asked as they took their seats.

'Not officially, but my guess would be North Africa. General Montgomery has taken over as commander, and we need a victory to raise spirits.'

'Agreed, and the last thing you needed was bad news before shipping out. Take it easy on Stan, though, this is especially rough on him. Remember he's lost Bill as well.'

'Damned shame. I liked him, and you can stop looking so worried, George. I was angry when I heard the news, but I've slept on it. We are going to have to face this situation over and over again before this war is over. I remember the quiet courage Grace showed at the death of her husband, and it's an example to all of us. And knowing her, when she was offered this mission there is no way she would refuse.'

'You're right. She was a remarkable girl.'

'Was?' Dan raised his eyebrows.

'Sorry – is a remarkable girl.'

'That's better. The important word here is "missing", and until they have proof they are dead, I'll hold on to that.' Dan pushed his empty plate away and stood up. 'Now, let's go and see Stan.'

Potter showed them straight in, and after the usual greetings, they three men sat down to talk.

'I was dreadfully sad to hear about Bill and Grace,' Dan said. 'What is being done to find them?'

Stan explained the situation, and they discussed what action could, and was being taken to trace them.

They had been deep in conversation for about an hour when Potter burst into the office. 'Sir, a dispatch rider has just delivered an urgent message for you from HQ. He said you were to have it at once.'

Stan took the sealed envelope and frowned at the large red words 'For immediate attention' written on it.

'Excuse me while I read this,' he said as he slit the letter open.

Dan watched a mixture of emotions flash across Stan's face as he read the contents of the message.

When he'd finished he put it face down on the desk and closed his eyes for a moment before opening them again and looking up. 'Grace is safe. She's made it to Gibraltar after crossing the Pyrenees and Spain.'

Dan felt a wave of relief and some pride when he heard that. He muttered softly under his breath, 'That's my girl.'

'Wonderful news!' George was smiling until he saw Stan's sombre expression. 'Is she all right? Is Bill with her?'

'Grace is unharmed, but she came alone. There's still no sign of Bill. We won't know the whole story until Grace arrives. They are going to get her back as soon as possible.'

'By sea, I expect. Don't give up on Bill yet,' George told him. 'They must have had a good reason for separating. He could be right behind her.'

'You're right, and it's a huge relief to know one of them is safe.' Stan stood up. 'Grace's parents must be given the good news at once. Shall we all go, gentlemen, and give the neighbours something to talk about as three ranking officers descend upon the house?'

They walked out of the office, smiling, buoyed up with the chance to give good news for a change.

Ted's mouth dropped open when he saw them standing outside, his eyes fixing on the tall man. 'Oh, it's so kind of you all to come and it will do Jean good to see you again, Dan. Er . . . you're all smiling.'

'That's because we've got good news,' Stan told him. 'Grace is safe!'

'Thank God! Come in – come in.' Then he turned and

ran down the passage, shouting, 'Jean! Grace is safe. She's alive! Jean, where are you? We've got guests. Dan's here as well. Jean!'

She came running down the stairs and threw her arms around her husband, laughing and crying at the same time. 'Is she all right? Where is she?'

'I don't know yet. Look who's here to give us the wonderful news.'

She rushed up to them and shook Stan's hand, kissed George on the cheek and hugged Dan. 'Where have you been, young man? We've missed you.'

'They're keeping me busy.'

'I don't doubt it.' She gazed at the officers crowding the passage and shook her head. 'We'd better go into the front room.'

'The kitchen will do, Jean,' Dan said, taking her arm. 'I could do with a cup of your excellent tea.'

She smiled up at him. 'Grace really is safe?'

'Yes, and when I see her I'll give her a good talking to for worrying us all like this.'

'And she'll tell you to mind your own business,' Ted laughed.

'Ah, but she can't do that now she's in the army.' Dan tapped his shoulder. 'I'm an officer. Any cheek and I can have her charged with insubordination.'

Jean was busy making the tea and turned round to look at Dan. 'You do that, young man, and you'll have us to deal with. Do you know Dan brought Grace home one evening and they were both covered in mud?'

'We'd been on manoeuvres with the Home Guard that

day.' Dan had an amused expression on his face. Jean was never going to forget that.

'Well, at least you're clean this time. Sit down everyone. The tea is ready.'

They were laughing while they shuffled the chairs so they could all sit down.

'Can you tell us where Grace is?' Ted asked Stan as he handed round the cups of tea Jean had just poured.

'We haven't got much information at the moment, but I'll tell you what we know. First, I must have your promise to keep this information to yourselves.'

'We promise.' Jean and Ted both nodded.

'I received the news this morning that Grace has arrived in Gibraltar.'

'Gibraltar!' Ted gasped. 'What the blazes is she doing there?'

'She came from France, over the Pyrenees, through Spain and into Gibraltar.'

'That's incredible!' Jean looked at Stan. 'With the captain?'

'As far as we know she came alone, but we are more hopeful now that Bill won't be far behind.' Stan didn't let his concern for Bill show, not wanting to spoil their joy at knowing their daughter was alive.

Ted was shaking his head. 'That girl of ours has some courage.'

'That's why Bill took her with him. He needed someone who wouldn't let him down if things got nasty, and he knew she would keep her wits about her. When Grace arrives home I must ask you not to press her for details.

Too many lives depend upon her silence. You understand?'

'We will keep this to ourselves,' Ted promised. 'Will we ever know the whole story?'

'Most unlikely.'

'I don't care about that.' Jean began refilling the empty cups. 'Our girl is safe and coming home. That's all that matters. We won't ask questions or expect her to talk about it. She will need rest and some normal home life without being constantly reminded of what she has been through. She will be given leave, won't she?'

'Of course,' Stan told them. 'Once the debriefing is over she can come home for as long as she needs. I'll let you know when she is back in this country. It will probably be a week or so.'

'Thank you all so much for bringing us this good news. When Brian was killed all Grace received was a telegram – so impersonal.' Jean smiled at Stan. 'But you took the trouble to come in person. We really appreciate that kindness.'

'And I'm delighted to be able to come again with much better news.'

'I'll come again when Grace is home,' George told them.

'You are always welcome,' Ted replied. 'I'm sure Grace would like to see you as well, Dan.'

'I doubt I'll be here. I'm on embarkation leave at the moment.'

'Oh, dear.' Jean looked concerned. 'You be careful, young man, wherever you're going.'

'I will.'

The men took their leave then and walked out to the

waiting car. When they reached it Stan turned and stared at Dan, a smirk on his face. 'Young man?'

'So?'

'How can anyone call a great six-and-a-half-feet brute like you "young man"? You must be thirty at least.'

'He's twenty-eight actually,' George told him with a wide grin on his face. 'And he's only six feet four. At least he was the last time we measured.'

'You'd better measure again, George. He's still growing!'

'Do you think so? Have you got a tape measure with you?'

'Will you two stop analysing me and get in the car! The neighbours are beginning to wonder what three army officers are finding so funny. They'll be rushing into Ted and Jean's house to find out what's going on. Jean likes me and in her eyes I am a young man.' A devilish look crossed Dan's face. 'If you two elderly gentlemen would get in the car I might consider buying you lunch.'

'Watch it, young man. We outrank you.'

'Get in, Stan, and you, Uncle.'

'How do you manage him?' Stan asked as he climbed in the back of the car with George, leaving Dan to sit in front where there was more room for him.

'He's quite docile really – as long as he's giving the orders.'

'Good officer material then,' Stan chuckled. 'He'll probably end up as a brigadier by the end of the war. That's if he stays alive, of course.'

'I'll survive,' Dan told them. 'I have plans.'

'Really?' Both men lent forward eagerly.

'And what might they be?' George asked.

'None of your business!'

'Not a brigadier, George – it will be a general.'

'Without a doubt.'

'Oh, you two have really cheered me up!' Stan told them, laughing. 'Grace is safe and that could mean Bill will turn up soon as well. Take us somewhere we can get a bottle of champagne, General. I feel like celebrating.'

Laughter filled the car, and when Dan glanced at the driver he saw he was having terrible trouble not to roar with laughter. He sat back and smiled. It had been a good morning and he could ship out with an easy mind.

Chapter Twenty-Five

There were five officers sitting behind a large table when Grace took her seat. Three she didn't know, but was relieved to see Stan and one of her instructors from the training centre. Both of them smiled encouragingly at her, but the others were serious and watching her intently. She lifted her chin just a little higher, determined not to show how hard this was going to be for her.

'Welcome back,' the one chairing the debriefing said. 'I'm Brigadier Nelson . . .'

He introduced everyone else, but Grace didn't take in the names.

'We want you to give a full and detailed account of everything that happened on this mission.'

Grace drew in a silent breath. The fact that she was here and Bill wasn't was tearing her apart. She had left him behind and that was something she couldn't forgive herself for.

'When you're ready.'

'Sorry, sir, I was just sorting out my thoughts.' There was only one place to start and that was from the moment they landed in France. Grace began to speak; her voice firm and clear.

It took almost an hour to relate all that had happened, and when she had finished she looked at the officers. Now the questions would come.

'We'll take a break here for refreshments.'

'Thank you, sir. May I leave the room for a moment?'

He inclined his head. 'Ten minutes.'

Grace hurried to the ladies' room, relieved to find it empty. That had taken more out of her than she thought it would. She splashed cold water on her face, took several deep breaths, and only when she felt in full control again did she make her way back to the debriefing.

They were talking among themselves when she returned, but stopped as soon as she entered the room. She was given a welcome cup of tea and sipped it, longing for this ordeal to be over.

'Do you know what the chateau was being used for, and what the explosion destroyed?'

'No, sir. I never saw Captain Reid again.'

'So you left without knowing what had happened to him,' one of the other officers said.

His remark hurt, but Grace tried not to let it show. 'I was following orders, sir. I was told to avoid capture, because if Captain Reid was caught they could use me to make him talk.'

'Even so, you left before finding out what had happened

to him, or what the chateau was being used for.'

Grace bristled at the man's tone. 'I was following orders! With the area swarming with German troops searching for you it would be dangerous to disobey orders. Not only for Captain Reid and myself, but for the many others who were helping us. I don't suppose you have ever been in that situation, sir, so I realise it is hard to understand.'

There was silence but Grace didn't lower her gaze. They could do what they liked with her; she didn't care. After what she had gone through no one was going to intimidate her.

'Quite right.' Stan glared at the offending officer. 'Captain Reid is an experienced operator and would know exactly what had to be done if things went wrong. It would have been imperative that his companion was safe. With only himself to worry about he will have had more chance of surviving.'

'I agree,' the chairman said firmly. 'Let's move on. You said you came over the Pyrenees. Did you make the journey on your own?'

'No, sir, I had a guide as far as Spain; an English man by the name of Harry.'

There were puzzled looks the other side of the table as they all turned to the SOE instructor. When he shook his head, the chairman turned to Grace again.

'What do you know about him?'

'Nothing. He was waiting at the house when we arrived. Captain Reid knew him, though, and called him Harry. The captain told me that if there was trouble I was to find Harry and he would help me.'

'And he took you over the mountains?'

Grace nodded. 'Once we were over the border he turned back and told me he was going to find Captain Reid.'

Stan let out a pent up breath. 'Did Bill give Harry your codes?'

'I don't know, sir, but he seemed to know him well, so he might have done. The Germans had found our wireless set, though, so we couldn't send any messages. When we went to the chateau I don't believe Captain Reid expected to come out again.' Grace struggled to keep her emotions out of her voice. 'He was insistent that I left the chateau if he wasn't back by twelve.'

'A sensible decision.' The chairman gave Grace an understanding smile. 'And I suspect that was not an easy order to obey.'

'No, sir, I wanted to stay, but I trusted Captain Reid. He'd told me it was imperative that I got away.' She sat up a little straighter, longing for this to end. 'I followed his orders and did just that.'

'How did you get to Gibraltar without money?' one of the officers asked.

'Harry gave me what little he had, and when I needed more I worked as a waitress in a cafe until I had enough for the train fare. That's why it took me so long to get home.'

The man in charge looked at the others. 'I think you will agree that this is a story of determination, resilience and courage, gentlemen. It is unfortunate that we still do not know what was in the chateau. However, after listening to Lance Corporal Lincoln's account of her escape we can hope that Captain Reid will also return. We do know, however, that there was something important there and the captain put his life at risk to destroy it, trusting that his companion would escape. Whoever this Harry was, Captain Reid trusted him enough to ask for help if it was needed. He played a vital role in Lance Corporal Lincoln's escape, and he deserves our gratitude.'

When they all nodded agreement, he turned back to Grace. 'Thank you. You have behaved in an exemplary manner, and I am sure you are now ready for some leave. Welcome home, and well done.'

'Thank you, sirs.' Grace stood up, saluted smartly and marched out of the room. Once outside her legs threatened to give way and she held on to a small hall table for support. Her mind was numb. The sea crossing had been rough and the moment she had arrived they had whisked her to the debriefing, giving her no chance to rest before the grilling. She was so tired.

'Grace.' Stan gripped her arms to hold her up. 'Let's get you home.'

'No,' she shook her head. 'Take me to my digs in Aldershot, please. I would like to rest before travelling home.'

'I understand. My car is outside.'

'Can we get a cup of tea and a sandwich first? I haven't had much to eat.'

'Of course. They've got a canteen here.' He watched as she straightened up, and then walked beside her to the canteen. He didn't help her because he knew she would have hated that. This girl was going to stand on her own two feet, no matter what she had been through. After watching her in that room his admiration had grown and he now understood what George and Dan recognised in her. Bill also saw it. Courage. Bloody courage!

While they were in the canteen the SOE instructor came over. When Grace went to stand up he made her sit down again. 'I'm glad you are still here. You were a good student and I felt sure you would do well. You have proved my instinct correct. I am proud of you.'

Grace grimaced. 'I'm not proud of myself. I left Bill behind.'

'That is exactly what you had to do. You played your part and got Bill into the chateau. You could not help him after that and you did what he needed you to do, and that was to get out of there alive. Do not reproach yourself, Grace.'

'Thank you, sir, but it's hard.'

'I know, but these are dangerous times. In years to come we will look back and only then recognise the sacrifices made by individuals. I know Bill well, and if there is any way of getting out alive, he will have found it. You relax and rest now.'

As the instructor walked away, Stan scowled. 'I didn't like the glint in his eyes when he was talking to you. I have a nasty feeling we haven't seen the last of him.'

Grace didn't bother to comment, she was too weary to work out what he meant.

'Ready?' he asked when he saw her plate was empty. 'Or would you like another sandwich?'

She shook her head, stood up and walked with him

to the waiting car. She settled in the back and closed her eyes for a moment, listening to the hum of the tyres on the road. It was strangely comforting.

'Sleep if you want to,' Stan told her softly. 'You must be worn out after your journey and debriefing. They might have given you a day to recover.'

'They were anxious to see if I had any information about the chateau. If you have further questions about Bill, could you leave it for a short time, sir? I've done all the talking I want to for a while.'

'You told me everything you knew at the debriefing, so relax now.'

They were soon back at Aldershot, and when Stan went to help her out of the car, she smiled. 'I'm all right, sir.'

'Just trying to be a gentleman,' he joked. 'You are officially on leave now so go home as soon as you feel rested enough. Take as much time as you need.'

'Thank you, sir.' She saluted and walked in to the house.

'Potter!' Stan called as he strode into the office. 'Tell the medics I need a female nurse here at once!'

'Are you ill, sir?'

'Not for me. Why are you still standing there? Don't come back without one!'

Potter turned and ran from the office.

Stan paced the room. Grace said she was all right, but he wasn't too sure about that. At the debriefing she had given a clear, unemotional account of the mission without a hint of how she was feeling. Her journey to Gibraltar had been skirted over as if it was unimportant, but he'd seen that brief crack in her composure when the debriefing had finished. Any fool could see that her escape from France had been tough. She'd had a guide over the Pyrenees, but once over the border Harry had left her to make her own way across Spain. And who the hell was Harry? Was he the one who had sent that message? Dammit Bill! Was the mission a success or failure? If you don't come back this is going to haunt us forever.

'Sir.'

Stan spun round to face the military nurse standing in his office. He had been so lost in thought he hadn't heard anyone come in. 'Ah, thank you for coming so quickly. Lance Corporal Lincoln has just returned from a hazardous mission and is exhausted. She was checked by a doctor on her return and is physically fit, but I would like you to keep an eye on her for a few hours. Let her sleep, but when she wakes make sure she has something to eat and drink.'

'I understand, sir. If she's in a communal billet it might be wise to move her to the hospital.'

'She's in a room of her own.' Stan handed the nurse the address, a slight smile on his face. 'When she sees you she will tell you to leave, saying she doesn't need you. Ignore her. You are there on my orders and she can take it out on me later.'

'Sounds like she has a strong character.'

'I doubt she would be alive today if she didn't possess a strong, determined character.'

'Anything else I should know, sir?'

'No, that's it. Her name is Grace, by the way.'

The nurse was just leaving when George arrived. 'Is Grace all right, Stan?'

'Just exhausted. The nurse is a precaution. I want someone around should she need them.'

'Very thoughtful of you. How did the debriefing go? You look done in.'

'Sit down and have a drink with me and I'll tell you all about it. It's quite an amazing story.'

Chapter Twenty-Six

The next morning when Stan walked into the office he stopped in astonishment. Grace was at her desk going through the post.

'What the devil are you doing here?'

'I work here, sir.'

'Don't you be cheeky with me, Sergeant!'

'It's Lance Corporal, sir.'

'I've just promoted you. Where's Potter?'

'He's gone to get some fresh milk and more supplies. Why have you promoted me?'

'Because you deserve it. A "thank you, sir," would be nice.'

'Thank you, sir.'

'Did you always speak your mind with your lawyer boss?'

'He encouraged me to do so.'

'Then he has a lot to answer for.' Stan began to laugh. 'Ah, but I've missed you. Nevertheless, you shouldn't be here. You are officially on leave. Potter has another week before returning to his unit. Go home. Your parents are anxious to see you.'

'I know they are, but I would rather stay here for a while.'

Stan sat beside her. 'I know you are worried about Bill, but the moment there is any news I will come and tell you. You have my word on that, so go home. See your family and go out with your friends, learn to laugh again. Whatever the outcome of this mission, you did everything you were asked to do. We are all proud of you, and Bill will be too when he finds out what you endured to escape. I know you feel you shouldn't have left him behind, but that was exactly what you had to do, and Bill wouldn't have been pleased if you'd stayed around trying to help him. You would have put both of your lives in danger by doing that.'

'So I keep being told, but it doesn't help. He gave me strict instructions, though, and he'd also asked Harry to get me out if things went wrong. I did as ordered, but reluctantly. When I finally reached Gibraltar I should have been elated, but I wasn't. I was safe, but Bill and Harry were still in danger. It's hard to dismiss that.'

'I wonder who this Harry is.'

Grace shook her head. 'I really don't know, but if it hadn't been for him I might still be there trying to avoid capture.'

'I hope I can shake his hand one day and thank him.

You said he went back to find Bill. Do you think he can?'

'If anyone can find him then Harry will.'

'That's comforting to know.' Stan stood up. 'Now get out of here, Sergeant, and that's an order. By the way, what did you do with the nurse?'

'I sent her back to the hospital, sir.'

He looked up at the ceiling. 'I don't know why I bother.'

'It was a kind thought, but I didn't need her.'

The door opened and George strode in, smiling with pleasure when he saw Grace. 'Welcome home, my dear, but what are you doing here? Has he got you working again already?'

'Don't blame me! She won't damned well go on leave. You tell her, George. She might obey you. I'm wasting my breath.'

'All right!' Grace stood up, hands raised in surrender. 'I'm going.'

George looked at his watch. 'I've got a couple of hours free. Get your bag and I'll take you home.'

'It's already packed and it won't take me long to collect it.' She reached the door and looked back at Stan. 'You promise?'

'You have my word.'

She nodded, went out, and closed the door softly behind her.

'What was that about?' George asked, frowning.

'I think she wanted to stay here in case there's any word about Bill. She isn't going to be able to relax until she knows what's happened to him. It's important she gets away from here, though.'

'I agree. I fear the war has a long way to go yet, and that girl has already had her share of heartaches. Sitting on the sidelines is hard, Stan. I applied to return to active duty, but all I've done is swap one desk for another. I guess Dan was right when he hinted that we were too old.'

'Maybe, but there are many twists and turns to come and we could get our chance – or you could. You're younger than me and have had battle experience. Have you heard from Dan yet, by the way?'

'No, he might still be at sea.'

Stan nodded. 'Thanks for taking Grace home. There's another reason I want her out of the way for a while. I think the SOE could be after her.'

'That wouldn't surprise me. They are on the lookout for suitable candidates, and they know she would be right for the job after this mission. What will you do?'

'I would like to tell them they can't have her, but it would have to be Grace's decision. I'll try to keep them away from her until she has come to terms with what has happened. This is no time for her to be making hasty decisions.'

'Don't forget to point out that she is a valuable member of your intelligence team and would be hard to replace.'

'Absolutely, and when Bill gets back he might need her help again.'

'If they want her they will have to approach you first, so tell them all that before she makes a commitment. Keep me informed, Stan.'

'Will do.'

Grace arrived back then and stood in the doorway. 'All ready.'

'I don't want to see you for at least ten days,' Stan told her sternly.

'Right, sir.' She walked with George to the car he had ordered, and climbed in the back. 'Thanks for the lift. Will you come in when we get home?'

'Just for a few minutes. You don't have to worry, Grace, your parents are understanding people and they know they mustn't ask any questions. They love you and are just happy to have you home again for a while.'

'When Brian died I didn't want to talk about it and this is the same feeling. That debriefing drained me.'

'Now you need to rest, and the best place to do that is at home.'

She nodded and changed the subject. 'How is Dan?'

'All right – as far as I know. He's on a ship somewhere. My guess is he's heading for North Africa.'

'Ah, he'll be happy to be on the move at last.'

'I expect so.' George sighed. 'Dangerous place, though, with Rommel in charge of the Germans.'

'I know he has a fearsome reputation but he isn't invincible; neither is Hitler. It's going to be a long, hard struggle but we have to win. There isn't any other alternative and we will all do whatever is necessary to bring about their downfall.'

George looked at her and smiled. 'I agree with every word of that, but enough of the war. You are home safely and on leave. Take the time to clear your mind. Try not to dwell on the past or the future. The past is gone and we can't change it, and the future is yet to come. All we can have is this moment, so live it, Grace.'

She gave a little laugh. 'You sound just like my mother.'

'She's a wise woman.'

For ten days Grace slept, went to the cinema, read several books, and did all the normal things. She didn't talk about her experiences and her parents never asked. It would have helped if Helen had been home as well, but her family said she hadn't been on leave for some time. James and Tim were evidently away somewhere so she spent the time with her parents or on her own, but this time she didn't mind. It was just the kind of quiet time she needed. Every day she had hoped that Stan would come with news, but he never did.

The time at home had been a chance to get back to something like normal life where she didn't have to keep hiding for fear of being caught, but she was pleased to be back at Aldershot. At home there had been too much time to think and she needed work to keep her occupied. Potter had left everything neat and tidy for her and a folder full of reports to bring her up to date.

Stan marched in looking preoccupied, as usual. 'Good morning, sir.'

'Is it?' he muttered, not breaking his stride. At the door of his office he stopped and turned his head. 'Good Lord, have ten days gone already?'

'They have.'

'Ah, you look better. Did you enjoy your leave?'

'I did, thank you, sir.'

He nodded. 'Make a strong pot of tea and bring it to my office. We have work to catch up on.'

He was right, and it took them a week to deal with everything. Grace was finishing off the last report when the office door opened, and the words 'Can I help you' died on her lips. Standing there grinning was the man she had never expected to see again.

'Bill!' Overcome with joy she threw herself at him, laughing as he gave her a bear hug.

'Don't I get one of those as well?' asked a familiar voice.

'Harry! Oh, this is wonderful!' Grace was not normally a demonstrative person, but this was too much for her, and she cried out with pleasure as she rushed to greet him.

'What the devil's going on here?' Stan boomed, standing in the doorway. 'Where the hell have you been?'

'That's a pretty good description of the last few weeks, wouldn't you say, Harry?'

'Close enough.'

Stan couldn't hide his relief at seeing Bill again and slapped him on the back before approaching the other man and shaking his hand. 'So you're the mysterious Harry. I suspect we have a lot to thank you for. We really thought we'd lost these two. Grace! No more work today. We are going to celebrate! Come in to my office. I've got a bottle of whisky I've been saving for a special occasion.'

Stan only had two glasses so they used cups, but no one cared. They were all too happy.

'When did you arrive back?' Stan asked when they were settled.

'About two hours ago. We hitched a lift on a plane from Switzerland.'

'How on earth did you get there, Bill?' Grace asked.

'With difficulty,' Harry said dryly.

'But why come that way?' Stan wanted to know. 'You were closer to Spain, surely?'

'We tried that, but after the damage I'd caused they were determined to catch me, and brought in extra troops. Harry managed to get you to Spain before the area was flooded with more troops and tracker dogs, Grace. It was too risky to go that way so we had to head for Switzerland. Harry had to come with me because he'd borrowed a home-made wireless set and tried to send a message. The SS nearly caught him. He managed to get away, but not before they had seen him. He had to disappear after that.'

'That answers the puzzle of the strange message we picked up. What was in the chateau, Bill?'

'I found a huge, well-camouflaged building in the grounds. It was a communication centre, full of the finest equipment I've ever seen, and the men in there were very busy. There's no telling what information they were gathering. I couldn't leave that so I found an armaments store and made a bomb. It went up beautifully, and should put them out of action for some time.'

'How did you get out of there?' Grace wanted to know.

'I couldn't, but fortunately the grounds were huge and I was able to dodge the search parties for several days. I

288

survived on grapes, berries, and anything else I could find. Once the frantic activity had quietened down I stole an ordinary German uniform from the sleeping quarters and jumped on a lorry leaving the chateau.'

'That's how I found him,' Harry continued. 'I guessed he must still be in there and was searching for a way in when I saw a soldier jump off a lorry and dive into the undergrowth by the road. I crept up on him and there was Bill sitting in a ditch.'

Bill grinned. 'That's the second time he nearly shot me. I don't think Harry likes Germans.'

'Of course I don't! They invaded my country.'

'Your country?' Stan frowned. 'But you're English, aren't you?'

'I was educated at Cambridge University, but I'm French. Free French.'

Grace stared at him, absolutely stunned. 'I'd never have guessed it. Your accent is perfect. I have a friend who is working as an interpreter for the Free French. Helen, you might have met her.'

'Not that I recall, and if she's as beautiful as you I would certainly have remembered.'

Grace laughed. 'You didn't pay me compliments like that when I arrived back at the farm scratched and filthy.'

'I was so relieved to see you I thought you were the most beautiful girl ever.'

'Stop flirting with Grace,' Bill reprimanded. 'You'll have to stand at the back of a long line.'

'There he goes again!' Grace shook her head. 'He's only just arrived back and is talking nonsense already.'

'And now you are back you'll have to attend a debriefing.'

'Not me,' Harry told them and standing up. 'I have my own outfit to report to.'

'I'll need your name for my records,' Stan said.

Harry bent and kissed Grace's cheek. 'See you again sometime, lovely one. And Bill, try not to get into trouble again. Oh, and my name is Harry. Just Harry.'

Wiping the sweat from his eyes, Dan paused and looked around. How many of his men had he lost in that battle? It had begun with an enormous gun barrage that had lit up the night sky and shattered the silence of the desert. What had followed had been twelve days of fierce fighting. They had finally won the battle of El Alamein and Rommel was in full retreat.

Dan spotted a few of his men slumped down on the ground and leaning against a wall. When he approached they began to stand up. 'Stay where you are,' he said, sitting down beside them.

The sergeant among them grinned. 'We've got Rommel on the run this time. He'll have a job to come back from this beating.'

'They're badly weakened and we should now be able to push them out of Africa.' Dan studied the men all around, looking for any he could recognise. It wasn't easy, though, because they were all dirty and dishevelled. 'Have you any idea how many of ours have survived, Sergeant?'

'We haven't done a tally yet, sir. Would you like us to do that now?'

'No, get yourselves sorted out first. When you've cleaned up and had something to eat, come and find me. We'll do it together.'

'Right you are, sir.'

Dan hoisted himself up and strode towards the hastily set up operations section. The loss of even one man was too many in Dan's opinion, and he feared that battle had been costly – but a huge success. He would need to keep reminding himself of that. They had taken a battering at home with Dunkirk, the desperate fight in the air and the Blitz. A victory was badly needed and now they had one. The once considered invincible had been shown to be vulnerable, and that should give a spark of hope to everyone.

'It's such a long time since we've heard that sound.' Grace smiled up at George as they stood outside listening to the church bells ringing. To mark the victory at El Alamein, Churchill had ordered all church bells to be rung. They had been silent since the outbreak of war.

Bill joined them. 'Dan's out there, isn't he, George? Have you heard from him yet?'

'I expect he's been in the thick of the fighting. It will be a while before we hear from him. He's not much of a letter writer anyway.'

Stan came out of the office just as the last peals faded away. 'Clever idea to ring the bells. That gives everyone a taste of victory, making them even more determined to finish the war off.'

'It will be back to Europe next,' Bill remarked.

'There's a lot to be done before that,' George pointed out. 'When we go in again there will be no turning back. There cannot be another Dunkirk, so everything must be carefully planned. I would say there's no chance of launching an invasion for at least a year.'

Chapter Twenty-Seven

When Grace looked back she couldn't believe eighteen months had passed since she had returned from France. Preparations for the invasion were well under way, and the country was crowded with troops and equipment, and more were still pouring in. Camps were springing up everywhere; tanks were hidden in trees and ships waiting in the harbours around the coast. Efforts were being made to camouflage as much as possible, but it was a huge task. An even greater concern was how to keep all this activity a secret, especially the location of the proposed landings. A great deal of work and thought had been put into the need to trick Hitler into believing the invasion would be in a different place to the one planned.

Stan and Grace were returning from an intelligence meeting when they were waved off the road. They got out of the car and watched as a convoy of lorries came past carrying newly arrived American troops. When they saw Grace they began to whistle and shout out to her. Laughing, she came smartly to attention and saluted them. This caused even more hilarity.

The convoy seemed never ending, and following them were tanks.

'My God!' Stan murmured. 'There isn't room on this small island for any more, surely. It's going to need a miracle to keep this build-up a secret. If Hitler doesn't already know then he must be asleep!'

'Let's hope he is. We've had a few miracles in this war so far, like plucking the army off the beaches at Dunkirk, beating the Luftwaffe in the air, surviving the Blitz, and not forgetting El Alamein and the seamen in the Atlantic. We'd have starved without their bravery.'

Stan looked down at Grace and smiled. 'All true, but you forgot one. The miracle of getting you and Bill back from France.'

She shrugged. 'I would say that was luck on my part and Bill's skill at undercover work. Will he be going over with the troops?'

'He's going in with the second wave where he can be of the most use. Dan's back from North Africa and will be going in first, as usual. He's a colonel now.' Stan grinned. 'George is trying hard to be included and he'll probably succeed. He's younger than me and has battle experience.'

'James and Tim arrived home last month after serving in Malta for a while. They'll be needed. It looks as if the two of us will be the only ones left behind.'

'We'll have our part to play, though. Have you seen your friend Helen lately?'

'Not for nearly two years. It's worrying, but if anything had happened to her we would have been told.'

'That's true. Ah, the road is clear at last.'

When they arrived back at Aldershot, George marched into the office, all smiles. 'Come to let you know I'm leaving here today.'

'Where are you going?' Grace asked.

'Now you know I can't answer that, Grace.'

'Of course not. Silly question.'

'You've got your wish then, George?'

'Yes. I got thrown out of Dunkirk and I want to go back. You two take care of yourselves while I'm away.'

'And you be careful.'

'I will, Grace.' He kissed her cheek, shook hands with Stan, and left.

'We are going to have a lot of people to worry about, aren't we?'

'I'm afraid so. Before you start typing up the report of today's meeting, put the kettle on, Grace. I'm gasping for a cup of tea.'

'I expect you're finding the weather a bit different from North Africa,' Bill said to the tall man standing beside him.

Dan nodded and gazed up at the dark, leaden sky, feeling the rain on his face. 'Wish it would clear enough for us to get going. I hate hanging around like this. It's unsettling for the men to be sitting on the ships for so long, not knowing if we're going tonight or not.'

The harbour was filled with men and ships, as were many others along the coast. Bill sighed. 'Just look at that! The Germans must know we're coming. Assembling such an enormous invasion fleet can't have gone unnoticed, surely. This country is groaning under the weight of troops and armaments.'

'They know we're coming but let's hope they have believed all the misinformation you've been feeding them so they don't know where or when. Surprise is the key to success for this operation.'

'Well, they won't be expecting us in this kind of weather. Though it doesn't seem quite as bad . . .'

Suddenly there was activity everywhere and a soldier ran up to Dan. 'H-Hour now, Major Chester!'

Dan was immediately moving. 'See you in Berlin, Bill.'

'I'll be there!'

Long legs took Dan with speed to the ship, glad all the waiting was over. He was going back at last. And they damned well wouldn't drive him out again! This time they would be staying. Retreat was out of the question.

Bill stayed where he was and watched the huge armada making its way out of Southampton and knew the same was happening at Dartmouth, Portland, Portsmouth and Shoreham. He would be going with one of the follow up-forces. He knew Germany was now a very different country to the one he and Dan remembered, and he hoped they both survived to meet up and see for themselves. It would be painful and sad, no doubt, but Hitler and his regime had to be defeated.

* * *

It was nearly dawn but Stan and Grace were still in the office waiting for news. When the phone rang Stan snatched it up eagerly, and Grace waited, hardly able to breathe with the tension they were feeling.

'It's underway!' he said, replacing the phone and looking at the calendar. June 6th. 'You might as well get some sleep now. There's nothing else for us to do and there won't be any news for a few hours.'

'I don't think sleep will be possible. What are you going to do, sir?'

'Rest for a couple of hours and then go to the ops room and wait for the reports to start coming in.'

'Can I come with you?'

'Admittance is restricted or the place would be full to bursting. I'll write you up for seven days' leave.'

Grace knew it was useless to refuse. She wouldn't be needed for a while. All she could do was wait, and she might as well do that at home with her parents. They would be excited, but she knew too many men involved in this invasion to be able to relax. She had seen a little of what conditions were like in France and could picture the opposition the troops would probably face.

Stan was already writing out the leave authorisation and when he handed it to her he smiled. 'By the time you return we will have a clearer picture of the situation. Go home and try to relax. The build-up to the invasion has been a trying time.'

'Thank you, sir.'

There wasn't any need to rush home because Grace knew both of her parents would be out, so she hung around for a while and arrived home near six o'clock that evening. She was pleased to find her mother at home. It was nice to be greeted instead of walking into an empty house.

'How wonderful!' Jean exclaimed, giving her daughter a hug. 'How long have you got?'

'Seven days. Is Dad at work?'

Jean nodded. 'He won't be home until later. We've just heard the exciting news that the invasion is under way. Let's have a nice cup of tea before you unpack your bag. I do miss our little chats.'

Grace laughed, feeling some of the tension of the last few days easing away.

'You look tired, darling,' her mother remarked as she poured the tea.

'We've been busy and haven't had much sleep. I'll catch up on it while I'm home.'

'I expect you've known about the invasion for some time.'

'Yes. The bad weather held it up which was worrying for everyone, but they were finally able to go ahead.'

Jean sighed. 'Everyone is naturally very excited and is saying that the war could be over by Christmas. I hope they are right, but I can't help thinking about all those young men. You probably have a better idea than most of us, so do you think it could be over that quickly?'

'It's too soon to say, Mum. I don't think it's going to be that easy, though.'

'No, you are right, but we can hope for a speedy victory. Tell me what you've been up to. The last time you were on leave you were worried about someone you'd been working with. Is he all right now?'

Grace raised her eyebrows.

'Don't look at me like that, Grace. I know you weren't allowed to tell us anything, but I'm not daft. One night you were restless and I sat by your bed for a while. You cried out the name "Bill". You were very distressed.'

'You didn't tell me.'

'No, darling. I haven't mentioned it to anyone – not even your father. Whatever it was, you needed to come to terms with it yourself, and I knew you would. Can you talk about it now?'

'The only thing I can tell you is that Bill is all right.'

'Good. You were very worried about him. What is he like?'

'Tall, good-looking, late twenties I would say.' Grace smiled. 'When I first met him I thought he was flippant, always joking and never taking anything seriously, but I was wrong. That is the face he presents to the world, and I saw a very different man when we worked together. He is intelligent, efficient and a very brave man.'

'You sound as if you think a lot of him.'

'I do.'

Jean studied her daughter carefully. 'Perhaps we could meet him sometime?'

'Maybe, but it won't be for a while.'

'I take it that means he's involved in the invasion.'

'Mum, everyone I know is taking part; James, Tim, Dan and even George.'

'George!' Jean exclaimed. 'I didn't expect him to go.'

'He's an experienced officer, and he wanted to go.'

Jean nodded and changed the subject abruptly. 'Do you know where Helen is?'

'No.'

'I thought you might have some idea as you work in Intelligence and must see a lot of secret information.'

'I do, but I don't know anything about Helen's work. All she has told me is that she is working as an interpreter for the Free French. I'm sorry I can't tell you anything more than that.'

'I shouldn't have asked.' Jean squeezed her daughter's hand. 'Why don't you go and unpack while I get dinner ready?'

Over the next week they listened avidly to the news reports of the invasion. The troops were beginning to move inland, much to everyone's relief. As Grace read the newspapers and tuned into the wireless every day, she knew the reports could not convey the real struggle each individual was experiencing. How were all those she cared about? Were they injured; were they alive? What about the people at the farm who had risked their lives for her – would they be all right? To have armies fighting desperately over your land must be terrible. Was Harry there? Of course he was – he would probably have been in the first wave. All those people were at the forefront of her thoughts, and one other she was dreadfully worried about.

Where are you, Helen? Are you still in France? If you are, please stay safe!

There were only two days of her leave left when James came to see her. The moment she set eyes on him she knew something was wrong. He looked drawn and ill. She took him into the kitchen and put the kettle on to make tea.

He sat down with a weary sigh. 'I'm glad you are home, Grace. Are your parents here?'

'They are both at work. Are you on leave?'

'Yes, and I've got bad news. Tim was killed two days ago. I saw him go down and he didn't stand a chance.'

Sadness swept over her. He had been such a lovely boy and so full of life. James must be devastated to have seen his friend killed like that.

'I'm so sorry, James. What a tragedy.'

He nodded and gulped his tea down. 'To have survived all the battles we've been in and then to be killed when the war could be entering its final stages is hard to take. Could you break the news to Helen for me, Grace?'

'Of course. Would you like to stay here tonight? I've still got two days' leave left.'

'That's kind of you, but I'm on my way to see Tim's family.' He stood up and hugged her. 'Wish I could stay, but I can't.'

'I understand.'

She stood at the door and watched him walk down the street. His head was high and stride confident, as always. Anyone passing him wouldn't know the pain he was feeling at this moment. He had seen many of his colleagues die, but he had been particularly close to Tim. She wondered if the scars they were all suffering would ever heal. When she thought about Brian she knew they would never

301

completely go away, but she had to learn to live with them.

Closing the door, she wiped a tear from her eyes, very aware that this might not be the last time such news arrived.

Grace's leave did not end on a happy note. Not only had she received the sad news of Tim's death, but on the last day London had a new threat to face. On 13th June Hitler began sending over unmanned flying bombs, and once again people had to endure the danger and destruction these noisy and unpredictable weapons were causing.

Chapter Twenty-Eight

'Sir, there's a young girl here asking to see an officer. Says she's English and has some important news.'

Dan looked up from the map he was studying and frowned. 'Did you check her papers?'

'Yes, sir, but they're French. If she is English then they must be false. She sounds English, though.'

'That doesn't mean much. I can sound German if I need to. Bring her in and let's see what this is about. Keep a guard on her.'

Dan folded the map and put it away; including any other papers he had spread about. No point taking chances in case she wasn't who she said she was.

The girl who entered was of average height with dark brown hair and eyes. She certainly didn't look English. 'What can I do for you?'

'It's what I can do for you that is important, Colonel. I

have come to tell you that there is a trap waiting for your regiment a mile down the road.'

'We've scouted that area and found nothing.'

'Two machine gun posts have been concealed in the hillside. They were set up during the night and when you advance they will be looking right down at you. It will be a massacre, Colonel.' She pulled a tattered map out of her pocket and spread it out on the makeshift table. 'This is where you are, and the guns are here. Not only are they well hidden, but they are hard to get to. We know because we tried to get a close look at dawn.'

'We? Are you with the resistance?'

'The men I'm with are. There's no harm in telling you now; I am SOE. If you could give us enough explosives we can try to knock them out before you move forward.'

It was a plausible story but Dan was still cautious. 'You can't expect me to give strangers explosives, surely? I will need to meet the rest of your group before taking any action.'

She nodded and put the map back in her pocket. 'I would have thought less of you if you hadn't shown caution. We have also learnt that lesson, Colonel. I'll take you to them, but you can only bring one soldier with you.'

It could be a trap, but then again she could be telling the truth. If that was the case, he had to take the chance. He nodded to the sergeant standing by the entrance of the wrecked building they were using. He acknowledged the silent command with a nod. 'Very well, take us to them.'

Waiting in a small copse a short way from the camp

were three men. Dan studied them carefully. They were all armed but showed no sign of aggression.

'Ah, you found a colonel. Well done, Helen,' one man said in perfect English and held out his hand to Dan. 'I'm Harry, sir. Free French. And you are?'

'Chester.' Dan shook his hand, and then his gaze fixed on the girl. She was also staring back at him. 'Your name is Helen?'

She looked him up and down and her smile widened. 'Ah, yes, you fit the description of Major Daniel Chester, formally of the War Office while recovering from an injury.'

He had never seen this girl before and there was only one way she could know that about him. 'Are you Grace Lincoln's friend?'

'I am.' She held out her hand. 'I'm pleased to meet you at last. Grace enjoyed working for you, and you helped her through a difficult time.'

'We helped each other.' He shook her hand and relaxed. They were genuine, and that meant the information was as well. 'Thank you for coming to us. If you would all come back to the camp with me we can work out what to do about this problem.'

The unusual sight of their colonel walking with a girl and three civilian men, all armed, caused a buzz of interest when they returned to the camp.

Dan headed straight for the damaged farm house they were using as a base and turned to his sergeant. 'Find Captain Bolton and Lieutenant Harris and ask them to come here at once. See if you can rustle up refreshments as well.'

'Yes, sir.'

The officers appeared almost immediately, along with mugs of tea and a pile of sandwiches quickly prepared by their cook. Helen and the men tucked in enthusiastically, not caring what the sandwiches contained.

'When did you last eat?' Dan wanted to know.

Harry shrugged and grinned, taking another sandwich. 'Can't remember.'

'You told me you were Free French, but you sound English and are not in uniform. Did you get separated from your unit?'

'I work alone, Colonel, and go where I'm needed. The uniform is a hindrance when I want to blend into the background. I carry it with me, though. And I sound English because I was educated there.'

'Ah, that explains it. I was educated in Germany.'

'So I've heard.'

Dan gave him a speculative look. 'And how do you know so much about me?'

'Someone must have told me.' Harry grinned and took another sandwich from the rapidly depleting pile.

That was all Harry was going to say and Dan knew it would be useless to ask more questions.

'Let's get down to work.'

They spent the next hour exploring ways of knocking out the gun emplacements. Then Dan ran a hand through his hair and shook his head. 'Whatever we do is going to be risky and damned difficult. They've chosen a good spot by the look of it.'

'Wish Bill was with us. He'd deal with them in no time

at all. I've never met a man so skilled at blowing up things.'

'Do you have any idea where he is?' Dan asked. 'He sounds just like the man for the job.'

'I haven't the faintest idea, and that man can't be found unless he wants to be.'

'Who is he?' Dan was intrigued.

'Captain William Reid masquerades as British Intelligence, but he's really a spy, like Harry.' Helen laughed softly at Dan's astonished expression. 'Ah, I see you know him.'

'We've met, but I'm having a hell of a job believing this. France is a big country and the chances of our meeting like this must be astronomical!'

'True, but here we are; and here you are stuck unless we can disable those guns. If you try to go another way it will mean leaving that trap for someone else to fall into.' Harry rubbed his chin thoughtfully. 'Whatever the risks are, we have got to deal with this. We'll need plenty of explosives. It's the only way, Colonel.'

'I agree. I'll get a team together and go with them.'

The room erupted with protest.

'Sir!' the lieutenant stepped forward. 'With the brigadier dead you are our highest ranking officer. We are trapped here unless we can move forward and meet up with the other regiments. The men trust your leadership, sir. You are needed here.'

The two resistance men, who had remained silent until now, shook their heads. 'You give us the explosives and we will do this. It is for us to put those guns out of action. We find them – we destroy them.'

'Leave it to us, Daniel. The men are experienced and

have more chance of getting up that hill unnoticed.'

'I can't let you go alone. This is our fight as well.'

'What about a compromise?' Harry suggested. 'Let us have two of your best demolition men. Not you, though. Your men are right. Your place is here.'

'Very well. I agree, but reluctantly.'

Dan heard the officers breathe an audible sigh of relief and could understand their concerns. Their situation was not good and it was imperative that they meet up with the others. The last thing any of them wanted was to find themselves surrounded and captured. He hated to stand on the sidelines, though, especially in a dangerous situation like this, but for the time being he was in command and had no choice in the matter.

'Sergeant, find Adams and Walker. Harry, you go with him and explain the problem to them. Take their advice; they are experts, and then come back here.'

When the men left, Dan turned to Helen. 'Would you like more sandwiches?'

'No, thank you.' She gave a grim smile. 'It looks as if you've had a tough time getting this far.'

Dan nodded. 'And if you hadn't come to us we could have been cut down before getting any further. Somehow we have to fight our way out of this because I won't be captured again!' he growled. 'We will be moving after midnight, no matter what the situation. We have to!'

'We'll do what we can to help.'

'You have probably already saved our lives by alerting us to the guns.'

The men returned and Dan ran through the task with

his men to make sure they fully understood what had to be done. 'Have you got everything you need?' he asked.

'Yes, sir. If we can get close enough without being seen, we will deal with those guns.'

'The light is just beginning to fade, so good luck to all of you.'

Dan's men saluted and then hauled packs onto their backs before filing out.

'Helen, you can stay here,' Dan said when she headed after the men.

She turned her head. 'I go with them.'

'You don't have to risk your life as well.'

'Daniel, I have risked my life every day for more than two years. I am an excellent shot with good night vision. I can give them cover while they are working. See you later.' She waved before disappearing.

'That's a brave girl,' the captain remarked. 'Hope they succeed.'

'If they don't then we will have to try again because we will be moving out soon. We can't stay here much longer. Tell the men to be ready. If the way is cleared we'll move out at once.'

'Yes, sir.' Both officers saluted and hurried out, leaving Dan and the sergeant alone.

Dan sat on a wooden box and rested his head against the wall. Waiting was always hard. If the brigadier had still been alive he could have gone with them, instead he had to delegate and let others take the risks.

'Why don't you snatch some sleep, sir?' the sergeant told him. 'I'll wake you if you're needed.'

'I won't be able to sleep until we're safely out of this place. You can if you want to.'

The sergeant shook his head.

'Let's take a walk round then and see how preparations are going for the move.' Dan hauled himself to his feet.

They spent the next hour touring the camp and talking to the men. They were naturally curious and concerned about the situation so Dan gathered them together and explained fully what was happening. All of a sudden there was a loud explosion, followed by another and another. The men were all on their feet staring at the flames leaping into the air as trees caught fire on the hill.

'Looks like they did it, sir,' one of the men shouted.

'Lieutenant!' Dan yelled. 'Get ready to move out now while there's confusion on that hill.'

The men moved with such speed that they were on their way in only five minutes and making their way towards the blaze. They moved in complete silence in case there was trouble lurking ahead of them. They had gone some way when Dan saw movement in a clump of bushes beside the road. He lifted his hands and everyone stopped quickly, and formed a defensive position. The breath hissed out of him in relief when he saw Adams and Walker step out grinning. They were followed by Helen, Harry and the two resistance men. They all appeared to be in good spirits and unhurt, which took a weight off Dan's shoulders.

'We've dealt with the guns, sir, and as many of the Germans as we could, but we think there are still a few hiding up there. They might cause a bit of trouble, but we should be able to deal with them all right.'

'Well done!' Dan shook hands with the Frenchmen and thanked them. Then he smiled at Helen and Harry. 'You've probably saved a lot of lives, and we are grateful. What are you going to do now?'

'Stay with you until you meet up with the others. We'll scout ahead so you won't know we're there unless we spot trouble, then we'll alert you.'

Dan nodded. 'We are in your debt.'

Helen gave a quiet laugh. 'You shouldn't say things like that, Daniel. We might want to collect one day.'

'Anything – anytime,' he replied.

'Oh, I can see why Grace liked working with you so much.' She lifted her hand in a wave and the group melted away.

If there were Germans still on the hill they made no move to attack the troops and they passed that spot without incident. They made good progress for three days, meeting only sporadic resistance. There had been no sign of Helen or her companions as they moved forward, but Dan was sure they were out there. Then one evening Helen and Harry appeared.

'There's a large contingent of British troops over the next rise,' Harry told Dan. 'I'm leaving you now to rejoin my unit. I want to be with them when Paris is liberated. The information I have is that it could happen within the next couple of weeks.'

'Good luck, Harry.' Dan shook his hand. 'It's been good to meet you, and thanks for your help.'

'My pleasure.' Harry hugged Helen and spoke quietly in her ear, then turned and strode away.

'Where are the others?' Dan wanted to know.

'They have returned to their villages.' She looked up at Dan. 'About that favour?'

'Name it.'

'My work here is finished and I need to send a message to get picked up. When we reach your troops would you persuade them to let me use their wireless set?'

'Of course. You'll be glad to get home.'

Helen nodded and sighed. 'I've been lucky to avoid capture for so long, Daniel. Many others have not been so fortunate.'

Dan studied the slim girl in front of him, noting just how weary she was. 'I'll see you get home, Helen.'

'Thank you.'

Chapter Twenty-Nine

Paris was liberated on August 25th 1944, and that night they had a party in the mess. Grace sat with an untouched drink in front of her and watched the smiling faces as they celebrated. Her thoughts went back to the time she had worked for James. On occasions like this she would have been circulating, doing her job of seeing that the party went smoothly. It was a role she had enjoyed and she had felt useful, needed. She'd had an interesting job, a husband she loved and the future had looked good. All that had been wrenched from her and so many others. She shook herself mentally. It was useless to dwell on the past. That life was gone and would never return, not even when the war was over.

Snap out of it, Grace, she told herself sternly. *This is a night to celebrate, not dwell on what had been. So you're feeling lonely and useless with everyone close to you away – admit it! You've done all that was asked of you, so damned well finish your drink and join in the celebration!*

Grace had just taken a sip of her drink and summoned up a smile when a corporal came up to her.

'Sergeant Lincoln, Major General Haydon wants you to return to the office immediately.'

'Thank you, Corporal.' Once outside, Grace started to run. What had happened? Stan wouldn't have sent for her tonight unless it was very important.

'That was quick,' Stan remarked when she rushed into the office.

'What's wrong, sir?' she asked, slightly out of breath.

'Nothing is wrong.' He smiled. 'I have to go somewhere and I need you to accompany me. I hope you didn't mind leaving the party?'

'No, sir.' Grace relaxed; he was smiling. 'Where are we going?'

'You'll see. Do you still keep a bag packed and ready?' She nodded.

'Go and collect it, then. We are leaving at once.'

Thirty minutes later they were in the car and heading for London. Stan turned and smiled at her. 'I do like a day full of good news, for a change.'

'I'm pleased you've have had a good day,' she joked. 'Can you share some of it with me, sir? My thoughts have been a little gloomy this evening.'

'You'll have to wait a while longer, Captain.'

'Sergeant, sir.'

'You have just been promoted again.' He handed her

a packet. 'Put these on your uniform as soon as possible.'

Grace was stunned. 'What have I done to deserve this again?'

'It's for your excellent service, and we need you as an officer.'

'Why?'

'So you can go into places normally off limits to you.' Stan gave an amused chuckle. 'There are plans and I have been given my instructions.'

'What plans?'

'Do you ever stop asking questions? I'm not saying anything else. George sends his love, by the way.'

'You've heard from George! How is he?'

'He's fine, so is Bill, Dan and—'

'And?' When he just grinned, Grace sighed. 'You are being very irritating today, sir.'

'Yes, aren't I? Ah, we've arrived.'

The car stopped and Grace looked out, unable to believe her eyes. 'This is my house! What are we doing here?'

'Questions – questions! Take a look at the people coming out of the front door.'

Everyone was smiling and waving, and then one person stepped to the front and Grace was scrambling to get out of the car. 'Helen!' she cried, running to greet the friend she hadn't seen for such a long time. 'You're home at last!'

Jean immediately took charge. 'Come inside everyone. There's food and drink laid out in the front room. Will you join us, Major General Haydon?'

'I would love to, and the name is Stan.'

Already sitting in the front room was Helen's grandmother, bursting with pride and happiness. Ted handed round glasses of beer. 'Sorry we haven't anything stronger. But it will do to toast Helen's safe return to us.'

When this was done, Grace turned to Stan. 'Thank you, sir. How did you know?'

'I received a message to say Helen was on her way home. I checked and discovered she had arrived today.'

'Thank you again, sir.'

'It's my pleasure, Captain.'

Ted heard that and said, 'Captain?'

'I've been promoted again, Dad.'

'My word, this is turning out to be a day for celebrations. Listen, everyone! Grace is now a captain!'

She accepted the congratulations, laughing. 'I think there is some devious reason for this promotion, but I haven't found out what it is yet.'

'Devious – me?' Stan pretended to be shocked. 'The Intelligence Service never does anything underhand.'

This remark produced roars of laughter, and Ted asked, 'Oh, and who convinced Hitler the invasion would be in the Pas-de-Calais instead of Normandy?'

'I haven't the faintest idea,' he said, giving Grace a sly wink and then finishing his beer. Putting down the empty glass he went round the room and shook hands with everyone to take his leave.

'I can only let you have two days with your friend,' he told Grace.

'I'm grateful for that, sir.'

The party went on until the early hours of the morning,

and it wasn't until after lunch that the friends had time to themselves. The morning rain had stopped and the sun was out, so they decided to catch a bus to Hyde Park.

They ambled along in silence for a while until two soldiers saluted Grace as they passed.

'You nearly missed that,' Helen laughed.

'They took me by surprise. I'd forgotten I'm an officer now. Nudge me if that looks like it's happening again.'

'I will.' Helen sighed. 'This is lovely just strolling along in a beautiful park with nothing to worry about.'

'You must be happy to be back.'

Helen nodded. 'I stayed longer than planned, but I'm glad I did. We managed to be of help to the allies.'

'Can I ask how you got out?'

'I joined up with some British soldiers and their officer arranged it for me. That was good of him, but then your Daniel is a good man.'

'Pardon?' Grace stopped walking and stared at her friend.

'I said Colonel Daniel Chester is a good man.'

Grace could hardly believe what she was hearing. 'You met Dan out there?'

'I did and I probably helped to save his life.' Helen laughed at Grace's astonished expression. 'Aren't you going to thank me?'

'Be serious, Helen! Tell me what this is all about.'

'Can't. I've only told you this much because you were out there at one time. I expect it was Daniel who got the message through to Stan.'

'Well, I'm blowed!'

'Aren't you going to ask how he is?'

'If you helped to save his life then I take it he is fine.'

'He is.' Helen sighed dramatically. 'Such a dynamic man.'

'Hmm.' Grace found an empty seat and sat down, patting the seat beside her for Helen. 'Tell me who else you met.'

'Sorry, that's classified.' Helen closed her eyes and lifted her face to the sun. 'What are you going to do when the war is over? Will you go back to the law firm you worked for before this mess began?'

'I don't think I could. We've seen and done so much, I can't imagine returning to the lives we had. I like army life and might consider staying in. What about you?'

'If all goes well I will be returning to France and getting married.'

'Oh, you've met someone. Is he French?'

'Yes, but the war isn't over yet and nothing is certain.'

'If you do marry a Frenchman your grandmother will be delighted. I hope it all works out for you.'

'Me too. What about you. Have you met anyone special?'

'Quite a few special men have come into my life, but I have no plans to marry again. I might one day, but at the moment I can't see any chance of that happening.'

'Not even James. He seems fond of you and you for him.'

Grace shook her head. 'We are friends now and that's all. I have some sad news for you, Helen. I should have told you before but didn't want to spoil your homecoming. Tim was killed during the invasion.'

'Oh, that's terrible.' Helen was clearly shocked. 'He was such a likeable boy. James must be devastated.'

'He was very upset when he came and told me. Let's hope the war is over soon to stop all this senseless killing of young men.'

'Amen to that! But I really don't think it will be this year. Winter is fast approaching and that could make things even harder.'

'So it looks as if we will have to wait until next year.'

'Most likely. The men out there have a huge task on their hands and crossing the Rhine into Germany won't be easy.'

'I expect you saw a lot of the fighting while you were there. Do your family know where you've been all this time?'

'I haven't said anything, of course, and they haven't asked, but they must have guessed. I did consider staying to the end, but there wasn't a lot more I could do. The escape route I was working on was no longer needed.'

'Is that what you were doing?'

'Most of the time. I was one link in a very long chain to help downed airmen get back home.'

'Did you help Tim? I always felt he knew something about you but wasn't letting on.'

Helen nodded. 'He was brought to us. It is sad to find out he was killed after all that.'

'Yes, it's tragic.' Grace sighed. 'So it looks as if we will both have to wait and watch, hoping for the fighting to end soon. And when it does, the work of rebuilding shattered countries and lives will begin. The problem of displaced persons will be enormous. If I stay in the army I might be able to help in some way.'

'Don't commit yourself yet, Grace. They might put pressure on you to sign up for years, but wait and see how things work out. Do you remember in the beginning how we wanted to do something worthwhile and had no idea what that could be?'

'I do, and I believe we have done that in ways we never imagined.'

'We have, and that's why I'm urging you to wait. Something quite unexpected might come up and you will need to be free at that point.'

Grace smiled at her friend. 'You have changed. Before the war I was always the one urging caution. I had a job to stop you running headlong into things.'

'I've had to learn to sum up a situation carefully before taking action. But then, none of us will ever be the same, will we?'

'Change was inevitable, and perhaps that isn't a bad thing. Some of the things we've had to face have, hopefully, made us stronger to cope with whatever life throws at us.'

'I'm sure they have. It seems strange to be sitting here talking about the end of the war. It's been going on for so long it has become our entire life.'

Grace nodded. 'Did we have a life before the world went crazy? It's hard to remember what it was like.'

'If I cast my mind back I think it was happy, carefree, and the only problem we had was what picture to go and see.'

'I'm sure it wasn't quite like that,' Grace laughed. 'Nice way to remember it, though.'

Helen grinned and pulled Grace to her feet. 'Let's walk again and see how many times you get saluted.'

They set off smiling happily, the serious conversation pushed aside and just glad to see each other again.

Chapter Thirty

Christmas 1944 came and went. There had been an air of hope and expectancy that the coming year would finally see the end of the war in Europe.

Grace stopped on her way to the camp to admire clumps of primroses on a grassy bank, dancing in the March breeze. It was as if they were saying 'Look at us, there is still beauty to be seen'. Such a small thing but it lifted Grace's spirits. The constant stream of information now coming in told of mass bombing, fierce fighting and terrible atrocities being uncovered.

There was no sign of Stan when she arrived, so she settled down to deal with the pile of reports on her desk.

An hour later he arrived. 'I've just heard some good news! The allies have crossed the Rhine. The Nazis are finished, Grace. It can only be a matter of weeks now.'

'That is good news. It will be such a relief when the fighting is over.'

'It's been a long, hard war.' Stan stood by her desk. 'Have you made any plans for the future?'

'Not really.'

'I'm going to ask you not to rush to get demobbed. There is going to be a great deal to do, and your language skills will be useful.' He gave a lopsided grin. 'I could see you are promoted again.'

'No, thank you, sir.' Grace laughed at the expression on his face. 'Captain is fine with me. I promise I won't do anything hasty. I have been considering staying in the army anyway, so I'll wait and see what happens.'

'Good.'

When he disappeared into his office, Grace shook her head in amusement. She certainly didn't want another promotion. If she did decide to stay in the ATS there could be a time when she had to return to a woman's outfit, and a higher rank might make it difficult for her. Of course, the Intelligence Service could ask her to stay, but she wasn't going to bank on that. Her options would need careful consideration, but they had to finish the war first.

That finally happened on May 7th when Germany surrendered unconditionally and May 8th was declared VE Day. The country went wild. Hitler was dead and the long years of war were over. People were dancing in the streets and there were celebrations going on everywhere.

Helen and Grace were both on leave so they made their way to Trafalgar Square to join in the fun. As it got dark, lights were turned on everywhere. After years of making sure not even a crack of light showed, it was a wonderful sight.

'Hey, Captain!' A laughing Canadian soldier caught Grace and spun her round. 'Will you and your friend help me and my buddies to celebrate? Where can we go to get a drink? Somewhere nice because we wouldn't take an officer to a dump.'

'Grace!' Helen appeared with the soldier's friend. 'Come on. We're going to the Savoy Hotel.'

'It will be packed!'

'So will everywhere, but we'll get in all right.' The Canadian let out a piercing whistle and four more of their friends appeared. 'These beautiful girls are taking us somewhere we can get a drink.'

Another piercing whistle brought over two more soldiers, and by the time they reached the hotel they had acquired three British, two French and four Americans, all looking for a place to get a drink and have a party.

Grace had been right. The place was packed, but everyone was in such a good mood that no one complained when they pushed their way in.

Somehow the soldiers managed to get to the bar and order drinks. Their group had grown even larger in that time. The drinks arrived with two British soldiers, two sailors and an airman.

The noise was deafening and it was almost impossible to hear what anyone said. A glass of champagne was put on the table in front of her, and when she looked up to thank the person she leapt to her feet in delight.

'James! Helen, James is here.' Grace hugged him

and Helen pushed her out of the way to take her turn.

'Hey, you know each other.' One of the Canadians slapped James on the back. 'Join us; we're gonna have one hell of a party tonight.'

'There are four of us.'

'Bring them all over. "The more the merrier", they say.'

It was dawn before Grace and Helen made their way back home. They were tired and their sides ached from laughing so much. It had been a hilarious night.

'Hope no one salutes me because I'll fall over if I try to salute back.' Grace giggled and that set them off laughing again.

'It was good to see James there, wasn't it, Grace? I noticed you managed to have a talk with him. Was he offering you a job with him again?'

'There is a job for me at the law firm if I want it, but James has decided to stay in the air force. Flying has always been his passion, so he's going to make that his career – for the time being anyway.'

'I don't blame him. Now the war is finally over I expect many people are deciding what they are going to do.'

'Good heavens!' Grace exclaimed when they reached their street. 'Everyone's still up and lights are blazing in every window. The war in Europe really is over.'

They didn't crawl out of bed until midday. Everyone else was still asleep so Grace and Helen sat in the kitchen working their way through a pot of strong tea.

'I'm going back to France in two days' time, Grace.'

'So soon?'

'Yes, I need to check on some people to see they are all right, and several of our group were captured. I want to find out what happened to them, if possible. Then I'll go to Paris to meet up with Maurice.'

'Is that the man you're going to marry?'

Helen nodded. 'We arranged this before I left France. His home is there and he's waiting for me.'

'What's he like? You haven't said much about him. Do you have a photo?'

'Sorry, no photos, and you'll have to wait until you meet him to see what he's like. I think he's gorgeous.'

'I'm sure you do,' Grace teased. 'I'll give you my opinion when I've seen him. Will you marry here?'

'No, in France, and we'll be living there. My family are so excited about that, and grandmother is thrilled, of course. She can't stop smiling.'

'Of course she can't. Her favourite granddaughter is marrying a Frenchman and going to live in the country of her birth. I hope you will have room for me to come and visit? Providing Maurice agrees, of course.'

'He will be delighted. We shall expect you to come often, and we'll visit you wherever you end up.'

'If I do stay in the army I could be posted anywhere, but I'll write every week.'

'Me too.' Helen smiled at her friend. 'So, our adventure continues with a new life for both of us.'

'Not the one we could possibly have imagined, but here's to a peaceful and happy future.' They raised the tea cups in salute.

* * *

It had been hard saying goodbye to Helen knowing they were now going their separate ways. They had been constant companions from the time they were born, except for the years apart during the war, but Grace was happy for her friend. She deserved a lot of happiness after what she had done.

Two weeks had passed since VE Day and Grace had now made up her mind to stay in the ATS.

Stan swept into the office. 'Go and pack a bag. We're off to Berlin tomorrow. Make sure you've got your dress uniform and an evening frock. Nip home and get one if you have to.'

'I don't have anything like that,' she protested. 'I haven't needed dressy clothes for a long time, sir.'

'You'd better go and buy one then.'

'Where? I don't have any clothing coupons.'

'Ah, I never thought of that. I'll see what I can sort out, and don't leave the office for a while yet.'

He disappeared into his office and closed the door. Grace smiled and went back to work. What on earth was he on about? Her dress uniform would be appropriate for anything they might attend. The last time she had worn an elegant gown had been when she had been posing as an SS officer's girlfriend. Never mind about that, though. They were going to Berlin and that was an exciting prospect.

An hour later the office door burst open and piles of boxes walked in. At least that's what it looked like because the man carrying them could hardly be seen. A woman guided him to the desk where he dropped the boxes just as Stan came out of his office.

'Where's the young lady you want me to dress, Stanley?'

'Standing right beside you, Gregory.'

Gregory turned his full attention to Grace, frowning as he walked round her. 'Stand still, dear,' he ordered when she tried to keep him in view. 'Dear, dear, these uniforms don't do anything for the female form. Take off your jacket, dear.'

If he said 'dear' once more she would slosh him, Grace decided. 'My name is Captain Grace Lincoln!'

'Very nice, dear. Now, remove your jacket, please, dear.'

Grace spun round to face Stan and was even more annoyed to see he was finding it difficult not to dissolve into helpless laughter. 'Who is this man, sir?'

'A designer.'

'A designer!' Gregory squeaked, highly offended. 'I dress the best, the beautiful and the highest in the land. I could make a hippopotamus look elegant!'

This was ridiculous. Grace's annoyance faded a little as she began to see the funny side and couldn't resist teasing this man with such a high opinion of himself. 'You are too modest.'

'Ah, sadly that is one of my faults.' He broke into a smile as if she had paid him a compliment. 'But I am sure we can do something with you, don't you think, Adel?'

'You will work your usual magic, Gregory. The hair is pretty – what we can see of it, and she has good bone structure.'

'Hmm.' Gregory reached out and expertly removed the pins from Grace's hair, letting it tumble around her shoulders. 'Hmm, promising, but it depends on the figure hidden by that terrible uniform. Take it off, dear.'

'I am not getting undressed in here!'

'Use my office,' Stan offered, quickly stepping aside. 'I'll see no one comes in.'

'Bring the top two boxes in, Stanley,' Gregory ordered as he swept into the other office.

As Grace passed Stan she hissed quietly, 'You'll suffer for this . . . sir!'

The boxes were immediately put on the desk and as the door closed behind Stan, she could hear him laughing.

She endured another critical scrutiny and many dears before Gregory came to a decision.

'Red, I think . . . Yes, red. It's in the top box, Adel. I thought that might be the one from the description Stanley gave me.'

Grace was horrified. 'I am not wearing red!'

'I'm not suggesting scarlet, dear, but a deep ruby red. You have a hint of red in your hair, which is quite glorious by the way. It's a crime to have it screwed up like you do.'

'Army regulations.'

'Yes, well, they have their rules I suppose, but you must wear it down when you can. Ah, here is the gown.' He took it from his assistant and held it up against Grace. 'Quite perfect. Let's hope Stanley guessed your size correctly. We haven't time for major alterations.'

Adel helped Grace into the gown and it fitted perfectly. Then there was another lengthy examination.

'Shoes, Adel. You have a decent height, around five feet seven or eight, but we will make you a little taller. The gold strappy ones, Adel. What size are you, dear?'

'Six.' Grace was looking down at the gown wishing there

329

was a mirror in the office. It was lovely and very comfortable, but she was sure he'd made a mistake with the colour. She never wore red, and what on earth were they going to be doing in Berlin for Stan to insist she had something like this?

The shoes also fitted, making her around three inches taller.

'Walk up and down, dear.' He watched to see how the gown moved around the hem. 'Quite a transformation, don't you think, Adel? She has good posture.'

'Perfect, Gregory. Your choice of gown and colour is impeccable, as ever.'

He bristled with pride at the compliment. 'Go and show Stanley, dear.'

Feeling rather self-conscious, Grace walked into the other office.

'Here is your Cinderella, Stanley. Does she meet with your approval?'

'My word, you look beautiful and that colour is stunning on you. Well done Gregory.'

'It was a pleasure, Stanley. Oh, and do try not to clutter it up too much with army decorations or whatever.' He collected up the boxes and headed for the door.

'Wait a minute!' Grace stopped him. 'How much does all this cost? I'm positive I can't afford it.'

'You don't have to, dear,' Gregory informed her. 'It's all been taken care of.'

Grace stared at the door after he had left, and then spun round to face Stan. 'What did he mean? Who is paying for this? The gown must cost a fortune, and I dread to think how expensive the shoes are. I can't allow someone else to pay for them. If I can't afford them myself then they must be returned!'

'Gregory owed me a favour, so stop fretting and just enjoy the clothes. You are going to have to blend in with some important people and their wives.'

'What on earth are we going to be doing in Berlin?'

'Working. Now, get changed and go and pack. We're leaving at five in the morning.' Stan opened the door to leave and looked back. 'I shall be proud to be your escort, though I doubt I shall have that pleasure for long. See you in the morning, *dear*.'

'I've got to stop over in Paris,' Stan told Grace when they were waiting for the transport plane.

'Oh, Helen's there. She's going to marry a Frenchman, and I haven't met him yet. Would there be time for a quick visit, sir? I have the address.'

'I'm sure we could fit it in if the meeting doesn't last too long, and I'll come with you.'

'Thank you, sir.' Grace boarded the plane with a smile on her face, excited about the visit.

When they arrived they went straight to the meeting which, fortunately, only lasted two hours.

'Right.' Stan glanced at his watch. 'They've provided us with transport, but it will only be a quick visit. Our plane for Berlin leaves at four o'clock.'

The driver knew Paris well and they were soon outside a smart building, and Grace hoped Helen and Maurice were in. It would be a shame to miss this opportunity to see them. The apartment they wanted was on the first floor and Grace almost danced with relief when Helen opened the door.

'What a lovely surprise!' Helen hugged Grace and shook hands with Stan. 'Come in. What are you doing in Paris?'

'We are on our way to Berlin, but we had to stop over for a meeting. This is only a flying visit, I'm afraid,' Stan explained.

'Maurice! Look who's here,' Helen called.

When he came into the room, Grace stared at him in astonishment. 'Harry!'

'Hello, Grace.' He held out his arms and she rushed to hug him.

'You two have been playing games with me, haven't you? But this is wonderful!'

They were both laughing at the surprise they had sprung on Grace, and Helen said, 'You promised to tell me what you thought of him.'

'He's gorgeous, of course.'

Harry turned to Stan and shook his hand. 'Good to see you again. Can you stay for dinner?'

'That isn't possible, but another time, perhaps.'

'You will always be welcome, Stan. Bring Bill with you some time.'

'I'll do that.'

They could only stay for an hour and were soon heading back to the airfield and on their way to Berlin.

Chapter Thirty-One

'There used to be a good cafe just there. It was cheap and the meals enormous. Just what us young boys needed.'

Dan glanced at the man who had come to stand beside him. 'Bill, I'm pleased to see you made it.'

'You too. Your office told me where to find you.' Bill looked around and shook his head. 'What a mess! It's hard to find the places I once knew so well.'

'I agree. I've been walking the streets for the last couple of hours and the place is unrecognisable. And to add to the chaos the city has been divided up between the allies.'

'Churchill and Roosevelt had to come up with a plan acceptable to all of the allies, and you can bet that wasn't easy. Damned shame Roosevelt didn't live to see the end of the war.'

'Yes it is. But dividing the city up like this makes me

uneasy. This could be a recipe for trouble in the future.'

'That's why I'm staying here for a while. What about you?'

'I'm on my home soon but I'll probably be back at some time.' Dan began walking and Bill fell into step beside him. 'The rebuilding of Europe is going to be an enormous task. People are scattered all over the place with nowhere to go. It's tragic.'

'The cost was high, but the Nazis had to be stopped from taking over Europe. If they had defeated Britain then there was no telling where they would have stopped.'

'Yes, it had to be done.' Dan stopped in front of a ruined building. 'I had a friend who lived here. Wonder what happen to him and his family? They were nice people, but then they might have been seduced by Hitler and become ardent Nazis. I don't think walking these shattered streets, remembering the past, is a good idea, Bill. Come back with me and I'll buy you a drink. We can toast our good fortune in surviving.'

'You're on!' Bill grinned. 'Stan's on his way here and is bringing Grace with him.'

'Yes, I know.'

'Of course you do. Did you arrange it?'

'Me? Why would I do such a thing?'

'Remind me never to play poker with you,' Bill laughed. 'I see you've been bumped up to brigadier and have been given a medal for the way you saved your men and got them back to the rest of the troops.'

'That medal belongs to a young SOE girl who saved us from being slaughtered. I've put in a report to make damned sure she gets one as well. There was also a Frenchman with her who spoke perfect English, but I don't have any details about him.' Dan glanced at Bill. 'I'm hoping you can help me there. He knew you.'

'That sounds like Harry. I don't know his real name, but I'll try and find out for you.'

'Thanks, I would appreciate that. Let's get that drink.'

The officers' mess wasn't busy and they had just been served with drinks when Stan marched in.

'Good, you're here. I'm glad to see you are both in one piece.' Stan looked at their glasses of beer and grimaced. 'Mine is a double whisky, Dan.'

Bill was on his feet, staring at the door. 'Where's my Grace? You didn't come without her, did you?'

'I left her to settle in with the women. You'll see her tonight – and she isn't *your* Grace.'

'I can dream, can't I? How is she?'

'The same as ever. Continually asking questions and telling me how to do my job. She's damned good army material.'

Dan laughed softly and got up to order Stan's drink and another two beers.

'That's better.' Stan declared when the drink was put in front of him. 'Tell me who is coming to this gathering tonight.'

'Representatives of all the allies, their wives and guests. It's a diplomatic exercise,' Bill explained. 'The idea is to get everyone together so they can be nice and friendly over a few drinks.'

Stan gave a cynical laugh. 'With all of them in the same

room it means we shall have to be on our best behaviour. Good job I've got Grace with me. I believe she's been used to this kind of thing when she worked for James. You'd never believe the trouble I had persuading her to let Gregory find her a suitable gown. I thought she was going to throw him out of the office.'

'Stan! You didn't? Not Gregory.' Bill shook his head before bursting into laughter. 'I wish I'd been there.'

'It was quite hilarious.' Stan was also laughing now. 'He kept calling her "dear", and you can imagine how she reacted to that. Dan, you would have to meet the man to understand. Anyway, his choice was impeccable and she looked lovely when he'd finished.'

'I can't wait to see her again.' Bill glanced across at Dan. 'It will be a pleasure for all of us.'

Stan finished his drink and stood up. 'I'd better go and unpack now. We'll see you tonight.'

There was a rap on the door and when Dan opened it he found Bill standing outside. 'Stan isn't ready yet so I thought we might as well go together.'

'I'm part of the reception group so I have to be there early.'

'That's all right. It will give me a chance to sum up the situation and perhaps try out my Russian.'

Dan stepped aside to let Bill in. 'You speak Russian as well? Is there anything you can't do?'

'Hmm. Let me see. Oh, yes, I don't have much luck finding a nice girl who will settle down with me.'

'You'll never settle down.' Dan buttoned up his

jacket and made sure his appearance was in order.

'Perhaps you're right.' Bill followed Dan out, and as they marched along he said, 'How long is it since you've seen Grace?'

'The last time was at a party to celebrate my return to my regiment.'

'But that was years ago! Are you telling me you haven't met her since?'

'I am. I haven't seen her for four years.'

'Why, for heaven's sake? And don't tell me you're not interested because I know differently.'

'I had my reasons,' Dan replied as they walked into the building. 'I'll be busy for a while, but I'll see you later. You can buy me a drink. I might need it.'

Bill grinned and walked into the room to see who had turned up early.

Grace was nervous which was surprising. She'd done this kind of thing many times before. They had all been lawyers, barristers and judges then. Tonight it would be officers and politicians from different countries, but not something she should find daunting. There would be people there she knew, and Stan had told her George had just arrived. It would be lovely to see him again, and Bill. Would Dan be there? She hadn't asked, and why would she? Not once in all these years had he bothered to contact her, but she had worried about him, as well as all the others. The fact that he had just walked away without a glance back had hurt. They had worked well together for that short time and had fun. He'd declared that they were friends, but friends kept in touch . . .

And why on earth was all this nonsense coming into her head now?

There was a knock on the door and Stan called out, 'Time to go, Grace.'

'I'm ready. Come in, sir.'

He nodded approval when he saw her. 'Stick with me tonight. I might need your skill with languages. My French is passable but I never could master German.'

'I won't let you out of my sight,' she promised.

'I must make the most of tonight,' he told her as they walked to the venue, 'because I have just had orders through that you won't be working for me any more.'

'Why?' she asked, not pleased with that sudden news. 'Where am I going? Why are they moving me?'

'Questions,' Stan sighed. 'You have been transferred to another officer.'

'Who?'

'You'll meet him tonight.'

Grace didn't like the sound of this, but couldn't ask more questions because they had arrived.

'Smile, dear.' He laughed softly. 'Gregory would be proud of the way you look in one of his gowns, even if we have had to add a couple of things to make it clear you are an officer.'

'I still think my dress uniform would have been suitable.'

They stopped by the sergeant major who was announcing the arrivals and Grace looked into the hall. It was already crowded and all the women were wearing evening gowns.

'See what I mean,' Stan whispered.

'It's hardly appropriate in the middle of war-torn Europe,' she complained.

'This evening is purely a diplomatic affair, and I'm sure you know what they are like.'

'Yes, I do,' she had to agree, as they reached the sergeant major. He raised his voice to announce the arrival of Major General Haydon and Captain Lincoln.

Pinning a smile on her face, Grace entered the room with Stan.

When he heard the names, Dan slowly turned his head towards the door and was shocked at his reaction to seeing Grace again after so long. He felt as if he had been kicked – hard. This wasn't the young girl he had laughed with and manhandled over the army assault course. This was a woman who had grown through all she had experienced, and held herself with elegance and confidence. Grace was the right name for her.

She moved along the line, quietly helping Stan with the languages when needed. When she reached Dan, he smiled. 'Hello, Grace.'

'Good evening, Brigadier,' was all she said and continued walking.

At that moment he knew he had made a mistake. He'd been so sure he was doing the right thing. He was a damned fool.

As soon as everyone had arrived and his job on the reception committee was finished, Dan found Bill. 'I'll have that drink now, and make it a strong one.'

'Ah, someone isn't happy. Doesn't Grace look beautiful? She was like that in France and the German officers were tripping over themselves to meet her. She provided the distraction I needed to slip away unnoticed. I couldn't have done it without her. Was she pleased to see you?' Bill asked innocently.

'Her greeting was as warm and welcoming as an arctic storm. Are you going to get me that drink?' Dan snapped.

'At once, sir!'

Bill soon returned with a large brandy and watched the tall man empty the glass in two swigs. 'Feel better now?'

Dan gave a wry smile. 'No, but I'd better not drink any more of that stuff. I need to keep a clear head.'

'So, our Grace is mad at you. What are you going to do about it? I only ask because if you are going to give up—'

'Don't even think about it, Bill.'

'Why the devil didn't you step in when you had the chance, Dan?'

'That's just what I'm asking myself!' Dan looked at his empty glass and grimaced as he put it down. 'Ah, well, one more battle to fight.'

Dan strode across the room until he reached Grace, Stan and George.

'Ah, Dan. Quite a crowd gathered here.' Stan turned to Grace. 'Meet your new boss.'

Just for a moment her eyes blazed, then her composure returned and she inclined her head in acknowledgement.

Dan admired her self-control. She was clearly not at all happy about being assigned to him, but she was in the army and had to obey orders. 'I'll expect you in my office by eight o'clock tomorrow.'

'Yes, sir.'

Chapter Thirty-Two

That night Grace tossed and turned, ashamed of the way she had acted towards Dan. There was no reason why he should have kept in touch with her. They had worked together for only a few weeks and then they had gone their separate ways. She had admired his determination to get fit enough to return to his regiment, and his kindness and understanding had helped her through those painful weeks after Brian had been killed. He had greeted her tonight with obvious pleasure and used her Christian name. And what had she done? She had insulted him. And now she knew why!

She thumped her pillow in exasperation. Over the years she had listened to George, Bill and Stan talking about him and what he was doing and she had pretended not to care. But the moment she had seen him tonight the truth had become clear. Gradually, bit by bit she had fallen in love with him. The first thing she had to do in the morning was apologise without letting him know about her feelings for him. That would be too embarrassing for both of them. If he'd wanted to take their friendship any further he would have contacted her. Four years of silence told her everything she needed to know.

The morning finally came and Grace followed the instructions she had been given to find his office. A young girl was already there, but before Grace could say anything, Dan came out of his office.

'Punctual, as always,' he said briskly. 'There's a desk in my office you can use.'

He held the door open for her and closed it behind them. She turned to face him. 'Sir, I must apologise for my conduct towards you last night.'

He took a step towards her and then stopped, his gaze sweeping over her tired face. 'Go ahead then.'

He was clearly angry and wasn't going to make this easy for her. And why should he?

'I'm sorry I spoke to you so sharply. It was rude of me and I am ashamed. I can offer no reasonable excuse for my lack of manners. I apologise, sir.'

'Cut out the, "sir", Grace, and tell me what the blazes that was all about.'

'For some reason I was angry you hadn't bothered to contact me even once over the last four years. That was absolutely ridiculous, for you had no reason to do so. I can see that now.' He'd demanded an explanation and she hoped that was good enough because she really couldn't say more without giving herself away.

He took another step forward. 'I couldn't. I didn't dare see you again.'

'That doesn't make sense. George kept in touch, so did James and Bill. Did I do something wrong when we worked together?'

'Of course not. I count those weeks as some of the best I have ever spent.'

Now Grace was completely at a loss to understand what he was saying. 'Then why did you walk away? The last thing you said to me was that we were friends, and I felt as if we had indeed become friends.'

'Then I had better explain, but you might not like what I am going to tell you. If it embarrasses you, tell me and I will never mention it again.'

Now Grace was worried. 'Whatever it is, I think you had better tell me.'

'When you came to work for me I was not happy. I had lost men in France, I was injured and stuck in a desk job, but you worked quietly, efficiently and never once complained. Your husband had only recently been killed, and when I saw how courageous you were in dealing with the pain, it helped me to sort my own feelings out. I very quickly realised something else. I had fallen in love with you.'

Grace gasped. This was the last thing she had expected.

He gave a wry smile at her reaction. 'It shocked me as well, and I couldn't do a damned thing about it because you were grieving for the loss of a husband you had loved. When I returned to my regiment I knew I would be off fighting again somewhere and there was always the chance

I wouldn't survive.' He was right in front of her now. 'That is the reason I stayed away, Grace. I loved you too much to inflict something like that on you again. This war has made it impossible for me to ask you out, take you to restaurants for intimate dinners or spend long days together. My love for you has not changed over the long years of separation and I want you in my life. Whether it is as a friend, lover or as my wife, is up to you. I hope it will be the latter, but the choice is yours.'

Her head was spinning. Now she understood why he had kept away. He'd only been thinking of her.

'Which of the three is it to be, Grace?' he asked when she didn't answer.

She looked up at him, moisture filling her eyes. 'It has taken me a long time to realise that I love you, but I do, and the third option sounds perfect.'

He immediately closed the remaining space between them and gathered her in his arms. When the long, passionate embrace came to an end, he whispered, 'Thank heavens. I really thought I didn't stand a chance after staying away for so long, but you had needed a couple of years to recover from your loss, and by then I was in the desert fighting. I had to wait.'

'You took a chance. I might have married in that time.'

'It was a risk I felt I had to take. I watched your progress through the war and I must admit you gave me some scary times, but you came through uninjured and still single. As soon as the fighting was over I knew I had to get us together again as quickly as possible.'

'So you arranged for me to come here?'

Dan nodded. 'We will be returning to England in two days' time, and a month later I will be posted back to Berlin. It will be a rush I know, but would you agree to put in for demob so we can marry quickly? As a civilian and my wife I can arrange for us to have married quarters here.'

'Can you do that?'

'I'm an officer and good at giving orders.'

'Ah, I know that only too well,' she laughed.

He smiled down at her. 'I'm not giving orders now. I'm asking. How do you feel about leaving the army?'

'I did consider staying because I had no idea what to do with my life now the war is over.' She reached up and kissed him. 'I didn't know you were going to ask me to marry you. I'll put in for demob as soon as we arrive home. We have wasted enough time.'

He gave a sigh of relief. 'Thank you, my love. It's been a long wait, and I thought this day would never come, but I endeavoured to take each day as it came, and that got me through.'

'That was the only way to get through the long dreadful war,' Grace agreed. 'But, now, this day is ours.'

Hold on to Your Dreams

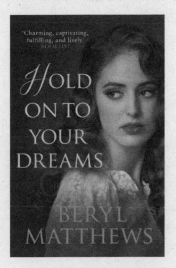

London, 1899. As she prepares for a glittering ball that will usher in the new century, twenty-year-old Gertrude Melrose considers her good fortune. Attractive, intelligent, with a loving family, her only concern is for her brother Edward, who seems intent on squandering his inheritance at the gaming tables.

A few days later the Melrose family's happiness is shattered when Edward's debts threaten to destroy their prosperity. Edward is disowned by his father, and the family must face up to their changed circumstances. But with the support of her friend David, and Alexander Glendale, one of Gertie's spurned suitors, Gertie finds the strength of character to fight for her family and, ultimately, to hold on to her dreams.

The Forgotten Family

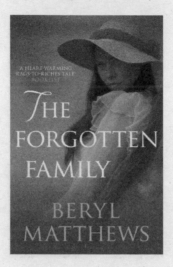

London, 1890. Queenie Bonner is only two years old when she is taken from her large family in the slums to a big house in the country. She is frightened and confused, begging to be taken back, but she is told that this is now her home. She yearns for her nine brothers and sisters, especially Harry, who is her favourite. Albert and Mary Warrender rename her Eleanor and bring her up as their daughter.

As time passes Eleanor forgets about her other family and loves Mary and Albert as her mother and father. But fifteen years later, when Mary dies, Albert tells her about the Bonners. With Albert's help, she sets about tracing her forgotten family. Eight are traced, but one remains missing. There is no sign of Harry. She knows she will never rest until he is found. But where is he?

London's East End, 1919. Robert Hunter is eagerly awaiting the return of his father from the war. Next door Ruth Cooper's family is also preparing to welcome home her dad, who by some miracle managed to survive the sinking of his ship in the battle of Jutland. Both youngsters try their best to understand the many physical and mental scars borne by their returning loved ones.

After five years of separation and anxiety and, for Bob, the worry of caring for his frail mother, emotions are running high. But Alf Hunter, traumatised by the action in the trenches, returns a changed man. When he takes to drink to numb the horrors of war, Bob must put his own happiness on hold to support his family.

Diamonds in the Dust

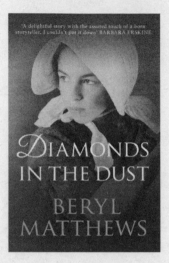

London, 1920. The three Bentley children are used to fending for themselves. Their widowed mother has been forced to take a night job at Grant's clothing factory, and sees them only at breakfast and on Sundays. But at nearly eighteen, and with a job as a housemaid to help make ends meet, Dora is well able to look after her younger siblings Tom and Lily.

Then one morning their mother fails to appear for breakfast, and when Dora is told by the gatekeeper at Grant's factory that no one by the name of Harriet Bentley has ever worked there, the children grow worried. They know their mother loves them, and cannot believe she would deliberately deceive them. With the help of a neighbour, a former policeman who was badly injured during the War, Dora and her siblings start to investigate.